A Text Book of

CORE JAVA

FOR

M.C.A. : MANAGEMENT : SEMESTER - II

SUBJECT CODE : IT23

AS PER NEW REVISED SYLLABUS

RASIKA RAHALKAR

MC.S. (Computer Science), NET

Lecturer, M.E.S.'s Abasaheb Garware College

Pune

NIRALI PRAKASHAN

ADVANCEMENT OF KNOWLEDGE

N3188

Core Java (MCA - Sem. II) **ISBN 978-93-5164-984-7**

First Edition : January 2016

Published By :

NIRALI PRAKASHAN

Abhyudaya Pragati, 1312, Shivaji Nagar
Off J.M. Road, Pune – 411005
Tel - (020) 25512336/37/39, Fax - (020) 25511379
Email : niralipune@pragationline.com

✦ DISTRIBUTION CENTRES

PUNE

Nirali Prakashan : 119, Budhwar Peth, Jogeshwari Mandir Lane, Pune 411002, Maharashtra
Tel : (020) 2445 2044, 66022708, Fax : (020) 2445 1538
Email : bookorder@pragationline.com, niralilocal@pragationline.com

Nirali Prakashan : S. No. 28/27, Dhyari, Near Pari Company, Pune 411041
Tel : (020) 24690204 Fax : (020) 24690316
Email : dhyari@pragationline.com, bookorder@pragationline.com

MUMBAI

Nirali Prakashan : 385, S.V.P. Road, Rasdhara Co-op. Hsg. Society Ltd.,
Girgaum, Mumbai 400004, Maharashtra
Tel : (022) 2385 6339 / 2386 9976, Fax : (022) 2386 9976
Email : niralimumbai@pragationline.com

✦ DISTRIBUTION BRANCHES

JALGAON

Nirali Prakashan : 34, V. V. Golani Market, Navi Peth, Jalgaon 425001,
Maharashtra, Tel : (0257) 222 0395, Mob : 94234 91860

KOLHAPUR

Nirali Prakashan : New Mahadvar Road, Kedar Plaza, 1st Floor Opp. IDBI Bank
Kolhapur 416 012, Maharashtra. Mob : 9850046155

NAGPUR

Pratibha Book Distributors : Above Maratha Mandir, Shop No. 3, First Floor,
Rani Jhanshi Square, Sitabuldi, Nagpur 440012, Maharashtra
Tel : (0712) 254 7129

DELHI

Nirali Prakashan : 4593/21, Basement, Aggarwal Lane 15, Ansari Road, Daryaganj
Near Times of India Building, New Delhi 110002
Mob : 08505972553

BENGALURU

Pragati Book House : House No. 1, Sanjeevappa Lane, Avenue Road Cross,
Opp. Rice Church, Bengaluru – 560002.
Tel : (080) 64513344, 64513355,Mob : 9880582331, 9845021552
Email:bharatsavla@yahoo.com

CHENNAI

Pragati Books : 9/1, Montieth Road, Behind Taas Mahal, Egmore,
Chennai 600008 Tamil Nadu, Tel : (044) 6518 3535,
Mob : 94440 01782 / 98450 21552 / 98805 82331,
Email : bharatsavla@yahoo.com

niralipune@pragationline.com | www.pragationline.com

Also find us on f www.facebook.com/niralibooks

PREFACE

It gives me an immense pleasure in presenting this book, 'Core Java. This book has been designed to serve as a text book for students of Master of Computer Application (MCA), Semester – II.

The goal of presenting this book is to introduce and explain the basic concepts of Core Java as well as some of the Advanced Java techniques. I have tried to incorporate a large volume of programs on all the chapters. This will surely help students to understand the practical aspect of this language along with theory. This book will assist students to write complete software application using Java as a programming language. If you are familiar with Core Java, you will find the book to be an accelerated guide and a comprehensive reference for Advanced Java.

This book has been written which reflects the newly revised syllabus. The book has its own features. I have tried to keep the language as simple and lucid as possible. It highlights important concepts by giving suitable examples wherever necessary. It comprises a wide collection of methods and constructors along with syntax and their appropriate explanation.

A special attention has been paid to develop the interest about today's most popular Java programming language in students. Throughout the book, I have taken all the efforts not to distract a student from his objective of learning this new language.

There are many people who have helped me a lot while constructing this book.

I thank Prof. Gautam Bapat for the friendly manner in which he reviewed our script and suggested improvements from time to time, we must say he has done the editing, exceptionally well for our book.

I thank Mrs. Aabha Athavale, Mrs. Anita Panajkar for their important inputs time to time. Mr. Akbar Shaikh painstakingly attended to all the details to make this book appear good. I also thank Ms. Chaitali Takale and Mr. Ravindra Walodare,

Suggestions and positive criticism to improve this book are most welcome!!!

Author

SYLLABUS

1. **Fundamentals of OOP** **[Weightage 5] [Sessions 2]**
    - What is OOP
    - Difference between Procedural and Object Oriented Programming
    - Basic OOP Concept - Object, Classes, Abstraction, Encapsulation. Inheritance, Polymorphism
2. **Introduction to JAVA** **[Weightage 2.5] [Sessions 1]**
    - History of Java
    - Features of Java
    - Difference between C++ & JAVA
    - JDK Environment
    - Java Virtual Machine
    - Java Runtime Environment
3. **Programming Concepts of Basic Java** **[Weightage 5] [Sessions 2]**
    - Identifiers and Keywords
    - Data Types in Java
    - Java coding Conventions
    - Expressions in Java
    - Control Structures, Decision Making Statements
    - Arrays and its Methods
    - Garbage Collection and finalize() Method
4. **Java Classes** **[Weightage 10] [Sessions 4]**
    - Define Class with Instance Variables and Methods
    - Object Creation of Class
    - Accessing Member of Class
    - Argument Passing
    - Constructors
    - Method Overloading
    - static data, static methods, static blocks
    - this keyword
    - Nested and Inner Classes
    - Wrapper Classes
    - String (String Arrays. String Methods, StringBuffer)
5. **Inheritance** **[Weightage 10] [Sessions 4]**
    - Super Class and Subclass
    - Abstract Method and Classes
    - Method Overriding
    - final Keyword
    - super Keyword
    - Down casting and Up casting
    - Dynamic Method Dispatch

6. **Packages and Interfaces** **[Weightage 10] [Sessions 4]**
   - Importing Classes
   - User Defined Packages
   - Modifiers and Access control (Default, public, Private, Protected, Private Protected)
   - Implementing Interfaces
   - User Defined Interfaces
   - Adapter Classes
7. **Exception Handling** **[Weightage 7.5] [Sessions 3]**
   - Types of Exceptions
   - try, catch, finally, throw, throws keywords
   - Creating your Own Exception
   - Nested try Blocks
   - Multiple Catch Statements
   - User Defined Exceptions
8. **Java Input Output** **[Weightage 7.5] [Sessions 3]**
   - Java I/O Package
   - File Class
   - Byte / Character Stream
   - Buffered Reader / Writer
   - File Reader / Writer
   - Print Writer
   - File Sequential / Random
   - Serialization and De serialization
9. **Multithreading** **[Weightage 10] [Sessions 4]**
   - Multithreading Concept
   - Thread Life Cycle
   - Creating Multithreading Application
   - Thread Priorities
   - Thread Synchronization
   - Inter Thread Communication
10. **Abstract Window Toolkit** **[Weightage 10] [Sessions 4]**
    - Components and Graphics
    - Containers, Frames and Panels
    - Layout Managers
      (a) BorderLayout
      (b) Flowlayout
      (c) GridLayout
      (d) CardLayout
    - AWT all Components
    - Event Delegation Model
      (a) Event Source and Handlers
      (b) Event Categories, Listeners, adapters
    - Anonymous Class

11. Applets **[Weightage 5] [Sessions 2]**

- Applet Life Cycle
- Creating Applet
- Displaying it using Web Browser with appletwiewer.exe
- The HTML APPLET Tag with all attributes
- Passing Parameters to Applet
- Event Handling in Applet
- Advantages and Disadvantages of Applet Vs Applications

12. Swing **[Weightage 5] [Sessions 2]**

- Features of Swing
- Model view Controller Design Pattern
- Swing Components
- JButton
- JRadioButton, JtextArea, JComboBox, iTable, JProgreNsBar
- JSlider, JDialog

13. Java Collection Framework **[Weightage 12.5] [Sessions 5]**

- Collections Overview
- The Collection Interfaces
  (a) Collection Interface, List Interface, Set Interface,
  (b) SortedSet Interface
  (c) The Collection Classes
  (d) ArrayList Class, LinkedList Class, HashSet Class, TreeSet Class
  (e) Accessing a Collection via an Iterator
- The Map Interfaces
  (a) Map Interface, SortedMap Interface
  (b) The Map Classes
  (c) HashMap, TreeMap
- The Legacy Interfaces
  (a) Enumeration Interface
  (b) The Legacy Classes
- Vector Stack Hashtable

CONTENTS

Chapter 1...

FUNDAMENTALS OF OOP

Contents ...

1.1 What is OOP

- Since invent of computers, programmers have tried many programming approaches. These include techniques such as ***modular programming, top-down programming, bottom-up programming*** and ***structured programming***. The main intention of all these techniques was to handle the complex tasks with more reliability. These techniques became very popular in last two decades. People started considering structured programming is a powerful approach to write complex programs. However, as the program grew much larger, even structured programming approach failed to give the desired results.
- Object-Oriented Programming (OOP) is an approach to develop and organize programs. It has eliminated some of the pitfalls of conventional programming methods. Not all languages are suitable to implement OOP concepts. Languages that support OOP are Smalltalk, Ada, Objective C, C++ and Object Pascal. C++ is basically a procedural language with object oriented features added as an extension. Java is a pure Object-Oriented Programming language.

- OOP treats the data as the main element in the program development and it does not allow the data to flow more freely around the system.
- It ties data and functions that operate on it more closely together and protects it from unintentional modification by some other functions.
- OOP approach decomposes the problem in to number of entities known as ***objects***. We can define ***data*** and functions (***methods*** in Java) around these entities.

1.2 Difference between Procedural and Object Oriented Programming

Procedural Programming:

- Procedural programming uses a list of instructions to tell the computer what to do step-by-step. It relies on - routines or subroutines. A procedure contains a series of computational steps to be carried out. Procedural programming languages are also known as top-down languages.
- This programming is spontaneous in the sense that it is very similar to how you would expect a program to work. If you want a computer to do something, you should provide step-by-step instructions on how to do it. It is, therefore, no surprise that most of the early programming languages are all procedural. Examples of procedural languages include Fortran, COBOL and C, which have been around since the 1960s and 70s.

Object-Oriented Programming

- Object-oriented programming, or OOP, is an approach to problem-solving where all computations are carried out using objects. An object is a component of a program that knows how to perform certain actions and how to interact with other elements of the program. Objects are the basic units of object-oriented programming. A simple example of an object would be a person. Logically, you would expect a person to have a name. This would be considered a property of the person. You would also expect a person to be able to do something, such as walking. This would be considered a method of the person.
- A method in object-oriented programming is like a procedure in procedural programming. The key difference here is that the method is part of an object. In object-oriented programming, you organize your code by creating objects, and then you can give those objects properties and you can make them do certain things.
- A key aspect of object-oriented programming is the use of classes. A class is a blueprint of an object. You can think of a class as a concept, and the object as the representative of that concept. So let's say you want to use a person in your program. You want to be able to describe the person and have the person do something. A class called 'person' would provide a blueprint for what a person looks like and what a person can do. Examples of object-oriented languages include C#, Java, Perl and Python.

Table 1.1

	Procedure Oriented Programming	**Object Oriented Programming**
Divided Into	In POP, program is divided into small parts called functions.	In OOP, program is divided into parts called objects.
Importance	In POP, Importance is not given to data but to functions as well as sequence of actions to be done.	In OOP, Importance is given to the data rather than procedures or functions because it works as a real world.
Approach	POP follows Top Down approach.	OOP follows Bottom Up approach.
Access Specifiers	POP does not have any access specifier.	OOP has access specifiers named Public, Private, Protected, etc.
Data Moving	In POP, Data can move freely from function to function in the system.	In OOP, objects can move and communicate with each other through member functions.
Expansion	To add new data and function in POP is not so easy.	OOP provides an easy way to add new data and function.
Data Access	In POP, Most function uses Global data for sharing that can be accessed freely from function to function in the system.	In OOP, data can not move easily from function to function,it can be kept public or private so we can control the access of data.
Data Hiding	POP does not have any proper way for hiding data so it is less secure.	OOP provides Data Hiding so provides more security.
Overloading	In POP, Overloading is not possible.	In OOP, overloading is possible in the form of Function Overloading and Operator Overloading.
Examples	Example of POP are : C, VB, FORTRAN, Pascal.	Example of OOP are : C++, JAVA, VB.NET, C#.NET.

1.3 Basic OOP Concepts

1.3.1 Objects

- Object is the basic entity in real world. It may represent a person, a place, a thing or a virtual entity such as a bank account. We can look around to find objects in real world. Cat, dog, car, television, table, plant etc. are some of the examples of objects. These real world objects have two important characteristic – state (data or attributes) and behavior (code to manipulate that data). This means that each object has data and code to manipulate that data. For Example, A television has attributes (size (32" /40" /44"), brand

(Sony /Samsung /Philips), type (LCD /LED /Plasma), transmission (cable / satellite dish), volume, brightness, contrast, color etc.) and behavior (switch ON , switch OFF, set size, set type, set transmission mode, change channel, change volume, change contrast, set color etc.)

- Software objects are modeled after real world entities. They too have states and behavior. They maintain their states in one or more variables and implement behavior with methods. Method is a function that operates on the data of an object.
- You can represent real world objects using software objects. You might want to represent real world television as a software objects in some animation movie or a real world bicycle as a software object in the program that control electronic exercise bicycle.

1.3.2 Classes

- We just mentioned that objects contain data and code to manipulate that data. The entire set of data and code can be made a user defined data type using the concept of class. A ***class*** may be thought of as a '***data type***' and an ***object*** as a ***variable*** of that type. Once a class has been defined, we can create any number of objects belonging to that class. ***Class*** is thus a collection of objects of similar type. For example, mango, orange, apple are all members of class fruit. So mango, orange and apple are all objects of class fruit. All these objects share characteristics of class fruit.
- In object oriented terminology, we say that a television object is an instance of the class Televisions. All televisions have states (size, type, volume, brightness etc.) and behavior (switch ON, change volume, change brightness etc.) in common. However each television's state (data) is independent of the other. It can be different than that of the other televisions. This itself means that all television objects may have different values for the data variables. A ***class*** is a blueprint or prototype that defines these variables and methods common to all objects of the same kind.

1.3.3 Abstraction

- ***Abstraction*** refers to the act of representing essential features without including the background details. Humans deal with complexity through abstraction. For example, we drive car without knowing the complex internal working of it. It is sufficient to learn the basic techniques of driving a car. We need not know the details about the design of the car engine. The user is isolated from all this complexity by using the concept of abstraction.
- In Java Abstraction is achieved using Abstract classes, and Interfaces.

Abstract Class

- A class which contains the abstract keyword in its declaration is known as abstract class.
- Abstract classes may or may not contain abstract methods ie., methods with out body (public void get();)

- But, if a class have at least one abstract method, then the class must be declared abstract.
- If a class is declared abstract it cannot be instantiated.
- To use an abstract class you have to inherit it from another class, provide implementations to the abstract methods in it.
- If you inherit an abstract class you have to provide implementations to all the abstract methods in it.

1.3.4 Encapsulation

- ***'Encapsulation'*** is the mechanism that binds data and code that manipulate the data together and keep both safe from outside interference and misuse. Encapsulation is the most striking feature of the class. Encapsulation makes it possible for object to be treated like a 'black box'. We perform a task without any concern with the internal implementation. The data is not accessible to the outside world. Only those methods which are wrapped in the class can access it. For example, the television has a data variable such as '**volume**' and a method that operate on the same data variable as '**reduce-volume**'. Volume will only be reduced if we press the reduce volume button. Otherwise the volume will not be reduced. It means, we are hiding details about 'how to reduce the volume when someone presses the reduce-volume button' from the user as well as we are protecting our data from outside world. **Encapsulation is also known as "data Hiding".**
- To achieve encapsulation in Java
    - Declare the variables of a class as private.
    - Provide public setter and getter methods to modify and view the variables values.

  Below given is an example that demonstrates how to achieve Encapsulation in Java:

Program 1.1:

```
/* File name : EncapTest.java */
public class EncapTest{

private String name;
private String idNum;
private int age;

public int getAge(){
   return age;
}

public String getName(){
   return name;
}
```

```
public String getIdNum(){
   return idNum;
}

public void setAge( int newAge){
   age = newAge;
}

public void setName(String newName){
   name = newName;
}

public void setIdNum( String newId){
   idNum = newId;
}
}
```

- The public setXXX() and getXXX() methods are the access points of the instance variables of the EncapTest class. Normally, these methods are referred as getters and setters. Therefore any class that wants to access the variables should access them through these getters and setters.
- The variables of the EncapTest class can be accessed as below:

```
/* File name : RunEncap.java */
public class RunEncap{
public static void main(String args[]){
   EncapTest encap = new EncapTest();
   encap.setName("Ameya");
   encap.setAge(27);
   encap.setIdNum("12343ms");
    System.out.print("Name : " + encap.getName() + " Age : " +
                                                   encap.getAge());
    }
}
```

- This would produce the following result:

```
Name : Ameya Age : 27
```

Advantages of Encapsulation:

- o The fields of a class can be made read-only or write-only.
- o A class can have total control over what is stored in its fields.
- o The users of a class do not know how the class stores its data. A class can change the data type of a field and users of the class do not need to change any of their code.

1.3.5 Inheritance

- ***Inheritance*** is the process by which one object acquires properties of another objects. For example, child always inherits properties of his parents, all cars inherit general, common properties from the class Vehicle. Thus inheritance mechanism supports the concept of hierarchical classification. As illustrated in Fig. 1.1, a class Vehicle is a parent class. Class Vehicle is inherited by 3 child classes 'Two Wheeler, Three Wheeler and Four Wheeler'. Class Two Wheeler is again further divided into two child classes such as Scooter and Bicycle. The principle behind this classification is that each child class shares common characteristics of the class from which it is derived. The child class may also contain its own properties along with the inherited properties.
- The concept of inheritance provides the idea of reusability. This means that we can add extra features to the existing class. This is possible by deriving a new class from the existing class. It contains combined features of both the classes. In Java, the derived class is called as 'subclass' and a parent class is called as 'super class'.

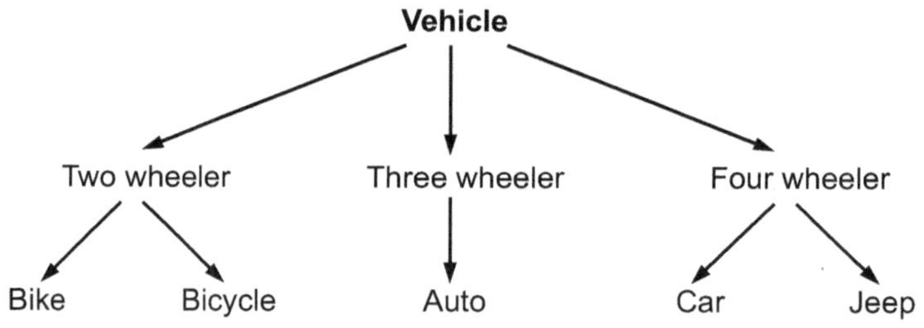

Fig. 1.1: Inheritance

1.3.6 Polymorphism

- ***Polymorphism*** means the ability to take more than one form. An operation may have different behavior in different instances. It allows one interface to be used for a general class of action. Consider an example of a function draw() which draws a shape. (functions in C++ are known as methods in Java. Hence we would use a word method instead of a word function here onwards.) Suppose we want to draw a circle, a rectangle and a triangle. If we would have used non object oriented programming language, we would have written three different methods with three different names for drawing these shapes. Lets say, drawCircle(), drawRectangle() and drawTriangle(). However, because of polymorphism in Java, a same name such as draw() can be shared by all these three objects. Polymorphism is extensively used in implementing inheritance.

Practice Questions

1. What is OOP?
2. What do you mean by Encapsulation? Explain with example.
3. Explain the following terms.
   (a) class
   (b) object
   (c) polymorphism
4. State the difference between Procedural and Object oriented programming.
5. Explain basic Concepts of OOPs?
6. What do you mean by Abstraction? Explain with example.
7. State difference between abstraction and encapsulation.
8. What is Inheritance in OOP?
9. Give any one example of polymorphism.
10. Explain basic OOPS concepts.

■■■

Chapter 2...

INTRODUCTION TO JAVA

Contents ...

2.1 History of Java

- Sun Microsystems decided to develop some special software that could be used to manipulate consumer electronics devices like TVs, VCRs, and some other electronic machines.
- A team of Sun Microsystems which was headed by 'James Gosling' started working on it.
- In the year 1991, a team invented a new language and announced it as 'Oak'. In the year 1995, 'Oak' was renamed as 'Java' due to some legal issues.
- 'Java' was based on existing languages like C and C++. But a team discovered that C and C++ had limitation in terms of reliability and portability. So they removed some of the features of C, C++ and made it as a simple, reliable, portable and powerful language.
- Java is a general-purpose, object oriented programming language.

2.2 Features of JAVA

- The inventor of Java wanted to design a language which could offer solutions to some of the problems from modern programming. The most striking feature of the language is that it is a ***platform neutral language***. Apart from this, there is a list of buzzwords which describes a full potential of the language. These striking features have made Java as the first application language of World Wide Web. It has also become a leading language for stand-alone applications.

Simple

- Java is designed to be easy to learn and use effectively for professional programmers. If you are an experienced programmer and know the basics of Object Oriented Programming, learning java is not that difficult at all.

Secure

- Whenever you download certain program, there is a risk of getting attacked by virus. Java achieved protection by confining an applet to the Java Execution Environment. It will not allow an applet to access other parts of computers. The ***bytecode*** mechanism helps ensure security.

Portable

- Portability is one of the major aspects of Internet. There are many computers and operating systems connected to the Internet. If a java program needed to be run on different machines, it is practically not possible to have different versions of java program for different computers. The ***same*** program should run on ***different*** computers. Java provided the ***bytecode*** mechanism to ensure portability.

Object Oriented

- Java is a truly object oriented language. Almost everything in java is an object. Java has a wide variety of classes. These classes are organized in various packages. We can use them in our programs while implementing inheritance. The object model in java is simple and easy to extend.

Robust

- Java has ability to create robust programs. It is a strongly typed language. It checks your code at compile time as well as at run time. It forces you to find few errors early in program to gain reliability. At the same time, it makes you free from having to worry about common programming mistakes.

Multithreaded

- Java supports multithreaded programming. This means that it can handle multiple tasks simultaneously. We can write program that do many things simultaneously.
- For example, we can listen to a song while scrolling a page up and down and at the same time an applet can be downloaded from a distant computer. This means, we need not wait for an application to finish one task before we start the other one. Java has easy-to-use approach towards multithreading. So we can concentrate on the specific behavior of a program rather than concentrating on synchronizing multiple tasks.

Architecture-neutral

- One of the main problems that a programmer may face is, if he writes a program today, will it run tomorrow – even on the same machine? Upgrades in operating systems, processors and system resources may make your program unable to execute even on the same machine. Java designers had a goal "**write once and run anywhere, anytime and forever**". **'Java Virtual Machine'** is an attempt to accomplish this demand.

Interpreted and High performance

- Java compiles the programs into an intermediate representation called '**Java Bytecode**'. This bytecode can be executed on any system which implements Java Virtual Machine. Java bytecode can be easily and directly translated into native machine code for very high performance by using **Just-In-Time** (JIT) compiler. This feature of Java runtime system helps us in creating platform-independent code.

Distributed

- Java is designed for the distributed environment of Internet. It has ability to share both data and programs on the network. It can access remote objects on the Internet very easily. It supports **Remote Method Invocation (RMI)**. This feature enables a program to invoke a method at remote location across a network.

Dynamic

- Java is a dynamic language. It is capable of dynamically linking in new class libraries, methods and objects. A java program carries enough run-time type information which is used to verify and resolve accesses to objects at run time.

2.3 Difference between C++ and Java

- Although Java was modeled after C and C++ languages, it differs from C and C++ in many aspects. It does not include a number of features available in C and C++. It also adds some new features. While C++ is a superset of C, Java is neither a superset nor a subset of C and C++. Some of the features of C and C++ have been overlapped in Java.
- Following are some of the major C++ features which were intentionally omitted from Java or were significantly modified.
    - o Java does not support operator overloading.
    - o Java does not support multiple inheritance of classes.
    - o Java does not use pointers.
    - o Java does not support global variables.
    - o There are no template classes in Java.
    - o Java does not have header files.
    - o Destructor function has been replaced by finalize() method in Java.

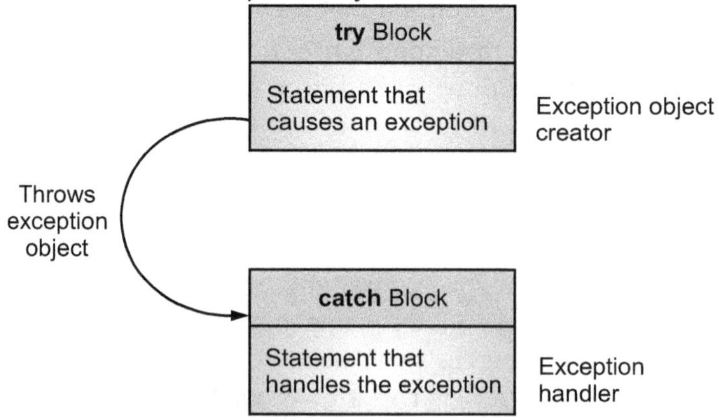

Fig. 2.1: Overlapping diagram for C, C++ and Java

2.4 JDK Environment

- Java Environment includes a large number of development tools, classes and methods. The development tools are part of the system called 'Java Development Kit (JDK). Classes and methods are part of the Java Standard Library (JSL), most commonly known as **'Application Programming Interface' (API).**
- Java Development Kit has a collection of tools for Java Development. They include:
  - javac
  - java
  - appletviewer
  - javadoc
  - jdb

Table 2.1: Java Development Tools

Tool	Description
Javac	The java compiler that translates javacode to bytecode file which java interpreter can understand.
Java	Java interpreter that runs applets and applications interpreting bytecode files. It launches a java application by starting Java Runtime Environment, loading a specified class and invoking that class's ***main*** method to run the program.
appletviewer	Enables us to run java applets. Normally applets are the programs those can be embedded in a web page and run in web browser. This is very useful tool which gives the same effect but on console.
javadoc	Creates HTML formatted documentation from java source code files.
Jdb	Java debugger that helps us in finding errors in java programs.

2.5 Java Virtual Machine

- **Java Virtual Machine (JVM)** is a program that interprets the intermediate Java byte code and generates the desired output. JVM is an imaginary machine that is implemented in software on the real machine. This 'Generic Machine' software can run on various existing computer systems. It is implemented on a wide variety of hardware platforms making Java as 'platform independent'. Byte code for JVM is stored in .class files. JVM is
  1. **A specification** where working of Java Virtual Machine is specified. But implement-tation provider is independent to choose the algorithm. Its implementation has been provided by Sun and other companies.

2. **An implementation:** Its implementation is known as JRE (Java Runtime Environment).
3. **Runtime Instance:** Whenever you write java command on the command prompt to run the java class, and instance of JVM is created.

Functions of JVM:

- The JVM performs following operation:
  - Loads code
  - Verifies code
  - Executes code
  - Provides runtime environment
- JVM provides definitions for the:
  - Memory area
  - Class file format
  - Register set
  - Garbage-collected heap
  - Fatal error reporting etc.

2.6 Java Runtime Environment

- JRE stands for "Java Runtime Environment" and may also be written "Java RTE."
- The JRE, or Java RTE, is developed by Sun Microsystems (the creator of Java) and includes the Java Virtual Machine (JVM), code libraries, and components, which are necessary to run programs written in Java. The JRE is available for multiple computer platforms, including Mac, Windows, and Unix.
- If the JRE is not installed on a computer, Java programs may not be recognized by the operating system and will not run. The JRE software provides a runtime environment in which Java programs can be executed, just like software programs that have been fully compiled for the computer's processor. JRE software is available as both a standalone environment and a Web browser plug-in, which allows Java applets to be run within a Web browser.
- **Java Runtime Environment (JRE)** facilitates the execution of programs in Java. It mainly includes the following components:
  - **Java Virtual Machine:** It is a program that interprets the intermediate Java byte code and generates the desired output. JVM is an imaginary machine that is implemented in software on the real machine. This 'Generic Machine' software can

run on various existing computer systems. It is implemented on a wide variety of hardware platforms making Java as 'platform independent'. Byte code for JVM is stored in .class files.

- o **Runtime Class Libraries:** These are the set of core class libraries that are required for the execution of the Java programs.
- o **User Interface Toolkits:** AWT and Swings are examples of tool kits that give support to the user to interact with an applications program.
- o **Deployment Technologies:** ***Java Plug-in*** enables the execution of Java applet on the web browser. ***Java Web Start*** enables remote deployment of an application.

2.7 Relationship between JRE, JVM and JDK

JDK (Java Development Kit)

- Java Developer Kit contains tools needed to develop the Java programs, and JRE to run the programs. The tools include compiler (javac.exe), Java application launcher (java.exe), Appletviewer, etc... Compiler converts java code into byte code. Java application launcher opens a JRE, loads the class, and invokes its main method.
- You need JDK, if at all you want to write your own programs, and to compile the m. For running java programs, JRE is sufficient. JRE is targeted for execution of Java files i.e. JRE = JVM + Java Packages Classes(like util, math, lang, awt, swing etc.) +runtime libraries. JDK is mainly targeted for java development. I.e. You can create a Java file (with the help of Java packages), compile a Java file and run a java file.

JRE (Java Runtime Environment)

- Java Runtime Environment contains JVM, class libraries, and other supporting files. It does not contain any development tools such as compiler, debugger, etc. Actually JVM runs the program, and it uses the class libraries, and other supporting files provided in JRE. If you want to run any java program, you need to have JRE installed in the system

Fig. 2.2: Relationship between JDK, JRE and JVM

- The Java Virtual Machine provides a platform-independent way of executing code; programmers can concentrate on writing software, without having to be concerned with how or where it will run.
- But, note that JVM itself not a platform independent. It only helps Java to be executed on the platform-independent way. When JVM has to interpret the byte codes to machine language, then it has to use some native or operating system specific language to interact with the system. One has to be very clear on platform independent concept. Even there are many JVMs written on Java, however hey too have little bit of code specific to the operating systems.

Practice Questions

1. Explain History of Java.
2. What are the key features of JAVA?
3. Explain the following terms:
   (a) Jdb
   (b) Javac
   (c) javadoc
4. State the difference between C++ and JAVA .
5. Write a short note on Java Runtime Environment.
6. What do you mean by Application programming API?
7. Write a short note on JVM, State its functions.
8. Describe Java Development Tools.
9. What is JDK?
10. Explain relationship between JVM,JDK,JRE.

Programming Questions

1. Write a program to declare a class EvenNumber which will find first n even numbers using constructor.
2. Write a program to declare a class OddNumber which will find first n odd numbers using constructor. (use if else)
3. Write a program to declare a class Natural which will print n natural numbers using constructor.
4. Write a program to declare a class Addition which will perform addition of first n even and odd number using constructor.
5. Write a program to declare a class Factorial which will find the factorial of n numbers using constructor.

6. Write a program to declare a class Fibonacci which will find n Fibonacci number using constructor.
7. Write a program to declare a class Hexadecimal which will find hexadecimal number of given number using constructor.
8. Write a program which will find binary number of a given number using constructor.
9. Write a program to declare a class Sum, which will find the sum of total digits of a number entered by user using constructor.
10. Write a program which will reverse a number given as command line argument.
11. Write a program to declare a class Exponential to find xy using constructor.

■■■

Chapter 3...

PROGRAMMING CONCEPTS OF BASIC JAVA

Contents ...

3.1 Identifiers and Keywords

3.1.1 Identifiers

- Identifiers are the words used by a programmer for naming classes, methods, variables, objects, labels, packages and interfaces in a program.
- Each variable has a name by which it is identified in the program. It's a good idea to give your variables symbolic names that are closely related to the values they hold. Variable names can include any alphabetic character or digit and the underscore _. The main restriction on the names you can give your variables is that they cannot contain any white space. You cannot begin a variable name with a number. All variable names are case-sensitive. MyVariable is not the same as myVariable. There is no limit to the length of a Java variable name.
- Java identifiers follow certain rules:
  - They can have alphabets, digits, underscore and dollar sign characters.
  - They must begin with a letter, a dollar sign ($) or an underscore (_). They must not begin with a digit.
  - Identifiers are case sensitive.
  - Identifiers must be meaningful and short enough to be quickly and easily typed.

3.1.2 Keywords in JAVA

- The Java programming language has total of 50 reserved keywords which have special meaning for the compiler and cannot be used as variable names. For technical reasons, the words false, null, and true aren't called keywords.
    - const and goto are resevered words but not used.
    - true, false and null are literals, not keywords.
    - all keywords are in lower-case.
- The following list shows the keywords grouped by category:

Access Modifiers:

1. **private:** Makes method or variable accessible only within its own class.
2. **protected:** Makes method or variable accessible to classes in same package or to subclasses of the class.
3. **public:** Makes class, method or variable accessible from any other class.

Class, Method and Variable Modifiers

1. **abstract:** Declares class that can not be instantiated, or method that have to be implemented by non-abstract subclass.
2. **class:** Indicates a class.
3. **extends:** Indicates a super class that subclass is extending.
4. **final:** Indicates that class is impossible to extend, method to override and variable to change value.
5. **implements:** Indicates a interface that the class is implementing.
6. **interface:** Indicates a interface.
7. **native:** Indicates that method is written in a platform dependent language.
8. **new:** Creates a new instance of a class by calling class's constructor.
9. **static:** Makes a method or a variable belong to a class as opposed to an instance.
10. **strictfp:** Used in front of a method or class to indicate that floating-point numbers will follow FP-strict rules in all expressions.
11. **synchronized:** Indicates that a method can be accessed only by one thread a time.
12. **transient:** Prevents fields from ever being serialized. Transient fields are always skipped when objects are serialized.
13. **volatile:** Indicates a variable may change out of sync because it is used in threads.

Flow Control

1. **break:** Exits a block of code in witch it is suitable.
2. **case:** Executes a block of code dependent of **switch** condition.
3. **continue:** Stops executing rest of loop's code(that goes after) and starts new iteration.

4. **default:** Executes a block of code if non of **switch** statements are true.
5. **do:** Executes a block of code one time, than based on **while** statement determines will it be executed again.
6. **else:** Executes a block of code when **if** condition is not true.
7. **for:** Executes a conditional loop on block of a code.
8. **if:** Executes a logical test.
9. **instanceof:** Determines if a object is instance of a class, a superclass or a interface.
10. **return:** Returns from method not executing any code that follows.
11. **switch:** Indicates a variable that will be compared to **case** statements.
12. **while:** Executes a block of code in loop if given logical test is true.

Error Handling:

1. **catch:** Declares a block of code that executes if exception occurs.
2. **finally:** Block of code that follows try block code and executes no matter how exception is handled.
3. **throw:** Used to pass an exception to method that called this method.
4. **throws:** Indicates a exception that can be thrown by a class or method.
5. **try:** Block of code that will be tried, but which may cause an exception.
6. **assert:** Evaluates a conditional expression to verify the programmer's assumption.

Package Control

1. **import:** Declares what packages or class to import in code.
2. **package:** Define to which package code in file belongs to.

Variable Keywords

1. **super:** Reference variable referring to immediate parent class(*super class*).
2. **this:** Reference variable referring to the instance of current object.

Primitives

1. **boolean:** A value indicating *true* or *false*.
2. **byte:** An 8-bit signed integer.
3. **char:** An Unicode character(16-bit unsigned integer).
4. **int:** An 32-bit signed integer.
5. **float:** An 32-bit signed floating-point number.
6. **long:** An 64-bit signed integer.
7. **double:** An 64-bit signed floating-point number.

Void Return Type Keyword

1. **void:** Indicates that method does not have return type.

Unused Reserved Words

1. **goto:** bad practice.
2. **const:** use **public final static**.

3.2 Data Types in JAVA

- Java is a strongly typed language. This means that every variable must have a declared type. There are **Eight** primitive data types in Java. Four are integer types, two are floating point types, one is character type and one is Boolean type.

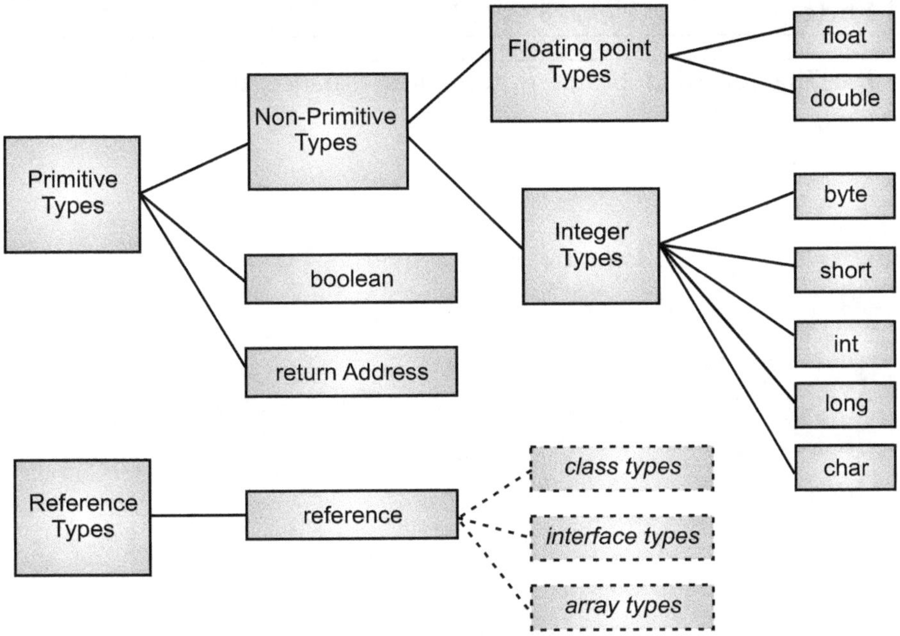

Fig. 3.1: Data types in Java

3.2.1 Integer Type

- Integer types can hold whole numbers such as 230, -56, 3456. Java supports four types of integers as shown in table 1.3. They are byte, short, int and long.
- Java does not support unsigned types. All Java values can be positive or negative.
- The following table shows the integer type, its memory size and the range of values it can store.
- It is advisable to use smaller data types whenever possible as wider data types take more time to manipulate. For example, instead of storing number 34 in an int type, it is always beneficial to store it in byte. This improves the speed of execution of the program.
- Long integers are always appended with L or l for example, 5678000L or 34567000l. Hexadecimal numbers have a prefix 0X or 0x,(for example, 0XCA45). Octal numbers have prefix 0, (for example, 012 is 10 in decimal number system)

Integer Types

- The integer types are for numbers without fractional parts. Negative values are allowed.
- Java provides four integer types as shown in Table 3.1.

Table 3.1

Type	Storage Requirement	Range (Inclusive)
int	4 bytes	–2,147,483,648 to 2,17,483,647 (just over 2 billion)
short	2 bytes	–32,768 to 32,767
long	8 bytes	–9,223,373,036,854,775,808 to 9,223,372,036,854,775,807
byte	1 byte	– 128 to 127

Program 3.1: The following program computes distance travelled by light using long variables.

```
class IntegerType
{
    public static void main(String args[])
    {
        int speed;
        long day;
        long sec;
        long dist;

        speed = 420000;
        day = 12000; // specify number of days here
        sec = day * 24 * 60 * 60; // convert to seconds
        dist = speed * sec; // compute distance
        System.out.print("In " + day);
        System.out.print(" days light will travel about ");
        System.out.println(dist + " miles.");
    }
}
```

Output:

```
In 12000 days light will travel about 435456000000000 miles.
```

- Clearly, the number itself is too large that the result could not have been held in an **int** variable.

3.2.2 Floating Point Type

- Floating point type holds numbers containing fractional parts such as 34.68 or -456.098.
- There are two types of floating point storages in Java. They are float and double. Float type values are single precision numbers and double type values are double precision numbers. The name double refers to the fact that this type stores the values that have twice the precision of the float type. (So we call it as double precision numbers.)
- Seven precision digits after decimal point may be enough in storing salary of an employee in Rupees and Paise but it won't be enough to store the experimental values in science laboratory. The only reason to use float type is to speed up the processing.
- Numbers of type float have 'F' or 'f' suffix (for example, 34.56F or 34.56f). Floating point numbers without suffix 'F' or 'f' are always considered as of type double. You can have an optional suffix 'D' or 'd' for double data type (for example, 345.67000D or 345.67000d).
- All mathematical functions such as sin(), cos(), sqrt(), etc. return double type values.
- There are three special floating point values to denote overflow and errors.
- Positive infinity (Double.POSITIVE_INFINITY): Result of dividing a positive number by 0 is positive infinity.
- Negative infinity (Double.NEGATIVE_INFINITY)
- NaN (Not a Number) (Double.NaN): Computing 0/0 or square root of a negative number gives NaN value.
- But these values are used rarely in practice.
- Table 3.2 shows the floating point type, size and range of values it stores.

Table 3.2: Floating Point types

Type	Storage Requirement	Range (Inclusive)
float	4 bytes	approximately ± 3.40282347E + 38F (6-7 significant decimal digits)
double	8 bytes	approximately ± 1.79769313486231570E + 308 (15 significant decimal digits)

Program 3.2: The following program computes an area of a circle.

```
class Circle
{
    public static void main(String args[])
    {
        double pi, rad, area;
        rad = 14.50;
        pi = 3.1416;
        area = pi * rad * rad;
        System.out.println("Area of circle is " + area);
    }
}
```

Since, radius of a circle and value of PI are in decimal values, we have used double data type to store their values. Since we have declared variables of type double, it displays values up to 6 decimal places.

Output:

```
Area of circle is 660.5214
```

3.2.3 Character type

- Java uses **char** data type in order to store character constants in memory.
- The char type takes 2 bytes in memory to store a single, individual character (for example, 'A' is a character constant with value as 65).
- Unicode characters can also be expressed using hexadecimal values from \u0000 to \uffff. (for example, '\u03C0' is used to store a greek letter 'Pi'(π)). A value which has a prefix '\u' denotes a Unicode value.
- Besides \u, there are several escape sequences which represents special characters. Table 3.3 shows escape sequences for special characters.

Table 3.3: Escape Sequences for Special Characters

Type	Storage Requirement	Range (Inclusive)
\b	Backspace	\u0008
\t	Tab	\u0009
\n	Linefeed	\u000a
\r	Carriage return	\u000d
\"	Double quote	\u0022
\'	Single quote	\u0027
\\	Backslash	\u005c

- Unicode encoding scheme was designed to solve some of the problems with traditional character encoding schemes such as ASCII in United States, ISO-8859-1 for Western European Languages, KOI-8 for Russian etc.
- It was designed with fixed 2 byte width sufficient to include all characters used in all languages in the world.
- Java was designed to use 16 bit (2 byte) Unicode characters, which was a major change over other programming languages which used 8 bit characters.

Program 3.3: The following program demonstrates char data type.

```
class CharacterDemo
{
    public static void main(String args[])
    {
        char c1, c2;
        c1 = 86;
        c2 = 'M';
        System.out.print("c1 and c2: ");
        System.out.println(c1 + "  " + c2);
    }
}
```

Output:

```
c1 and c2: V M
```

3.2.4 Boolean type

- The Boolean type has two values – true or false. It is used for evaluating logical conditions.
- Boolean data type can be denoted by a keyword **boolean** and uses only one bit of storage.
- All comparison operators return boolean type values.
- You cannot convert between integer and boolean values in Java. For example, In C++, value 0 is considered to be false and any non zero value is considered to be true. This is not the case in Java.
- Suppose I write a statement,

```
if ( x = 0)   //... meant x == 0
```

- In C++, this test compiles and runs evaluating to false but in Java, this test does not compile because integer expression 'x = 0' cannot be converted to a boolean value.

Program 3.4: Here is a program that demonstrates boolean data type:

```
class BoolTest {
public static void main(String args[]) {
boolean b;
b = false;
System.out.println("b is " + b);
b = true;
System.out.println("b is " + b);
// a boolean value can control the if statement
if(b) System.out.println("This is executed.");
b = false;
if(b) System.out.println("This is not executed.");
// outcome of a relational operator is a boolean value
System.out.println("10 > 9 is " + (10 > 9));
}
}
```

Output:

```
b is false
b is true
This is executed.
10 > 9 is true
```

3.3 Java Coding Conventions

What are the Coding Conventions?

- "Coding conventions are a set of guidelines for a specific programming language that recommend programming style, practices and methods for each aspect of a piece program written in this language."

Why do we need to learn coding conventions?

- It becomes mandatory to follow certain rule while coding so that even a new java programmer can walk through the code and can understand it. Following are the reasons why do we need to learn Java Coding Conventions-
  - Code Readability
  - Ease to grasp the code
  - Clean coding and better packaging of product.

1. **File extension of Java file:**
   - Java file has extension .java and byte-code will have .class and to use all these classes we can have java archive file with name .jar.
2. **Comment in Java**
   - **Single line comment:** For single line comment, one can use "//" and whatever we would write after this, would be ignored by compiler Example:

int B //this is one variable of integer type

Or use

/* this is just another line*/ but such single line comment always comes after a blank line.2. <strong>Multiline comment:</strong> When we want to comment in more than one line then we should use /*..........*/

3. **Methods:**
   - Method should start with lower case and if method contains multiple words then each inner words first letter should be in caps or in Upper Case. Along with this we should try to keep the name of method as verb. For example, calculateTotal, monthlySalary, dayOfMonth etc.
4. **Classes:**
   - Each class should start with first letter in Upper and again like method, if class name is made up of multiple words then each inner word's first letter should be in upper case. For example, Vehicle, HelloJava, EmployeeDetails, etc.
5. **Constructors:**
   - It will always be same as Class name. Constructor does not have any return type that's why we never write anything like void/any primitive data type as return type.
6. **Variables:**
   - It should start with lower case and like method if variable is made up of more than one words and first letter of each inner word would be in Upper Case. We should try to keep short name for variables and should avoid multiple word in variable name in code convention. Both, variables and methods seem similar. Only parentheses bring difference between a variable and method. For example, length, next_batch etc.
7. **Constants:**
   - Constant should be in complete Upper Case ex: SUNDAY, MONDAY.
8. **Structure of a Java Class**
   - Beginning comment
   - Package name and import statement
   - Class or interface declaration
   - Inside class order of variable

- Static variable should come first
- public variable
- protected variables
- private
- After variable declaration, Constructor should be declared
- Inside class, method should be in functional order there is no ordering of method on the basis of scope or access modifier

Example:

```
/*
*
* @author:Dwarika
* @purpose: this is a dummy class
* @copywrite: none
*
*
*/
package org.abodeqa.qa.demoproject.functional;
import org.abodeqa.qa.demoproject.test.Amazon;
public class DemoClass {
public static int staticint=0;
public int demoint= 3;
protected int proint= 4;
private int priint=5;
/* this is a constructor */
public DemoClass() {
}
//functionally we are going to call this method first so declare it first
private void firstMethod()
{
//body of method
}
//Second Method
public void secondMethod()
{
//body of method
}
}
```

9. **Each line of code should terminate with ";"**
10. **For Readability purpose**, try to keep each line at max 80 characters because many terminal does not support more than this.
11. **For readability we should wrap line of code if they are going beyond 80 characters**

    Some thumb rules for wrapping lines:

    - Break after a comma.For example

    ```
    functionName(firstParameter. secondParameter,
    thirdParameter,fourthParameter);
    ```

    - Break before an operator.

    ```
    variable = firstNumber*(secondNumber+firstNumber+thirdNumber
                                      +fourthNumber)*fifthNumber;
    ```

12. **Single declaration** in a line increase better readability and also support comment associated with declaration.

3.4 Expressions in Java

- An *expression* is a series of variables, operators, and method calls (constructed according to the syntax of the language) that evaluates to a single value.
- A Java Expression computes ("evaluates to") a value, typically based on other values of the same of different types
  - This is like a "formula" to compute a value
  - For years, you have likely been writing expressions in algebra, using them in Excel, in calculators, etc.

    Examples: "2*5", "1.0/3", "(a+b)*c", "a>b", "this.getConnectedAgent(i).name"
- In the process of computing the value, it may cause some changes to "program state" (e.g. change the value of a variable"
  - Assignment expression
  - Calling a method In most places AnyLogic
- In most places AnyLogic wants a value, we can give it a Java Expression.

Common Java Expressions

- Literal (3.5, 1, "my string", { 1, 2.71, 3.14, 0}, null)
- Comparison (a>b,a==b, a<=b)
- Mathematical Operators (+,-,/,*) Can be "overloaded" to mean other things (e.g. + as concatenation)
- "Dereferencing": Looking up field or value b in a reference to an object a: (a.b) (a is a reference to an instance of a class; b is a name of a field or method associated with the class of a, and thus with the object)

- Ternary operator: (predicate ? a: b)
- Potentially causes changes (Side effecting)
  - Assignment (a=b) Left hand side is some location (variable, field, etc.) and variants (a++, ++a, a+=2, a*=5)
  - Method call (function call): this.get_Main()

Additional Common Operators

- Boolean expressions
  - a&&b (logical and), a||b (logical or), !a (logical not)
- Indexing: a[20], a[getConnectionsNumber()-1]
  - Must value preceding must denote an array
- Method call: f(2,3)
- For strings strA+strB (concatenates strings)

Reading Java Expressions

- Generally, expressions are calculated from "inside out", and left-to-right
  Example:
  a.getConnectedagent(i).getName().length

- In this way expression forms string like structure (e.g. where the left components return values used by the right components)

Table 3.4

Expression	Action	Value Returned
aChar = 'S'	Assign the character 'S' to the character variable aChar	The value of aChar after the assignment ('S')
"The largest byte value is " + largestByte	Concatenate the string "The largest byte value is " and the value of largestByte converted to a string	The resulting string: The largest byte value is 127
Character.isUpperCase(aChar)	Call the method isUpperCase	The return value of the method: true

- The data type of the value returned by an expression depends on the elements used in the expression. The expression aChar = 'S' returns a character because the assignment operator returns a value of the same data type as its operands and aChar and 'S' are characters. As you see from the other expressions, an expression can return a boolean value, a string, and so on.

- The Java programming language allows you to construct compound expressions and statements from various smaller expressions as long as the data type required by one part of the expression matches the data type of the other. Here's an example of a compound expression:

  x * y * z

- In this particular example, the order in which the expression is evaluated is unimportant because the results of multiplication is independent of order; the outcome is always the same, no matter what order you apply the multiplications. However, this is not true of all expressions. For example, the following expression gives different results, depending on whether you perform the addition or the division operation first:

  x + y / 100 //ambiguous

- You can specify exactly how you want an expression to be evaluated, using balanced parentheses—(and). For example, to make the previous expression unambiguous, you could write:

  (x + y)/ 100 //unambiguous, recommended

- If you don't explicitly indicate the order in which you want the operations in a compound expression to be performed, the order is determined by the *precedence* assigned to the operators in use within the expression. Operators with a higher precedence get evaluated first. For example, the division operator has a higher precedence than does the addition operator. Thus, the two following statements are equivalent:

  x + y / 100

  x + (y / 100) //unambiguous, recommended

- When writing compound expressions, you should be explicit and indicate with parentheses which operators should be evaluated first. This pratice will make your code easier to read and to maintain.

3.5 Control Structures, decision making statements

3.5.1 Control Structures

- Normally statements in a Java program are executed sequentially i.e. in the order in which they are written. This is called sequential execution. Transferring control to a desired location in a program is possible through Control structure. Java allows mainly kinds of control structures, which include:

1. **Sequential Control Structures**

   o In sequential control structure program statements are executed from **top to bottom.**

Example:

```
sum=number1+number2;
average=sum/2;
System.out.println("Sum="+sum);
System.out.println("Average="+average);
```

2. Decision Control Structures

- Decision Control Structure allows **selection** of specific sections of code to be executed. There are **two types of decision control structures** simple if and Nested if.
  - **Simple Decision control structure**

```
int score=30;
if(score<75){
System.out.println("Failed");
}
else{
System.out.println("Passed");
}
```

  - **Nested Decision control structure**

```
int score=30;
if(score<75){
   System.out.println("Failed");
}
else if (score<85){
   System.out.println("Average");
}
else if (score<90){
   System.out.println("Above Average");
}
else{
   System.out.println("Excellent");
}
```

3. Repetition Control Structures

Repetition control structure allows the **repetition** of an action while some condition remains true.

There are two **types of repetition control structures** Sentinel loop and Counting loop.

- **do..while loop**

Example 1:

```
do{
   System.out.println("Try Again?:");
   try{tryAgain=br.readLine();}
   catch(Exception ex){System.out.println("Error:
                                                  "+ex.getMessage());}
   }while(tryAgain.equals("y"));
```

Example 2:

```
do{
    ctr++;
}while (ctr<=10);
```

- **while loop**

  Example 1:

```
String tryAgain="y";
while(tryAgain.equals("y")){
    System.out.println("Try Again?:");
    try{tryAgain=br.readLine();}
    catch(Exception ex){System.out.println("Error:
                                            "+ex.getMessage());}
}
```

  Example 2:

```
int ctr=0;
while(ctr<=10){
        ctr++;
}
```

- **for loop**

```
 for (int ndx = 0; ndx < 10; ndx++) {
        System.out.println(ndx);
}
```

3.5.2 Decision Making Statements

3.5.2.1 Introduction

- A Java program is a set of statements which are normally executed sequentially. In some situations, we have to change the order of execution of statements. The order will be executed based on some condition or decision.
- Java supports two decision making statements If and Switch.

3.5.2.2 If Statement

Simple If Statement:

- It is a powerful decision making statement to control the flow of execution of statements. It can be used to route a program execution through two different paths.

```
if (condition) statement1;
else statement2;
```

- Here statement 1 or 2 can be a single statement or a block of statements enclosed in curly braces. The condition returns a boolean value. 'else' clause is optional. Both statements will not be executed any time.
- For example,

```
if (marks >= 70)  grade = "First class with Distinction";
if (balance <= 0)
  message("Amount cannot be withdrawn");
else
  message("You can withdraw an amount");
```

Program 3.5: Program that demonstrates if-else control statement

```
class IfElse
{
   public static void main(String[] args)
   {
      boolean learning = true;
      if (learning)
      {
         System.out.println("Nirali Prakashan");
      }
      else
      {
         System.out.println("Pragati Prakashan");
      }
   }
}
```

Output:

```
Nirali Prakashan
```

Nested If Statement:

- When a series of decisions are involved, we may have to use more than one If-Else statement in nested form.
- For example,

```
if ( i == 10) {
  if ( j >= 5)
    { a = b; }
  else {a =  c;}
else a = d;
```

Else – If Ladder:

- This is another way of putting Ifs together.
- The If statements are executed top-down. For example,

Program 3.6: Program that demonstrates if-elseif control statement.

```
class NumberInWordDemo
{
   public static void main(String args[])
   {
int x = 3;
if(x < 0)
System.out.println("x is a negative number having value " + x);
else if(x == 0)
System.out.println("x is a zero number having value " + x);
else if(x == 1)
System.out.println("x is a positive number having value One");
else if(x == 2)
System.out.println("x is a positive number having value Two");
else if(x == 3)
System.out.println("x is a positive number having value Three");
   }
}
```

Output:

```
   x is a positive number having value
```

3.5.2.3 Switch Statement

- Java has built-in multi way decision statement known as **'switch'**. The switch statement tests the value of the given variable against a list of case values. If the match is found, code written for that case will be executed. Default statement is executed if none of the constant case value matches with the value of the variable.
- Break statement is used inside the switch statement to terminate the sequence.
- Break statement is optional. If you omit it, execution will continue into the next case.
- You can use switch as a part of case of an outer switch. This is called nested switch.
- No two case constants have same values in the switch statement.
- Switch is usually more efficient than a set of nested Ifs.

Program 3.7:

```
// A simple example of the switch.
class SampleSwitch {
public static void main(String args[]) {
for(int i=0; i<6; i++)
switch(i) {
case 0:
System.out.println("i is zero.");
break;
case 1:
System.out.println("i is one.");
break;
case 2:
System.out.println("i is two.");
break;
case 3:
System.out.println("i is three.");
break;
default:
System.out.println("i is greater than 3.");
}
}
}
```

Output:

```
i is zero.
i is one.
i is two.
i is three.
i is greater than 3.
i is greater than 3.
```

3.6 Arrays and its methods

- **'Array'** is a group of elements of same data type. All the elements stored in an array can be referred with the common name given for that array. Array can be created of any data type. It can have one or more dimensions. A specific element in an array is accessed by the index of an array.

One-dimensional Arrays

- To create an array in Java, you first create an array variable of desired type.

```
type var_name[]; // Array variable declaration.
```

Here, type defines which type of elements should be stored in an array.

For example, `int runs_scored[];`

- This is just the declaration saying that runs_scored is an array variable of type integer. No array actually exists. The value of the array is set to null. To link the actually physical array with the runs_scored variable, you have to use new operator. New operator allocates memory for arrays.

General Form:

```
ar_var = new type[size];
```

- Here, ar_var is the array variable that is to be linked with the physical array. Type is the data type of which elements should be stored in an array. Size is the number of elements in an array. The elements in the array that are allocated by new operator are initialized to zero automatically.

For example,

```
runs_scored = new int[10];
```

- Once this statement is executed, runs_scored array will refer to an array of 10 integer elements. All 10 elements are set to zero.
- All array index starts at 0. You can access a specific index of an array by specifying its index in a square bracket. For example,

```
runs_scored[4] = 94;
System.out.println(runs_scored[4]); //this line will display the
value stored at index 4.
```

- It is also possible to combine the declaration of array variable and allocation of an array as shown here:

```
int runs_scored[] = new int[10];
```

- Array can also be initialized when they are declared. Array initialize is a comma separated list of elements enclosed with curly braces.

For example,

```
runs_scored[] = {24, 45, 19, 56, 78};
```

- When this statement will be executed, an array will automatically be created large enough to hold these many number of elements enclosed in curly braces.
- So in the above example, an array will created of size 5.
- If you try to access the elements outside the range of an array, you will get runtime error as Java run-time system checks to see if all the array indices are in between the given range.

Program 3.8: A program for one dimensional array.

```
class Array {
public static void main(String args[]) {
int month_days[];
month_days = new int[12];
month_days[0] = 31;
month_days[1] = 28;
month_days[2] = 31;
month_days[3] = 30;
month_days[4] = 31;
month_days[5] = 30;
month_days[6] = 31;
month_days[7] = 31;
month_days[8] = 30;
month_days[9] = 31;
month_days[10] = 30;
month_days[11] = 31;
System.out.println("April has " + month_days[3] + " days.");
}
}
```

Output:

```
April has 30 days.
```

Multi-dimensional Arrays

- In Java, multi dimensional arrays are actually arrays of arrays. To declare multi-dimensional array variable, specify each index using a square bracket.

  For example,

  ```
  int twoD[][] = new int[3][3];
  ```

- This above statement allocates 3 X 3 two dimensional array (3 rows and 3 columns).
- It is also possible to initialize multi dimensional array.

  ```
  int twoD[][]={{1, 2, 3}, {4, 5, 6}, {7, 8, 9}}; // 3 X 3 matrix.
  ```

Program 3.9: A program for two dimensional array.

```
// Demonstrate a two-dimensional array.
class TwoDArray {
public static void main(String args[]) {
int twoD[][]= new int[4][5];
int i, j, k = 0;
for(i=0; i<4; i++)
for(j=0; j<5; j++) {
twoD[i][j] = k;
k++;
}
for(i=0; i<4; i++) {
for(j=0; j<5; j++)
System.out.print(twoD[i][j] + " ");
System.out.println();
}
}
}
```

Output:

```
0 1 2 3 4
5 6 7 8 9
10 11 12 13 14
15 16 17 18 19
```

3.7 Garbage Collection and finalize() Method

3.7.1 Garbage Collection

- Objects are dynamically allocated by using **'new'** operator. Now one question arises is that how these objects are destroyed and the memory is released for later reallocation. In some of the languages, dynamically allocated objects must be released manually with the help of delete operator.
- Java has a different approach while de-allocating objects. The de-allocation is done automatically. This technique is called **'Garbage Collection'**. When no reference to an

object exists, the object is assumed to be no longer required. The memory occupied by the object is released. All this is done automatically. No explicit deletion of an object is done in Java.

- Garbage Collection can not be forced explicitly. It occurs periodically if at all required during the program execution. We may request JVM for **garbage collection** by calling **System.gc()** method. But This does not guarantee that JVM will perform the garbage collection. This method is present in**System** and **Runtime** class.

Advantages of Garbage Collection:

1. Programmer doesn't need to worry about dereferencing an object.
2. It is done automatically by JVM.
3. Increases memory efficiency and decreases the chances for memory leak.

3.7.2 finalize() Method

- Sometimes an object needs to perform some action before it is destroyed. For example, if an object holds a non-java resournce like file handle, then you may want to make sure that these resources are freed before an object is destroyed. To handle such kind of situations, Java provides mechanism called **'finalization'**. To do this, you simple need to define finalize() method in a class. Java calls that method, whenever it is about to reclaim an object of that class. Inside the finalize() method, you can specify the required action to be taken care of. The **garbage collector** is a low priority thread that runs periodically, checking for objects that are no longer referenced.
- The finalize() method has a general form:

```
protected void finalize()
{
 //finalize() code is placed here.
}
```

- The keyword **protected** is an access specifier that prevents access to finalize() method outside its class. This method is called just prior to garbage collection.
- finalize() method is not called when an object goes out of scope.

Practice Questions

1. Write a short note on Identifiers in java.
2. What do you mean by keyword in java? List all the keywords in brief.
3. Explain the following terms.
   (a) Data Types in Java
   (b) Java Coding Conventions
   (c) Types of Control Structures

4. Define Java Expression. What are the common Java expressions?
5. Write a short note on: Importance of Control Structures in Java.
6. what is decision making structure in java? Explain following terms with example.
   (a) If Statement
   (b) Switch Statement
7. Explain Array's in JAVA with example.
8. Write a short note on: Garbage collection in java.
9. State finalize method in Java.
10. When finalize method is called in Java?

■■■

Chapter 4...

JAVA CLASSES

Contents ...

4.1 Define Class with Instance Variables and Methods

4.1.1 Defining a Class with Instance Variables

- When you define a class, you define its exact form and nature. You can define the data it contains (Properties) and the code that operates on the data (Methods). This type of grouping of attributes and methods is called as **'Encapsulation'**. A class is declared by the keyword **'class'**. A simple form of class definition is shown here:

```
class classname {
type instance_var1;
type instance_var2;
...
type instance_varN;
type method1(paralist){
body of method1 }
...
type method(paralist) {
Body of method }
}
```

- The data or variables defined within the class are called **'instance variables'**. The data type of a variable can be any primitive type. Type of method is the return type which will be the type of value returned by method. The instance variables and methods collectively are known as **'members of the class'**.

A simple class example.

```
class BoxDimension
{
   double width;
   double height;
   double depth;
}
```

4.1.2 Introducing Methods

- We have already seen, classes usually consists of instance variables and methods.
- The general form of a method:

```
type methodname(paralist) {
Body of method }
```

- Here type specifies type of data returned by the method. This can be any valid data type or even a class type that you have created. If method does not return a value, it will have a type void. The name is specified by *methodname.* This must be a legal identifier other than those already used in a current scope.

Method Returning a Value

- Methods that have a return type other than void will have a return statement that returns the value to the calling routine.
- The general form is as follows:

```
return value;  // the value is value returned.
```

Method that takes Parameter

- Paralist in a general form is a parameter list which is a pair of type and identifier separated by comma. Parameters are the arguments that are passed to the method when it is called. If the method has no parameters then the parameter list will be empty.

Program 4.1: A simple example of class defining methods

```
// This program includes a method PrintLine inside the MethodExample class.
public class MethodExample {
public static void PrintLine() {
System.out.println("This is a line of text.");
}
public static void main(String[] args) {
System.out.println("Start Here");
PrintLine();
System.out.println("Back to the Main");
PrintLine();
System.out.println("End Here");
}
}
```

Output:

```
Start Here
This is a line of text.
Back to the Main
This is a line of text.
End Here
```

4.2 Object Creation of Class

- When you create a class, you define new data type which can be used to create objects of that type. You can declare objects in two steps.
  1. You declare a variable of the class type. Its just a variable that refer to the object. It does not define an object.
  2. You acquire an actual copy of an object and assign it to the variable. This can be done with the help of new operator. **'new'** operator dynamically allocates memory for an object and returns a reference to it. This is nothing but the address of memory of the object.
- An object can be declared in one step like this:

```
Student s = new Student();
```

Where s is the object of class Student.

This can be done in two steps as follows:

```
Student s; // Variable declaration of type Student (Reference to object)
s = new Student(); // An object 's' is created of the type Student (Allocates memory to an object s).
```

- When the first line gets executed, s is declared as an object of Student. 's' contains value null as it is not pointing to the actual object yet. The next line actually allocates an object of Student class to 's'. After the second line gets executed, you can use 's' object as if it is the object of class Student.
- So the general form of object declaration is as follows:

```
class_var = new classname();
```

classname with parenthesis is called the **constructor** for the class. A constructor defines what occurs when an object is created. Constructor is an important part of class. Class can explicitly define its own constructor in its class definition. If no constructor is defined, Java will automatically provide a **default constructor**.

4.3 Accessing Member of Class

- In last chapter we learned to create objects, each object contain its own set of variables, we can assign values to these variables in order to use them in our program. Remember, all variables must be assigned values before they we used. Since we are outside the class, we cannot access the instance variables and the methods directly. To do this, we must use the concerned object and the dot operator as shown below:

```
objectname.variablename value;

objectname.methodname(parameter-list);
```

- Here objectname is the name of the object, variablename is the name of the instance variable inside the object that we wish to access, methodname is the method that we wish to call, and parameter-list is comma separated list of "actual values" (or expressions) that must match in type and number with the parameter list of the method name declared in the class. The instance variables of the Rectangle class may accessed and assigned values as follows:

rect1.length = 15;

rect1.width = 10;

rect2.length = 20;

rect2.width = 12;

- Note that the two objects rect1 and rect2 store different values as shown below:

	rec1		rec2
rect1.length	15	rec2.length	20
rect1.width	10	rec2.width	12

- This is one way of assigning values to the variables in the objects. Another way and more convenient way of assigning values to the instance variables is to use a method that is declared inside the class.

- In our case, the method getData can be used to do this work. We can call the getData method on any Rectangle object to set the values of both length and width. Here is the code segment to achieve this.

```
Rectangle recd = new Rectangle( ) ; // Creating an object
rect1.getData (15, 10);            // Calling the method using the
                                   object
```

- This code creates rect1 object and then passes in the values 15 and 10 for the x and y parameters of method getData. This method then assigns these values to length and width variables respectively. For sake of convenience, the method is again shown below:

```
void getData (int x, int y)
{
   length = x;
   width = y;
}
```

- Now that the object rect1 contains values for its variables, we can compute the area of the rectangle represented by rect1. This again can be done in two ways.
- The first approach is to access the instance variables using the dot operator and compute the a - That is,

```
int area1 = rect1_length * rect1.width;
```

- The second approach is to call the method rectArea declared inside the class. That is,

```
int areal - rectl.rectArea( ) ; //Calling the method
```

Program illustrates the concepts we discussed till now.

Program 4.2: Application of classes and objects class Rectangle.

```
class Rectangle
{
   int length, width;              //Declaration of variables
   void getData (int x, in y)      //Definition of method
   {
      length = x;
      width = y;
   }
```

```
    int rectArea                       //Definition of another method
    {
        int area = length * width;
        return (area);
    }
}
class RectArea                         // Class with main method
{
    public static void main (String args[ ])
    {
        int area1, area2;
        Rectangle rectl = new Rectangle();    //Creating objects
        Rectangle rect2 = new Rectangle();
        Recti.length = 15;                    //Accessing variables
        reeLl.width = 10;
        areal = rect1.length                  rect1.width;
        rect 2.getData (20, 12) ;             // Accessing methods
        area2 = rect2.rectArea();
        System.out.println("Area1 — " + area1);
        System.out.println("Area2 = " area2);
```

Output:

```
Areal = 150
Area2 = 240
```

4.4 Argument Passing

- Any valid Java data type can be passed as an argument into a method. These can be primitive data types such as int and float, or reference data types such as objects or arrays. Both primitive and reference data type arguments are passed by value; however. the impact on the calling method can be different depending on the passed data type.
- Where a primitive data type argument is being passed, the value of the argument is copied into the method's parameter. If the method changes the value of the parameter, then this change is local to the method and does not affect the value of the argument in the calling program. The following example illustrates this. The Employee class consists of just one method, increment, which adds W to a supplied argument of type int.

Program 4.3:

Employee

```
class Employee
{
    public void increment(int amount)
    {
        amount = amount + 10;
        System.out.println("amount within method:" + amount);
    }
}
```

The CreateEmployee application sets the variable amount to 500 and invokes the Employee class increment method with &Iowa as an argument.

CreateEmployee

```
class CreatEmployee
{
    public static void maie(String[] args)
    int amount = 500:
    Employee feed = new Employee();
    fred,increment(ammunt);
    System.out.println("amount outside method:" + amount);
}
```

The output of running the CreateEmployee application follows:

```
java CreateEmployee
amount within method: 510
amount outside method: 500
```

- So although the increment method has increased the amount to 510 the amount in the calling program remains at 500,
- If, however, the argument passed to a method is a reference data type, the memory address of the argument is copied to the method's parameter. Consequently, both the calling method argument and the called method parameter reference the same object. If the method changes the value of this object, then this change is reflected in the calling program. To illustrate this the second version of Employee has the increment method modified to accept an array argument, salary, of type int. The first element of salary is incremented by 10.

Employees – Second version

```
class Employee
{
   public void increment (int[] salary)
   {
      salary[0] = salary[0] + 10'
      System.out.println("amount within method: " +
      salary([0]);
   }
}
```

- In the second version of the CreateEmployee application, the argument passed to the increment method is an array, fredsSalary.

CreateEmployee - Second version

```
class CreateEmployee
{
   public static void main(String[] args)
   {
      int fredsSalary[] = new int [1];
      Employee fred = new Employee();
      fredsSalary[0] - 500;
      fred.increment(fredsSalary);
      System.out.println('amount outside method:"
      + fredsSalary[0]):
   }
}
```

The output of running CreateEmployee will now be as follows:

```
java CreateEmployee
amount within method: 510
amount outside method.: 510
```

4.5 Constructors

4.5.1 Introduction

- It is difficult to initialize all the class variables of the class each time an object of that class is created. If we can have all the setup done at the time when the object is created, it would be much simpler and easier. Java allows objects to be initialized when they are created. This automatic initialization is carried out with the help of constructor.

- Once defined, constructors are automatically called immediately after the object is created and before the new operator completes its job.
- Constructor initializes object as soon as it is created.
- It has the same name as that of the class.
- Constructors are syntactically similar to methods. They do not have return type including void.

4.5.2 Parameterized Constructors

- Objects may have different values. For example, two students should not have same roll numbers. So object must be unique and different. We need some way to initialize the variables with different values.
- We need a constructor which assigns the different values to variables when objects are created. Java provides constructor that takes arguments whose values will be assigned to variables.
- Constructors that have arguments are known as **'Parameterized constructor'**.

Program 4.4: A program that demonstrates the use of parameterized constructor.

```
class Student4{
 int id;
 String name;

 Student4(int i,String n){
 id = i;
 name = n;
 }
 void display(){System.out.println(id+" "+name);}

 public static void main(String args[]){
 Student4 s1 = new Student4(1,"Ameya");
 Student4 s2 = new Student4(2,"Shubhankar");
 s1.display();
 s2.display();
 }
}
```

Output:

```
1. Ameya
2. Shubhankar
```

4.5.3 Overloaded Constructors

- Java allows a class to have more than one method or constructor with the same name as long as the method signature or constructor signature differs in the parameter list. Parameters may differ in number of parameters or data type of parameters.
- Compiler chooses the correct form of constructor depending on the parameters provided in the constructor invocation. This technique is known as **'Overloaded Constructors'**.
- The class may contain more than one constructor. There is no limit on the number of constructors in a class.

Program 4.5: A program that demonstrates the use of overloaded constructors.

```
class Student5{
 int id;
 String name;
 int age;
 Student5(int i,String n){
 id = i;
 name = n;
 }
 Student5(int i,String n,int a){
 id = i;
 name = n;
 age=a;
 }
 void display(){System.out.println(id+" "+name+" "+age);}

 public static void main(String args[]){
 Student5 s1 = new Student5(1,"Ashwin");
 Student5 s2 = new Student5(2,"Gaurinandan",25);
 s1.display();
 s2.display();
}
}
```

Output:

```
1 Ashwin 0
2 Gaurinandan 25
```

4.6 Method Overloading

- Java allows a class to have more than one method or constructor with the same name, as long as the method or constructor signature (method or constructor declaration) differ in the parameters either the number of parameters or the data type of the parameter.
- The compiler choose the correct method or constructor based on the parameters provided in the method call or constructor invocation. This technique is called **overloading**.

What is Overloading for? Why is Overloading Useful?

- There are many times when you will be creating several methods that perform closely related operation under different conditions.
- For example, consider a simple method that is used to output a textual representation of its argument. This method could be:

```
println()
```

- Now suppose that you need a different print method for printing each of the int, float and string types. This is reasonable, because the various data types require different formatting and different handling.
- You could create three methods called printInt(), printFloat() and printString(). However, this is tedious as for every data type we should have the respective print method, and user has to remember number of the methods for every data type.
- The java programming language, along with several other programming languages allows you to reuse a method name for more than one method. This works only if there is something in the circumstances under which the call is made that distinguishes the method that is actually needed.
- In the case of three print methods, this distinction is based on the number and type of the arguments. By using the same method name, we end up with following methods.

```
public void println(int i)
public void println(float i)
public void println(String i)
```

- When you write code to call one of these methods, the appropriate method is chosen according to the type of argument or arguments you supply.
- So it is quite useful, for thinking about method names and for improving program readability, to be able to use one method name for several related methods requiring different implementations.

- However, you should restrict your use of overloaded method names to situations where the methods really are performing the same basic function with different data sets. Methods that perform different jobs should have different names.
- Two rules apply to overloaded methods:
  1. The argument list of the method must differ enough to allow unambiguous (confusion) determination of the proper method call. Normal widening promotions (For example: float to double) might be applied.
  2. The return type of the method can be different, but it is not sufficient for the return type to be only difference. The argument list of the overloaded method must differ.

Method Overloading

- Overloaded method is the method which has the same name but number of arguments may be different or if number of arguments are same then their data type must be different. Compiler will call the proper method depending on the type of argument and number of the arguments.
- If the two methods have same name, number of arguments, data type then compiler will issue ambiguity error. Overloaded method in java is example of polymorphism.
- Polymorphism is desirable feature of programming languages because it allows you to use the same methods for various input types.
- A polymorphic method is one that acts the same way on more than one input. When you use polymorphism through overloading you write a separate method for each input parameter type and give all these methods same name.
- For example:

```
1. void area(int radius)
   {
   calculate area of circle;
   }
2. void area(int base, int height)
   {
   calculate area of triangle;
   }
3. void area(int width, int length, int height)
   {
   calculate volume of cube;
   }
```

- When these three methods are used in one class depending on the input they will perform the operation.
    - The method No. 1 will be called when you call method with one input value of type int.
    - No. 2 will be called when you call method with two input values of type int.
    - No. 3 will be called when you call method with three input values of type int.

Program 4.6: Program for overloading method.

```
class Area
{
 double a;
Area()          // constructor
   {
     a=0;
   }
void cal_Area(int r)
{
    double pi=3.14f;
  a=pi*r*r;
  System.out.println(" The area of circle is =" +a);
}
void cal_Area(int b,int h)
{
   a=0.5*b*h;
  System.out.println(" The area of triangle is =" +a);
}
void cal_Area(int w,int h,int l)
{
   a=w*h*l;
  System.out.println(" The volume of cube is =" +a);
}
public static void main(String[] args) {
Area a1= new Area();
a1.cal_Area(2);   //calls method cal_Area(int r)
a1.cal_Area(4,5);    //calls method cal_Area(int r,int h)
a1.cal_Area(6,4,1); //calls method cal_Area(int w,int h, int l)
}
}
```

Output:

```
The area of circle is =12.56
The area of triangle is =10
The area of cube is = 24
```

☞ OVERLOADED METHOD

- A class can have more than one method with same name.
- Overloaded methods have different number of argument.
- If number of arguments is same then their data type must be different.
- It may have different return type.
- Performs widening of data types automatically
- Compiler will decide which method to be called on the basis of number of argument and their data types.

Program 4.7: Program for overloading.

```
class OverTest
{
   void a(byte a)
   {
   System.out.println(" method with byte called");
   }
   void a(short a)
   {
   System.out.println(" method with short called");
   }
   void a(long a)
   {
   System.out.println(" method with long called");
   }
   void a(int a)
   {
   System.out.println(" method with int called");
   }
   void a(float a)
   {
   System.out.println(" method with float called");
   }
   void a(double a)
   {
   System.out.println(" method with double called");
   }
   public static void main(String args[])
   {
   OverTest ob1 = new OverTest();
   OverTest ob2 = new OverTest();
   ob1.a(2);
   ob2.a(3.14);
   }
   }
```

Output:

```
   method with int called
   method with double called
```

- Keep in mind that by default java keeps every whole number as int and every number which contain the decimal point as double, so here it call method with integer and double argument respectively.
- To call a method having byte argument you must first convert the int value to byte by explicit casting as,
```
ob1.a((byte)2);
```
- To call a method having short argument you must first convert the int value to short by explicit casting as,
```
ob1.a((short)2);
```
- To call a method having long argument you must suffix the value with 'L' as,
```
ob1.a(2L);
```
- To call a method having float argument must suffix the value with 'f' as,
```
ob2.a(3.14f);
```
- Notice in the above example that there is no method with int as argument and when method is called on integer value as,
```
ob1.a(2)
```
here, java will not find the match so it will convert the int value to long and then it calls method having long argument.
- Conversion of the data type will takes place from the data type having low capacity to high as shown below.

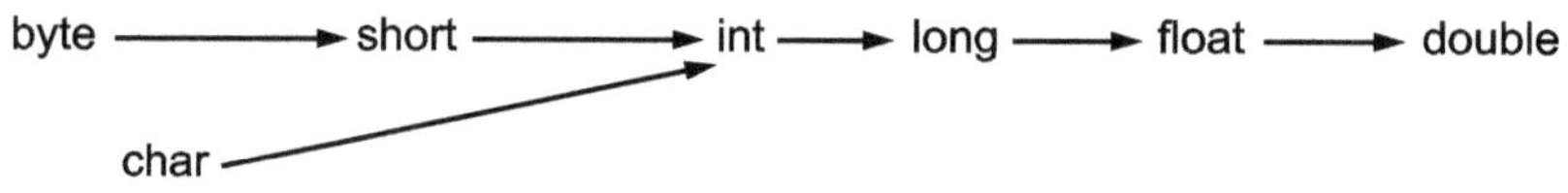

Fig. 4.1: Representing conversion of data type

4.7 Static Data, Static Methods, Static Blocks

4.7.1 Static Keyword

- You know that when a object (instance) of a class is created, if class has three variables p, q, r, in a class then all the objects of that class have their own copy of this variable separately.

```
class X
{
    int p, q, r;
}
class Y
{
    public static void main(String args[])
    {
        X ob1 = new X();
        X ob2 = new X();
        X ob3 = new X();
    }
}
```

- This three objects can be represented as,

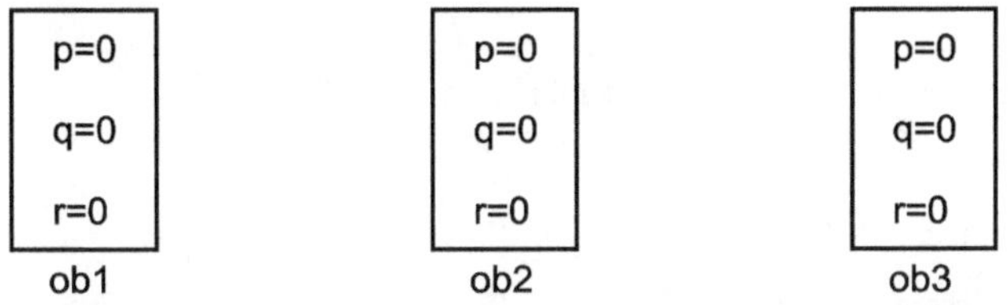

Fig. 4.2: Representing the various objects with variable

- In order to work with variable of the particular object, we must make a link between object and the variable as,

  ob1.p // p variable of the object.

- Here, if we want to perform operation on variable p, q or r then we need to create the object first, then and then only we can perform operation on this variables.
- There will be times when you will want to define a class member (variable or method) that will be used independently of any object of that class, i.e. can be used without creating the object. Such variables or methods are declared to be **static.**

4.7.1.1 Static Data

- Data members of a java class declared static are called class members.
- A class will be loaded before the creation of object. So if we are creating number of objects of class then before the creation of object a static variable will be created. Such variables will be shared between all the objects.
- Static data members are associated with class rather than object.
- So if some objects have some variables which are common then these variables or methods must be declared **static**. To create a **static** variable, precede its declaration with keyword **static.** Static variables need not be called on any object. As they are common.
- For example:

```
int h;            //normal variable
static int h;     //static variable
```

- When a data member is declared as **static**, it can be accessed before any object of its class are created. The most common example of **static** is **main()**. **main()** is declared as **static** because it must be called before any object of that class in which it is declared exist.

Program for static variables.

```
class X
{
    int p,q;
    static int r;
}
```

```
class Y
{
    public static void main(String args[])
    {
        X ob1 = new X();
        X ob2 = new X();
        X ob3 = new X();
    }
}
```

- In the above Program the variable **p** and **q** are declared as int variable whereas the variable **r** is declared as **static** variable. As mentioned above the static variable will be common between all the objects. It can be represented as,

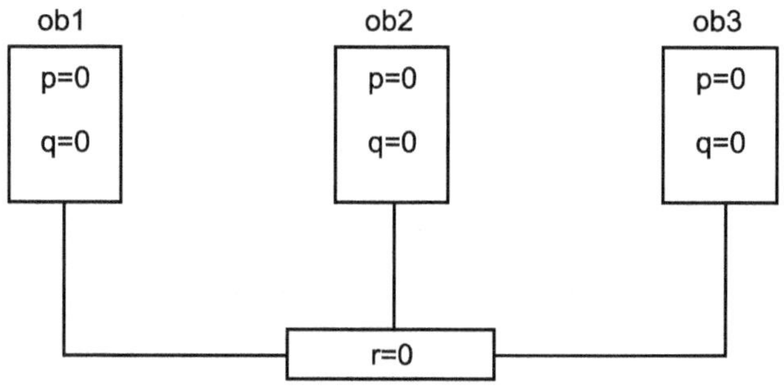

Fig. 4.3: Representing objects with static variable

- Just see the above Fig. 4.3. The static variable is common between all three objects. When we are accessing any variable as **p** we cannot access it directly without the reference of the object because **p** exist in all three objects. So to access the value of **p** we must link it with the name of the object.
- But the **r** is **static** variable and it is common between all the objects so we can access it directly. But when we are accessing it outside the class in which it is declared, we must link it with the name of the class i.e. with X as,

```
X.r=10;
```

Static Blocks:

- The instance variable of class are always initialised by the constructor. Java provide a special constructor that is used to initialise static variables.
- This special construct is known as *static initialiser.*
- Static initialiser is also known as static block. Which can be defined as:

```
static
{
    static variable =value;
}
```

- When class is loaded very first, the JVM will create the static variable and automatically calls static initialiser which assigns some value to the variable and then it creates object.

```
class X
{
   int p,q;
   static int r;
   static          //static initializer
  {
    r=100;
  }
}
class Y
{
   public static void main(String args[])
   {
      X ob1 = new X();
      X ob2 = new X();
      X ob3 = new X();
   }
}
```

☞**STATIC INITIALIZERS**

- A class can contain code in a static block that does not exist within a method body.
- Static block code executes only once, when the class is loaded.
- A static block is usually used to initialize static (class) attributes.

4.7.1.2 Static Method

- As we can declare the variable as **static,** very similar way the methods can be declared as **static.**
- To create a **static** method precede its declaration with keyword **static.**

```
static void display()
{
   //display something
}
```

- But there are some restrictions with the **static** method.
  1. Static method can call only other **static** methods, and
  2. They must only access **static** variable.

- If you need to do some computation in order to initialize your **static** variable, you can declare a **static** block which get executed exactly once when the class first loaded.
- Let us see one example which **calculates how many objects are created.**

Program 4.8: Program for calculation of how many objects are created.

```
class Countobj
  {
   static int count;     //static variable
   Countobj()
   {
   ++count;
   }
   static                //static initializer
   {
         System.out.println("Static block called");
         count=0;
   }
   static void display()   //static method
   {
      System.out.println("Object created are" + count);
   }
   public static void main(String args[])
   {
      Countobj.display();
      Countobj ob1= new Countobj();
      Countobj ob2= new Countobj();
      Countobj ob3= new Countobj();
      Countobj.display();
   }
}
```

Output:

```
object created are  0
Static block called
object created are 3
```

☞ **THE STATIC KEYWORD**

- The **static** keyword is used as a modifier on variables, methods.
- The static keyword declares the attribute or method is associated with the class as a whole rather than any particular instance of that class.
- Thus, **static members** are often called "**class members**," such as "**class attributes**" or "**class methods**".
- Static variables or methods are always invoked with the name of class in which they are declared.
- When the class is loaded the static variable will be created first.
- Static variable or methods are independent of object so they can be called before the creation of object of class.

4.8 this Keyword

- Sometimes a method will need to refer to the object that invoked it. To allow this, Java defines **'this'** keyword. **'this'** keyword can be used inside any method to refer to the current object. **'this'** is always a reference to the object on which the method was invoked.

  "this" keyword helps us to avoid naming conflicts.
- Here are few important points related to using this keyword

  this keyword represent current instance of class.
- You can synchronize on this in synchronized block in Java

  this keyword can be used to call overloaded constructor in java. if used than it must be first statement in constructor this() will call no argument constructor and this(parameter) will call one argument constructor with appropriate parameter.
- The following are different ways to use java this keyword
  1. Using with instance variable
  2. Using with Constructor
  3. Pass / Return current instance

1. Using With Instance Variable

- Using this keyword inside a method or constructor it will use instance variable instead of local variable, in the absence of this keyword it will use local variable,
- In the below example, parameter (formal arguments) and instance variables of class Student are same that is why we are using this keyword to distinguish between local variable and instance variable.

Program 4.9:

```
public class ThisExample {
    public static void main(String[] args) {
    Student student = new Student("Rockey", 65);
    }
}
class Student {
public int marks;
public String name;

// instance variable is used when creating object
public Student(String name, int marks) {
    this.name = name;
    this.marks = marks;
    System.out.println("Students name:"+this.name);
    System.out.println("Marks:"+this.marks);
}
}
```

Output:

```
Students name:Rockey
Marks:65
```

2. Using With Constructor

- The this() constructor call can be used to invoke the current class constructor (constructor chaining). This approach is better if you have many constructors in the class and want to reuse that constructor.
- Using this keyword inside constructor like following:

Program 4.10: //Program of this() constructor call (constructor chaining)

```
class Student13{
 int id;
 String name;
 Student13(){System.out.println("default constructor is invoked");}

 Student13(int id,String name){
 this ();//it is used to invoked current class constructor.
 this.id = id;
 this.name = name;
 }
```

```
void display(){System.out.println(id+" "+name);}
public static void main(String args[]){
Student13 e1 = new Student13(44,"Mangesh");
Student13 e2 = new Student13(222,"Rajesh");
e1.display();
e2.display();
}
}
```

Output:

```
default constructor is invoked
default constructor is invoked
44 Mangesh
222 Rajesh
```

3. Pass / Return Current Instance

- The this keyword can also be passed as an argument in the method. It is mainly used in the event handling. Let's see the example:

Program 4.11:

```
class S2{
void m(S2 obj){
System.out.println("method is invoked");
}
void p(){
m(this);
}

public static void main(String args[]){
S2 s1 = new S2();
s1.p();
}
}
```

Output:

```
method is invoked
```

- We can return the this keyword as an statement from the method. In such case, return type of the method must be the class type (non-primitive). Let's see the example:

Syntax:

```
return_type method_name(){
return this;
}
```

Program 4.12:

```
class A{
A getA(){
return this;
}
void msg(){System.out.println("Hello java");}
}

class Test1{
public static void main(String args[]){
new A().getA().msg();
}
}
```

Output:

```
Hello java
```

4.9 Nested & Inner classes

- It is possible to define a class inside another class. Such class is known as nested class. The scope for the nested class is bounded by the enclosing class. Therefore, if class B is defined inside class A, then class B does not have its own independent existence.
- A nested class can have an access to the members of the class in which it is nested.
- There are two types of nested classes: static and non-static.
- Static nested class has static modifier applied. It must access the members of its enclosing class with the help of objects as it is declared static. Static nested classes are very rarely used.
- The most important type of nested class is 'inner class'. An inner class is a non-static nested class. It has access to all of the variables and methods of its outer class. The following example illustrates how to define and use an inner class.

Program 4.13: Program that illustrates use of inner class.

```
class OuterClass
{
int outer_p = 50;
  void test()
  {
    InnerClass i = new InnerClass();
    i.disp();
  }
```

```
    class InnerClass
    {
      void disp()
      {
        System.out.println("Display outer_p: "+ outer_p);
      }
    }
  }
  class InnerClassDemo
  {
   public static void main(String args[])
   {
    OuterClass o = new OuterClass();
    o.test();
   }
  }
```

Output:

```
Display outer_p: 50
```

- In the above program, the InnerClass is defined within the scope of class OuterClass. Therefore any code in class InnerClass can access the variable outer_p which is a member of OuterClass. The main method of InnerClassDemo creates an instance of class OuterClass and calls its test() method. This method creates an instance of InnerClass and calls the disp() method.

Important:

- Inner class has access to all of the members of the enclosing class. But the members of the inner class are known only within the scope of the inner class and may not be used by the outer class.
- The difference between nested class and inner class is Inner class is a part of nested class. Non-static nested classes are known as inner classes.

Advantage of java inner classes

- There are basically three advantages of inner classes in java. They are as follows:
  1. Nested classes represent a special type of relationship that is it can access all the members (data members and methods) of outer class including private.
  2. Nested classes are used to develop more readable and maintainable code because it logically group classes and interfaces in one place only.
  3. Code Optimization: It requires less code to write.

4.10 Wrapper Classes

- Each of Java's eight primitive data types has a class dedicated to it. These are known as wrapper classes, because they "wrap" the primitive data type into an object of that class. The wrapper classes are part of the java.lang package, which is imported by default into all Java programs.
- The wrapper classes in java servers two primary purposes
  - To provide mechanism to 'wrap' primitive values in an object so that primitives can do activities reserved for the objects like being added to ArrayList, Hashset, HashMap etc. collection.
  - To provide an assortment of utility functions for primitives like converting primitive types to and from string objects, converting to various bases like binary, octal or hexadecimal, or comparing various objects.
- All Wrapper classes are immutable like the String class. Once created, cannot be changed and rather than being changed, a whole new object is created reflecting that change
- The following two statements illustrate the difference between a primitive data type and an object of a wrapper class:

```
int a = 35; Integer b= new Integer(44);
```

- The first statement declares an int variable named a and initializes it with the value 35. The second statement instantiates an Integer object. The object is initialized with the value 44 and a reference to the object is assigned to the object variable b.

Table 4.1

Primitive	Wrapper Class	Constructor Argument
boolean	boolean	Boolean or string
byte	byte	byte or string
char	character	char
int	integer	int or string
float	float	float, double or string
double	double	double or string
long	long	long or string
short	short	short or string

- Below is wrapper class hierarchy as per Java API.

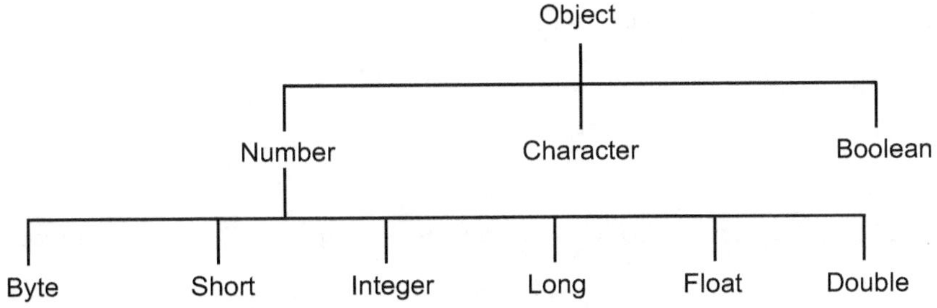

Fig 4.4: Wrapper Class Hierarchy

- The most common methods of the Integer wrapper class are summarized in below table. Similar methods for the other wrapper classes are found in the Java API documentation.

Primitive	Wrapper Class
parseInt(s)	returns a signed decimal integer value equivalent to string s
toString(i)	returns a new String object representing the integer i
byteValue()	returns the value of this Integer as a byte
doubleValue()	returns the value of this Integer as a double
floatValue()	returns the value of this Integer as a float
intValue()	returns the value of this Integer as an int
shortValue()	returns the value of this Integer as a short
longValue()	returns the value of this Integer as a long
int compareTo(int i)	Compares the numerical value of the invoking object with that of i. Returns 0 if the values are equal. Returns a negative value if the invoking object has a lower value. Returns a positive value if the invoking object has a greater value.
state int compare(int num1, int num2)	Compares the value of num1 and num2. Returns 0 if the values are equal. Returns a negative value if num1 is less than num2. Returns a positive value if num1 is greater than num2.
Boolean equals(Object intObj)	Returns true if the invoking Integer object is equivalent to intObj. Otherwise, it returns false.

Program 4.14: Primitive to Wrapper

```
public class WrapperExample1{
public static void main(String args[]){
//Converting int into Integer
int a=15;
Integer i=Integer.valueOf(a);//converting int into Integer
Integer j=a;//autoboxing, now compiler will write
                                        Integer.valueOf(a) internally
System.out.println(a+" "+i+" "+j);
}
}
```

Output:

```
15 15 15
```

Program 4.15: Wrapper to Primitive

```
public class WrapperExample2{
public static void main(String args[]){
//Converting Integer to int
Integer a=new Integer(3);
int i=a.intValue();//converting Integer to int
int j=a;    //unboxing, now compiler will write a.intValue()
            internally
System.out.println(a+" "+i+" "+j);
}
}
```

Output:

```
3 3 3
```

4.11 String

- String is nothing but a sequence of characters. Many languages implement string as an array of characters. But Java implements string as an object of type String. Once the String object is created, you cannot change the characters that comprise the string. But don't think it as a restriction. You can still perform all the operations on the String. The only thing is, whenever an operation is performed on the string and the string is modified, a new String object is created and all the changes are stored into that newly created object. This means that, the original version of the string remains unchanged. You must have had a question in mind, why all this??? This approach is used because, immutable and fixed strings are more efficient than changeable ones.

- A case where modifiable string is required, Java has two options: StringBuffer and StringBuilder classes. Both classes holds modifiable strings.
- String, StringBuffer and StringBuilder classes are part of java.lang package. All of these classes are final. This means that you cannot subclass these classes.

String Constructors:

1. String s1 = new String(); // Creates an empty string.
2. String s1 = new String(char chars[]); //Creates a string initialized by an array of characters.

   For example, Char ch[] = {'a', 'b', 'c', 'd'};

   String s1 = new String(ch); //Constructor initializes a string with 'abcd'.
3. String s1 = new String(char ch[], int strt_index, int no_chars); // Constructor that specifies a range of characters.

   Char ch[] = {'a', 'b', 'c', 'd'};

   String s1 = new String(ch,1,2); //initializes a string s1 with 'bc'.

   You can also construct a String object that contains the same string as another String object.
4. String s1 = new String(String obj);

   For example, char c[] = {'H', 'e', 'l', 'l', 'o'};

   String s1 = new String(c);

   String s2 = new String(s1);

   Both strings s1 and s2 will have the same contents as Hello.

String Literals

- We have seen several forms of constructors to create an instance of String class using new operator. But the easier way is to use a string literal. For each string literal, Java automatically constructs a String object.

  For example, String s1 = "Hello"; //Use of string literal.

String concatenation

- Java does not allow operators to be applied on String objects. One exception is '+' operator. This operator is overloaded as concatenation operator which concatenates two or more strings producing a resulting string. For example,

```
String s1 = "Hello";
String s2 = s1 + ", I am " + "Sonia..!!";
System.out.println(s2); //will print "Hello, I am Sonia..!!"
```

You can even concatenate strings with other types of data.

For example,

```
int a = 25;
System.out.println("I am " + a + "years old.");
```

Here, an int value of age is automatically converted into string. The above line will print as "I am 25 years old.".

- When Java converts some other type of data into String during concatenation, it calls valueOf() method defined by String class. This valueOf() method is overloaded for all primitive data types and Object. For primitive types, valueOf() returns a string which contains human readable form of the value. For objects, valueOf() calls toString() on the object.
- You can also override the default implementation of toString() method.

4.11.1 String Arrays

You can also create and use arrays that contain strings.

```
String book_names[] = new String[4];
```

The above string holds 4 string constants.

Program 4.16:

```
class StringOrdering
{
static String name[] = {"Nachiket", "Priyanka",
                                    "Chaitanya", "Ankush", "Gaurav"};
    public static void main(String [] args)
    {
        int size = name.length;
        String temp = null;
        for (int i = 0; i < size; i++)
        {
        for(int j = i+1; j < size; j++)
        {
        if (name[j].compareTo(name[i]) < 0)
        {
            //swaping two the strings
            temp = name[i];
            name[i] = name[j];
            name[j] = temp;
        }
        }
        }
```

```
            for (int i = 0; i < size; i++)
            {
            System.out.println(name[i]);
            }
        }
    }
```

Output:

```
Ankush
Chaitanya
Gaurav
Nachiket
Priyanka
```

4.11.2 String Methods

Following table shows various string functions along with its meaning and syntax.

Table 4.2

Method	Action performed
`s2 = s1.toLowerCase();`	Converts the string s1 to all lowercase
`s2 = s1.toUppercCase();`	Converts the string s1 to all Uppercase
`s2 = s1.replace('x', 'y');`	Replace all appearances of x with y
`s2 = s1.trim();`	Remove white spaces at the beginning and end of the string s1
`s1.equals(s2)`	Returns 'true' if s1 is equal to s2
`s1.equalsIgnoreCase(s2)`	Returns 'true' if s1 = s2, ignoring the case of characters
`s1.length()`	Gives the length of s1
`s1.ChartAt(n)`	Gives nth character of s1
`s1.compareTo(s2)`	Returns negative if s1 < s2, positive if s1 > s2, and zero if s1 is equal s2
`s1.concat(s2)`	Concatenates s1 and s2
`s1.substring(n)`	Gives substring starting from n^{th} character
`s1.substring(n, m)`	Gives substring starting from n^{th} character upto m^{th} (not including m^{th})
`String.ValueOf(p)`	Creates a string object of the parameter p (simple type or object)
`p.toString()`	Creates a string representation of the object p
`s1.indexOf('x')`	Gives the position of the first occurrence of 'x' in the string s1
`s1.indexOf('x', n)`	Gives the position of 'x' that occurs after nth position in the string s1
`String.ValueOf(Varaible)`	Converts the parameter value to string representation

4.11.3 StringBuffer

- It is a peer class of String which provides most of the functionality of String class. Strings are fixed length and immutable. In contrast to this, a StringBuffer represents mutable, growable sequence of characters. We can insert characters or substrings to the given string. We can even append it to the given string.
  StringBuffer constructors
  StringBuffer() // Default Constructor reserves room for 16 characters
  StringBuffer(int size) // Size defines the size of the buffer.
  StringBuffer(String str) // Sets the initial contents of the buffer.
- Some of the important methods are summarized here.

Table 4.3: StringBuffer class methods

Method	Description
strBuff.length()	Returns current length of the StringBuffer.
strBuff.capacity()	Returns total allocated capacity of the string buffer.
strBuff.ensureCapacity(25)	Preallocates room for 25 characters. Sets the size of buffer.
strBuff.setLength(12)	Sets the size of the string within a StringBuffer object.
strBuff.append(str)	Concatenates the String str at the end of the string buffer object strBuff.
strBuff.insert(n, str)	Inserts the string str at the nth position.
strBuff.reverse()	Reverse the characters of the string buffer object strBuff.
strBuff.delete(4,7)	Delete 3 characters from 4 till 6 (7-1)from the string buffer object strBuff.
strBuff.replace(5,7,"Bye")	Replaces one set of characters with another set.

Practice Questions

1. What is the Base Class of all Classes?
2. How to Create Object in a Class? What it is called?
3. Explain the following terms.
   (a) Accessing Members of a Class
   (b) Argument Passing in Java
   (c) Parameterized Constructors
4. What are the Constructors in Java? Explain types of Constructor with suitable example.
5. Write a shortnote on following terms.
   (a) Static Data (b) Static Methods (c) Static Blocks
6. What is String Concatenation? Explain with any one example.
8. Explain Nested and Inner Classes in java with suitable example.
9. What do you mean by Wrapper Class?
10. List out methods of string with their use.
11. Give any one example of String Array.
12. When to use StringBuffer and String?

Programming Questions

1. Write a program to declare class Date which will take today's date as input and find tomorrow's and yesterday's date.
2. Write a program to create a class Student having variables roll_no and name. Declare the constructor and define two methods one will take input and other will display output. Create one object of class, take input and display output.
3. Write a program to create a class Employee having variables empid and name. Declare the constructor and define two methods one will take input and other will display output. Create one object of class, take input and display output.
4. Write a program to create a class Point having variables x_cord and y_cord. Declare the constructor and define two methods one will take input and other will display output. Create one object of class, take input and display output.
5. Write a program to create a class Book having variables title and author. Declare the constructor and define two methods one will take input and other will display output. Create one object of class, take input and display output.
6. Write a program to create a class Employee having variables empid, name and salary Declare the constructor and define two methods one will take input and other will display output. Create two object of class, take input and display details of employee having highest salary.
7. Write a program to create a class Book having variables title, author and price. Declare the constructor and define two methods one will take input and other will display output. Create two object of class, take input and display details of book having lowest price.
8. Write a program to define the class company containing data members "name" and grade. Create two object, Initialize and display the information of object having grade "A".
9. Write a program to create a class Account having variable accno, accname, balance. Define deposit() and withdraw() methods. Create one object of class and perform the operation.
10. Write a program to create a class Student having variables roll_no and name. Declare the constructor and define two methods one will take input and other will display output. Create array of five object of class, take input and display output.
11. Write a program to create a class Employee having variables Empid, name and salary. Declare the constructor and define two methods one will take input and other will display output. Create array of five object of class, take input and display details of employee having highest salary.
12. Write a program to create a class Point having variables x_cord and y_cord. Declare the constructor and define two methods one will take input and other will display output. Create array of five object of class, take input and display output.
13. Write a program to create a class Book having variables title, author and price. Declare the constructor and define two methods one will take input and other will display output. Create array of five objects, take input and display details of Book having highest price.
14. Write a program to display total no. of object created.

■■■

Chapter 5...

INHERITANCE

Contents ...

5.1 Super Class and Subclass

Super Class

- In Java, like in other object-oriented programming languages, classes can be derived from other classes. The derived class (the class that is derived from another class) is called a subclass. The class from which its derived is called the superclass. It is a class which gives a method or methods to a Java subclass. A Java class may be either a subclass, a superclass, both, or neither.

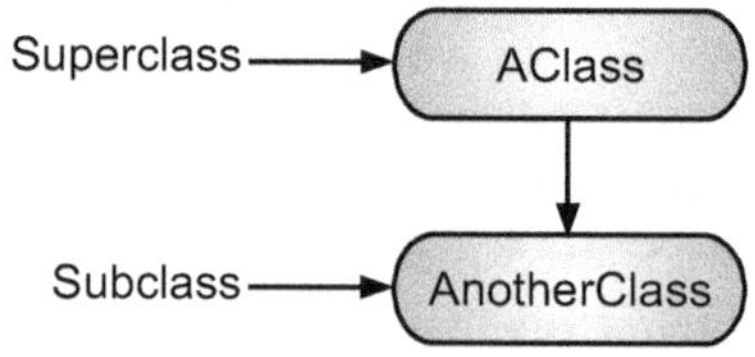

Fig. 5.1: SuperClass and SubClass

- The Cat class in the following example is the subclass and the Animal class is the superclass.

Program 5.1

```
public class Animal {
   public static void hide() {
     System.out.println("The hide method in Animal.");
  }
  public void override() {
      System.out.println("The override method in Animal.");
  }
}
public class Cat extends Animal {
  public static void hide() {
      System.out.println("The hide method in Cat.");
  }
  public void override() {
      System.out.println("The override method in Cat.");
  }
  public static void main(String[] args) {
      Cat myCat = new Cat();
      Animal myAnimal = (Animal)myCat;
      myAnimal.hide();
      myAnimal.override();
  }
}
```

Sub Class

- Subclass is created from existing class. In programming you often create a model of something (For example, an employee), and then need a more specialized version of that original model.
- For example, you might want a model for a manager. Clearly a manager actually is an employee, but an employee with additional features.
- Consider the following sample class declarations that demonstrate this:

```
public class Employee {
   public String name = "";
   public double salary;
   public Date birthDate;
   public String getDetailsl(){...} }
```

```
public class Manager {
    public String name = "";
    public double salary;
    public Date birthdate;
    public String department;
    public String getDetails(){....}
    }
```

- This example illustrates the duplication of data between the Manager class and the Employee class. Additionally, there could be a number of methods applicable to both Employee and Manager. Therefore, you need a way to create a new class from an existing class; this is called subclassing
- In object-oriented languages, special mechanisms are provided that allow the programmer to define a class in terms of a previously defined class.
- In the Java programming language, this is achieved by the keyword **extends** as follows:
  public class Manager extends Employee
  { private String department = " "; }

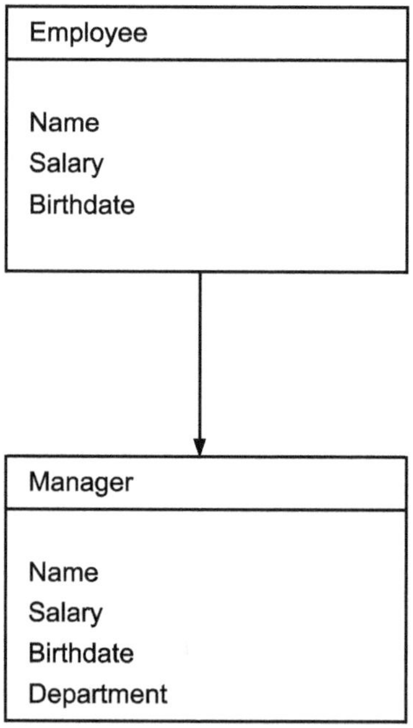

Fig. 5.2: SubClass

- Above Fig. 5.2, shows inheritance and is a relationship between Employee and Manager. Manager is–a Employee.
- To inherit a class, **extends** keyword is used. Say we have two classes **A** and **B**, and class **B** inherites the class **A**.

- Here, class **A** is called **superclass** because it is to be inherited and class **B** is called subclass. The following statement is used to inherit the super class by subclass.

  class B extends A

Program 5.2: Program for inheritance.

```
class A
{
    private int a,b;
    A()
    {
    a=10;
    b=20;
    }
    void display()
    {
    System.out.println("the value of a is" + a);
    System.out.println("the value of b is" +b);
    }
}
class B extends A       //B inherites A
{
private int k;
    B()
    {
    k=90;
    }
    void disp()
    {
    System.out.println("the value of k is" +k);
    }
}
class InheriteDemo
{
    public static void main(String args[])
    {
    A ob1 = new A();
    B ob2 = new B();
```

```
    System.out.println("The details of class A");
    ob1.display();
    System.out.println("The details of class B");
    ob2.display();
    ob2.disp();
     }
}
```

Output:

```
The details of class A
the value of a is10
the value of b is20
The details of class B
the value of a is10
the value of b is20
the value of k is90
```

- In above program, class **A** contains two variables **a, b** and one method **display()** which prints the value of **a** and **b**, and one constructor which initializes the variables **a** and **b**.
- The class **B** contains one variable **k** and one method **disp()** which displays the value of **k** and one constructor which initializes the variable **k.**
- In above program, class **A** is inherited by class **B** by keyword **extends.** When class **B** **extends** class **A** it gets all the properties of class **A i.e.** all the **variables** and **methods** declared as **public, protected.**
- Subclass includes all the members of the superclass but it cannot access those members of the superclass that have been declared as private. We can see it figuratively.

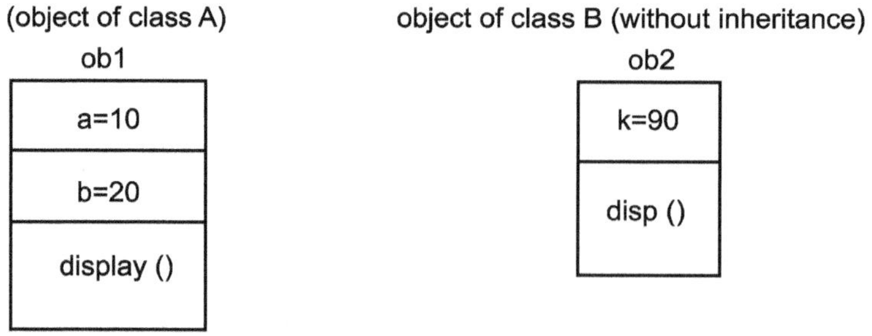

Fig. 5.3: Object Representation without Inheritance

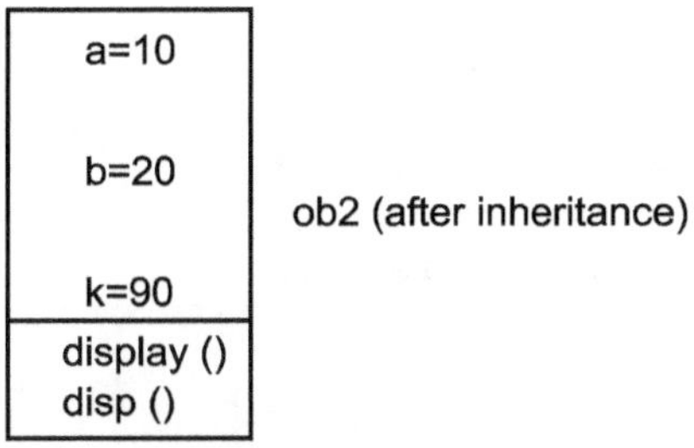

Fig. 5.4: Object After Inheritance

- As shown in the Fig. 5.4, the object of class **B ob2** has access to all the variables and methods of class **A.** So the statement is given below:

  ob2.display();

  it calls the display method of Class **A** because it is inherited by **B.**

Subclass Constructor

- A subclass can also explicitly call a constructor of its immediate super class. This is done by using the "super" constructor call. The subclass constructor uses the keyword "super" to invoke the constructor method of the superclass.
- A "super" constructor call in the constructor of a subclass, will result in the execution of relevant constructor from the super class, based on the arguments passed.
- The keyword "super" is used subject to the following conditions:
  1. "super" may only be used within a subclass constructor method.
  2. The call of superclass constructor must appear as the first statement within the subclass constructor.
  3. The parameters in the "super" call must match the order and type of the instance variable declared in the superclass.

Program 5.3: Program to illustrate the subclass constructor.

```
class A
{
    A( )
    {
        System.out.println("It is A()");
    }
```

```
    A (int x)
    {
        System.out.println("It is A (int x)");
    }
    int i = 10;
    public void f()
    {
    System.out.println("It is A f()");
    }
}
class B extends A   //class B is a subclass of class A
{
    int i = 20;
    B()
    {
        super(20);
        //this(10);
        System.out.println("It is B()");
        System.out.println("\t" + super.i);
        super.f();
        this.f();
    }
    B (int x)
    {
    }
    public void f()
    {
    System.out.println("It is B f()");
    }
    public static void main(String [ ] args)
    {
    B b = new B();
    }
}
```

5.2 Abstract Method and Classes

- Abstraction is a process of hiding the implementation details and showing only functionality to the user.
- Another way, it shows only important things to the user and hides the internal details for example sending sms, you just type the text and send the message. You don't know the internal processing about the message delivery.
- Abstraction lets you focus on what the object does instead of how it does it.
- A class that is declared with abstract keyword, is known as abstract class in java. It can have abstract and non-abstract methods (method with body).

```
abstract class A{}
```

- A method that is declared as abstract and does not have implementation is known as abstract method.

Example abstract method:

```
abstract void printStatus();//no body and abstract
```

Example of abstract class that has abstract method:

- In this example, Bike the abstract class that contains only one abstract method run. It implementation is provided by the Honda class.

```
abstract class Bike
{
  abstract void run();
}
class Honda4 extends Bike
{
   void run(){System.out.println("running safely..");}
   public static void main(String args[])
   {
      Bike obj = new Honda4();
      obj.run();
   }
}
```

Output :

```
running safely..
```

- Abstract class cannot be instantiated. This means, you cannot create an object of abstract class as the abstract class is not fully developed. As you cannot create an object, you cannot even define constructor and abstract static methods for the abstract class.

- Abstract class must be extended by some other class. The subclass that extends an abstract class must provide method definition for all of the methods declared in an abstract class. If the subclass does not provide method implementation for all the methods defined in an abstract class, that class must also be declared abstract.

When to use Abstract Methods and Abstract Class?

- Abstract methods are usually declared where two or more subclasses are expected to do a similar thing in different ways through different implementations. These subclasses extend the same Abstract class and provide different implementations for the abstract methods.
- Abstract classes are used to define generic types of behaviors at the top of an object-oriented programming class hierarchy, and use its subclasses to provide implementation details of the abstract class.

Program 5.4: Example of abstract class with normal method.

```
abstract class A
{
    abstract void callme();
    public void normal()
    {
        System.out.println("this is concrete method");
    }
}
class B extends A
{
    void callme()
    {
        System.out.println("this is callme.");
    }
    public static void main(String[] args)
    {
        B b=new B();
        b.callme();
        b.normal();
    }
}
```

Output:

```
this is callme.
this is concrete method.
```

5.3 Method Overriding

- In a class hierarchy, when a method in a subclass has same name and exact signature as the method in a super class, then the method in a subclass is said to override the method in super class.
- The version of the method defined by the super class will be hidden.
- If name and type signatures of two methods are not exactly same, then the two methods are simply overloaded.
- If you wish to access the superclass version of the method, then you can do this by using the super keyword.
- Overridden methods are another way to achieve polymorphism in Java.

Program 5.5: Program for overriding.

```
//Using run-time polymorphism
class Figure {
    double dim1;
    double dim2'
Figure(double a, double b){
    dim1 = a;
    dim2 = b;
}
double area(){
    System.out.println("Area for Figure is undefined.");
    return 0;
    }
}
class Rectangle extends Figure {
    Rectangle(double a, double b) {
    }
//override area for rectangle
double area() {
    System.out.println("Inside Area for Rectangle.");
    return dim1 * dim2
    }
}
```

```
class Triangle extends Figure {
   Triangle(double a, double b) {
   }
//override area for right triangle
double area() {
   System.out.println("Inside Area for Triangle.");
   return dim1 * dim2 / 2'
   }
}
class FindAreas {
   public static void main(String args[]){
      Figure f = new Figure(10, 10);
      Rectangle r = new Rectangle(9, 5);
      Triangle t = new Triangle(10, 8);
      Figure figref;
      figref = r;
      System.out.println("Area is" + figref.area());
      figref = t;
      System.out.println("Area is" + figref.area());
      figref = f;
      System.out.println("Area is" + figref.area());
   }
}
```

Output:

```
Inside Area for Rectangle
Area is 45
Inside Area for Triangle
Area is 40
Area for Figure is undefined
Area is 0
```

5.4 final Keyword

- The final keyword in java is used to restrict the user. The java final keyword can be used in many context. Final can be:
  1. variable
  2. method
  3. class
- The final keyword can be applied with the variables, a final variable that have no value it is called blank final variable or uninitialized final variable. It can be initialized in the

constructor only. The blank final variable can be static also which will be initialized in the static block only. We will have detailed learning of these. Let's first learn the basics of final keyword.

1. **Java final Variable:**

- If you make any variable as final, you cannot change the value of final variable(It will be constant).

Program 5.6: There is a final variable speedlimit, we are going to change the value of this variable, but It can't be changed because final variable once assigned a value can never be changed.

```
class Bike9{
 final int speedlimit=90;//final variable
 void run(){
  speedlimit=400;
 }
 public static void main(String args[]){
 Bike9 obj=new  Bike9();
 obj.run();
 }
}//end of class
```

2. **Java final Method:**

- If you make any method as final, you cannot override it.

Program 5.7:

```
class Bike{
  final void run(){System.out.println("running");}
}
class Honda extends Bike{
   void run(){System.out.println("running safely with 100kmph");}
   public static void main(String args[]){
   Honda honda= new Honda();
   honda.run();
   }
}
```

3. Java final Class:

- If you make any class as final, you cannot extend it.

Program 5.8:

```
final class Bike{}
class Honda1 extends Bike{
  void run(){System.out.println("running safely with 100kmph");}
  public static void main(String args[]){
  Honda1 honda= new Honda();
  honda.run();
  }
}
```

Output:

```
Compile Time Error
```

4. Inherit final Method:

- final method is inherited but you cannot override it.

Program 5.9:

```
class Bike{
  final void run(){System.out.println("running...");}
}
class Honda2 extends Bike{
   public static void main(String args[]){
    new Honda2().run();
   }
}
```

5. Blank or Uninitialized final Variable:

- A final variable that is not initialized at the time of declaration is known as blank final variable. If you want to create a variable that is initialized at the time of creating object and once initialized may not be changed, it is useful. For example PAN CARD number of an employee.
- It can be initialized only in constructor.

Example:

```
class Student
{
int id;
String name;
final String PAN_CARD_NUMBER;
...
}
```

6. Initialize Blank final Variable:

- We can Initialize blank final variable only in constructor.

Example:

```
class Bike10{
  final int speedlimit;//blank final variable
  Bike10(){
  speedlimit=70;
  System.out.println(speedlimit);
  }
  public static void main(String args[]){
    new Bike10();
 }
}
```

7. Static Blank final Variable:

- A static final variable that is not initialized at the time of declaration is known as static blank final variable. It can be initialized only in static block.

Example:

```
class A
{
  static final int data;//static blank final variable
  static{ data=50;}
  public static void main(String args[])
{
    System.out.println(A.data);
 }
}
```

8. final Parameter:

- If you declare any parameter as final, you cannot change the value of it.

```
class Bike11
{
  int cube(final int n)
{
   n=n+2;//can't be changed as n is final
   n*n*n;
  }
  public static void main(String args[])
{
    Bike11 b=new Bike11();
    b.cube(5);
}
}
```

Output:

```
Compile Time Error
```

5.5 Super Keyword

- In the above Program of inheritance, class B extends the A, the constructor of b initializes the a and b variable of the superclass A, in its constructor. This forms the duplicate code as it is in subclass as well as in superclass, if variable (here a and b) of the superclass are private then compiler will give error.
- There will be times when you want to create a super class that keeps the detail of its implementation to itself, (making it private). Sometime, the variable and methods of superclass are private, so they will be available to subclass but subclass cannot access it.
- In such cases there would be no way for a subclass to directly access these variables on its own. Whenever, a subclass needs a reference to its immediate superclass, it can do so by use of the keyword super.
- Super has two general forms:
  1. The first calls the superclass's constructor.
  2. The second is used to access a member, (variable or method) of the superclass that has been declared as private.
- A subclass can call the constructor of its superclass by use of **super** which have the following form:

```
super(parameter list);
```

- Parameter list specifies the parameter needed by constructor of the superclass.
- **super()** must be always the first statement executed inside a subclass's constructor.

Program 5.10: Program for super keyword.

```
class A
 {
 private  int j,i;
   A()
   {
   i=10;
   j=20;
   }
   A(int i1,int j1)
   {
   i=i1;
   j=j1;
   }
}
```

```
class B extends A
{
  int k;
   B()
   {
   super();
   k=30;
   }
   B(int i2,int j2,int k1)
   {
   super (i2,j2);  //calls argumented constructor of class A
   k=k1;
   }
}
class C
{
   public static void main (String args [])
     {
      B ob1 = new B ( );
      B ob2 = new B (10, 20, 30)
     }
}
```

- Observe the above Program when a object of class B is created with three arguments as:

  `B ob1 = new B(11,22,33);`

- It will call the constructor of **B** having three arguments and pass the value **11 to i2, 22 to j2 and 33 to k1**. As variable **i** and **j** are declared as private in class **A** they will not be available to class **B** for access which inherits the class **A**. So how **B** will initialize these variables. One alternate is to rewrite the same in constructor of class **B** and other is to use the **super.**
- We have used the keyword **super** over here. When the object of **B** is created, the value passes to variable **i2, j2, k1** of constructor, from here the value of **i2, j2** are passed to the constructor of the superclass through **super(i2,j2)** and copied into **i1, j1** of argumented constructor of class A which are then assigned to variable **i** and **j**.
- Observe over here that **super** have two arguments in the second constructor so here it will call the constructor of the superclass which have two arguments and pass these values to that constructor's variable. In first constructor it only calls the constructor without argument of the superclass with **super()**;

5.6 Downcasting and Upcasting

- Downcasting and upcasting are important part of Java, which permit us to build complicated programs using simple syntax, and gives us great advantages, like Polymorphism or grouping different objects. Java allows an object of a subclass type to be treated as an object of any superclass type. This is called Upcasting. Upcasting is done automatically,while Downcasting must be manually done by the programmer.
- Upcasting occurs when an object of one type is assigned to a variable declared with a supertype of the object. No explicit casting is needed:

```
Polyhedron p = new Cube (5);
```

- Downcasting, however, requires an explicit cast:

```
Cube c = (Cube) p;
```

- Upcasting and downcasting are NOT like casting primitives from one to other.
- To understand application of upcasting and downcasting please study following program:

```
interface A
{
  void display();
}
class B implements A
{
    public void display() {
        System.out.println("Am in class B");
    }

}
class C extends B
{

    public void display() {
        System.out.println("Am in class C");
    }
}
class ExampleClass {

public static void main(String[] args) {

        // Upcasting from subclass to super class.
        A aRef=new C();

        aRef.display();//Am in class C
        //Downcasting of reference to subclass reference.
        B bRef=(B) aRef;
        bRef.display();//Am in class C
    }
}
```

Applying Up-Casting

- The upcasting is casting from the ***child class to base class***. The upcasting in java is implicit which means that you don't have to put the braces (type) as indication for casting. In above program upcasting is applied where we create a new instance from class C and pass it to a reference of type A. Then we call the function display.

```
public static void main(String[] args) {
        // Upcasting from subclass to super class.
        A aRef=new C();
        aRef.display();//Am in class C
    }
```

Applying Down-casting

- The downcasting is the casting from ***base class to child class***. Below we continue on the previous upcasting snippet by adding to lines for downcasting where we down cast the aRef reference from type A to type B.

```
public static void main(String[] args) {
        // Upcasting from subclass to super class.
        A aRef=new C();
        aRef.display();//Am in class C
        //Downcasting of reference to subclass reference.
        B bRef=(B) aRef;
        bRef.display();//Am in class C
}
```

Output:

```
Am in class C
Am in class C
```

- The display function of class C is called because the type of object is class C

5.7 Dynamic Method Dispatch

- Dynamic Method Dispatch is the mechanism in which call to an overridden method is resolved at run time rather than at compile time. Dynamic Method Dispatch is related to a principle that states that a super class reference can store the reference of subclass object. However, it can't call any of the newly added methods by the subclass but a call to an overridden methods results in calling a method of that object whose reference is stored in the super class reference. It simply means that which method would be executed, simply depends on the object reference stored in super class object.

- Below program will clearly explain principle of Dynamic Method Dispatch

Program 5.11:

```
package ClassIllustration;
class A
{
 void callme()
 {
  System.out.println("Inside A's callme Method");
 }
}
class B extends A
{
 void callme()
 {
  System.out.println("Inside B's callme Method");
 }
}
class C extends B
{
 void callme()
 {
  System.out.println("Inside C's callme Method");
 }
}
class DynamicMethodDispatch
{
 public static void main(String args[])
 {
  A a = new A();
  B b = new B();
  C c = new C();
  A r;
  r = a;
  r.callme();

  r = b;
  r.callme();
  r = c;
  r.callme();
 }
}
```

- As you can see, Reference of class A stores the reference of class A, class B and class C alternatively. Every call to callme() method would result in execution of callme() method of that class whose reference is currently stored by a reference of class A. To compile the program

```
javac -d . DynamicMethodDispatch.java
```

- And to run the program

```
java ClassIllustration.DynamicMethodDispatch
```

- Here is the output that I received on executing this program on my machine

```
Inside A's callme Method
Inside B's callme Method
Inside C's callme Method
```

Practice Questions

1. What do you mean by Inheritance?
2. How do you restrict a member of a class from inheriting to it's sub classes?
3. How to derive Sub Class from Super Class? Explain with suitable example.
4. Does Java support Multiple Inheritance?
5. Write a short note on Abstract Classes and Method in java.
6. Explain the following terms.
   (a) Subclass Constructor
   (b) Abstract Method
7. Give any one example of method overriding.
8. Can we override a static method?
9. What is the importance of final Keyword in java. List different ways to use final keyword.
10. What does super keyword do? give any one example of it.
11. What is type casting? Explain up casting vs down casting?
12. Explain principle of Dynamic Method Dispatch in java.
13. Consider the following two classes:

```
public class ClassA {
    public void methodOne(int i) {
    }
    public void methodTwo(int i) {
    }
    public static void methodThree(int i) {
    }
    public static void methodFour(int i) {
    }
}
public class ClassB extends ClassA {
    public static void methodOne(int i) {
    }
    public void methodTwo(int i) {
    }
    public void methodThree(int i) {
    }
    public static void methodFour(int i) {
    }
}
```

   (a) Which method overrides a method in the superclass?
   (b) Which method hides a method in the superclass?
   (c) What do the other methods do?

■■■

Chapter 6...

PACKAGES AND INTERFACES

Contents ...

6.1 Importing Classes

6.1.1 Introduction

- One of the important Object Oriented Feature is the reusability of a code. We have achieved this feature by extending a class or implementing an interface in our program. If we want to reuse the code in some other program without actually physically copying it, then what can be the solution? The solution to this is to use the concept of package. The concept is similar to class libraries. The use of package is another way of achieving reusability in Java.
- Java groups variety of classes or interfaces together into packages. Grouping is usually done based on the functionality. Packages are nothing but containers for classes. Organizing classes into packages gives us various benefits. These are as follows:
  - Classes stored in the packages of other programs can be easily reused.
  - Two classes in two different packages can have same name. They can be referred with their fully qualified name.
  - They provide means to hide the classes.
  - They also provide means of separating design from coding.
- Java packages are divided into two categories- Java API packages and User defined packages.

6.1.2 Java's Built-in Packages

- The following table shows various built-in packages in Java.

Table 6.1: Java System Packages and their Classes

Package name	Contents
`java.lang`	Language support classes. These are classes that Java compiler itself uses and therefore they are automatically imported. They include classes for primitive types, strings, math functions, threads and exceptions.
`java.util`	Language utility classes such as vectors, hash tables, random, numbers, date, etc.
`java.io`	Input/Output support classes. They provide facilities for the input and output of data.
`java.awt`	Set of classes for implementing graphical user interface. They include classes for windows, buttons, lists, menus and so on.
`java.net`	Classes for networking. They include classes for communicating with local computers as well as with internet servers.
`java.applet`	Classes for creating and implementing applets.

6.1.3 Naming Conventions

- Packages can be named using standard Java naming conventions.
- Packages begin with lowercase letters so that user can differentiate package name from class name. All class names begin with upper case letters.
- A fully qualified class name can be given as follows:

```
import java.awt.Button;
```

- This statement uses fully qualified class name Button to import a Button class. Where java.awt is the name of the package in which a Button class is stored.
- Packages are usually designed in a hierarchical naming pattern. The levels in the hierarchy are separated by dots('.').
- Each package name must be unique. Duplicate names will cause run-time errors.
- Since multiple users work on the internet, duplicate package names are unavoidable. Java designers have recognized the use of domain names as prefix to the preferred package names.
- For example, `hyb.sbg.myPackage;`

  Here, hyb is city name. sbg is the name of organization and myPackage is the name of the package.

6.1.4 Accessing a Package

- As we have already shown, classes in a package can be accessed by a fully qualified name or it can be accessed by a short cut if we import the corresponding package. The general form of importing a package is as follows:

```
import package1[.package2].(classname|*);
```

- Here, package1 is the name of the top level package. Package2 is the name of the subpackage inside the top level package. There is no practical limit to the depth of hierarchy. Finally you can specify the name of the class explicitly or star(*) which tells the compiler that it should import the entire package. For example;

```
import javax.swing.JButton;

import java.awt.event.*;
```

- All of the standard Java classes are stored in a package called java. The basic language functions are stored in a java.lang package. This package is implicitly imported by the compiler for all Java programs. You do not have to import java.lang package in your program.

6.1.5 Finding Packages

- Packages are reflected into directories. Here arises one question that is how the java run-time system will find out where to look for a package that you have created.
  1. By default, Java run-time system finds it in the current working directory as its start. If your package resides in a current directory or in a subdirectory of the current directory, it will be found.
  2. You can specify a directory path or paths by setting a CLASSPATH environment variable.
  3. You can use –classpath option with java and javac to specify a path for your classes.

  For example, consider the following package specification:

```
package college;
```

- Java finds this package if the program is executed from a directory immediately above the college directory. If not, CLASSPATH must be set to include the path to college directory. The first approach is easy but the second approach lets you find the college package no matter in which directory your program resides.

6.1.6 Package Visibility

- Java provides many levels of protection to allow control over the visibility of variables and methods within classes, subclasses and packages. The three access specifiers, public, protected and private give various ways to produce many levels of access. The following table shows all combinations of access control modifiers.

Table 6.2: Class Member Access

	Private	No Modifier	Protected	Public
Same class	Yes	Yes	Yes	Yes
Same package subclass	No	Yes	Yes	Yes
Same package non-subclass	No	Yes	Yes	Yes
Different package subclass	No	No	Yes	Yes
Different package non-subclass	No	No	No	Yes

Program 6.1:

```
package package1;
public class Base
{
    long k = 10L;
    private long k_pri = 20L;
    protected long k_pro = 30L;
    public long k_pub = 40L;
    public Base()
    {
        System.out.println("base constructor");
        System.out.println("k = " + k);
        System.out.println("k_pri = " + k_pri);
        System.out.println("k_pro = " + k_pro);
        System.out.println("k_pub = " + k_pub);
    }
}
```

- This is file Subclass.java:

```
package package1;
class Subclass extends Base
{
 Subclass()
  {
        System.out.println("Subclass constructor");
        System.out.println("k = " + k);
        System.out.println("k_pri = " + k_pri);
                              //ERROR private so  accessed in class only
        System.out.println("k_pro = " + k_pro);
        System.out.println("k_pub = " + k_pub);
    }
}
```

- This is file Normal.java:

```
package package1;
class Normal
{
   Normal()
   {
      Base p = new Base();
      System.out.println("same package constructor");
      System.out.println("k = " + p.k);
      System.out.println("k_pri = " + p.k_pri);
                           //ERROR private so  accessed in class only
      System.out.println("k_pro = " + p.k_pro);
      System.out.println("k_pub = " + p.k_pub);
   }
}
```

- Following is the source code for the other package, **package2**. The two classes defined in **package2** cover the other two conditions which are affected by access control. The first class, **Base2**, is a subclass of **package1.Base**.
- This grants access to all of **package1. Base**'s variables except for **k_pri** (because it is **private**) and **k**, the variable declared with the default protection. Remember, the default only allows access from within the class or the package, not extra-package subclasses.
- Finally, the class **NormalOtherPackage** has access to only one variable, **k_pub**, which was declared **public**.
- This is file **Base2.java:**

```
package package2;
import package1;
class Base2 extends package1.Base
{
   Base2()
   {
      System.out.println("derived other package constructor");
      System.out.println("k = " + k);
                         //ERROR default so  accessed in package only
      System.out.println("k_pri = " + k_pri);
                           //ERROR private so  accessed in class only
      System.out.println("k_pro = " + k_pro);
      System.out.println("k_pub = " + k_pub);
   }
}
```

- This is file NormalOtherPackage.java:

```
package package2;
import package1;
class NormalOtherPackage()
{
   package1.Base p = new package1.Base();
   System.out.println("other package constructor");
   System.out.println("k = " + p.k);
                              //ERROR default so  accessed in package only
   System.out.println("k_pri = " + p.k_pri);
                                        //ERROR  private so  accessed in same
   //  class only
   System.out.println("k_pro = " + p.k_pro);
                                             //ERROR protected so  accessed in
   //subclass  only
   System.out.println("k_pub = " + p.k_pub);
}
}
```

- If you wish to try these two packages, here are two test files you can use. The one for package **package1** is shown here:

```
// Demo package package1.
package package1;
public class Demo
{
public static void main(String args[])
{
   Base ob1 = new Base();
   Subclass ob2 = new Subclass();
   Normal ob3 = new Normal();
}
}
```

- The test file for **package2** is shown next.

```
// Demo package package2.
package package2;
import package1;
public class Demo
{
   public static void main(String args[])
   {
      Base2 ob1 = new Base2();
      NormalOtherPackage ob2 = new NormalOtherPackage();
   }
}
```

6.1.7 Importing Packages

Program 6.2: A simple program that imports a package.

```
package MyPack;
/* Now, the Balance class, its constructor, and its show() method are
public. This means that they can be used by non-subclass code outside
their package.
*/
public class Balance {
String name;
double bal;
public Balance(String n, double b) {
name = n;
bal = b;
}
public void show() {
if(bal<0)
System.out.print("--> ");
System.out.println(name + ": $" + bal);
}
}
import MyPack.*;
class TestBalance {
public static void main(String args[]) {
/* Because Balance is public, you may use Balance
class and call its constructor. */
Balance test = new Balance("J. J. Jaspers", 99.88);
test.show(); // you may also call show()
}
}
```

6.1.8 Java API Packages

- Java packages are classified into two categories.
  1. Java API packages
  2. User Defined Packages.
- Java API provides large number of classes grouped into various packages according to their functionality. The most common packages defined in java are as shown below.

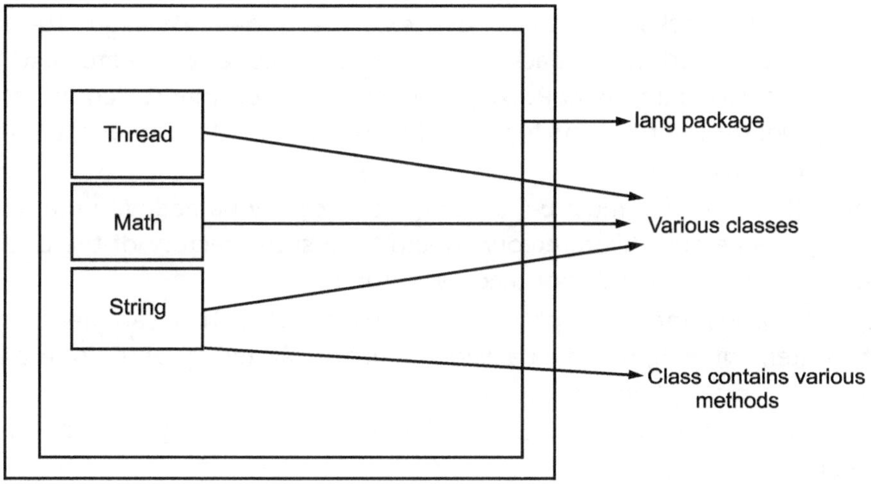

Fig. 6.1: JAVA API Packages

- The following table list some packages and their classes :

Table 6.3

Package Name	Contents	Classes
java.lang	Language support classes.These are the classes that java compiler uses and therefore they are automatically imported	String,Thread,Exception,ThreadGroup, Math,StringBuffer,Integer,Float,Double etc.
java.util	Language utility classes	Collection, Vector, Array, Date etc.
java.io	Input Output support classes	InputStream,OutputStream,Reader, Writer
java.awt	Set of classes for implementing GUI	Windows,Button,TextField,menus etc.
Java.net	Classes for networking,include classes for communication with local comp.	ServerSocket,Socket,InetAddress etc.
Java.applet	Classes for implementing applet	Applet etc.

6.2 User Defined Packages

6.2.1 Defining a Package

- Defining a package is very easy. You simply need to include a package keyword followed by the name of the package to be created at the start of the Java source file. Package statement should be the very first statement in your Java program (except comments and whitespaces). Here is the example:

```
package demoPackage;
public class FirstClass { //body of class }
```

- The name of the package in the above example is demoPackage. The class names FirstClass will be a part of the package. This piece of code will create FirstClass.java file and it will be saved in demoPackage directory under the current directory. When FirstClass program will be compiled, Java keeps the .class file under the same directory named demoPackage.
- Remember that .class file must be located in a directory named with the same name as the package name and this directory should be a sub-directory of the directory where the classes that will import this package are stored.
- Java also supports the concept of package hierarchy. This can be done writing a package statement with multiple package names separated by dots. For example,

```
package demoPackage.secondPackage;
```

- Here, the class is stored in a secondPackage and the package in turn, is stored in a demoPackage.
- A java file can have more than one class definitions. Only one of the classes in a Java file may be declared public. The filename for such java file will be the name of the class that is defined as public with .java extension.

6.2.2 How to create a Package

Program 6.3: Package demonstration

```
// A simple package
package MyPack;
class Balance {
String name;
double bal;
Balance(String n, double b) {
name = n;
bal = b;
}
void show() {
if(bal<0)
System.out.print("--> ");
System.out.println(name + ": $" + bal);
}
}
class AccountBalance {
public static void main(String args[]) {
Balance current[] = new Balance[3];
current[0] = new Balance("K. J. Fielding", 123.23);
current[1] = new Balance("Will Tell", 157.02);
current[2] = new Balance("Tom Jackson", -12.33);
for(int i=0; i<3; i++) current[i].show();
}
}
```

6.3 Modifiers and Access Control

- Once, you begin to program Java for a while, you will discover that making all your classes, methods and variables public can become quite annoying.
- The larger your program becomes and the more you reuse your classes for new projects, the more you will want some sort of control over their visibility.
- Modifiers are prefixes that can be applied in various combinations to the methods and variables within a class and some to the class itself.
- There is a long and varied list of modifiers. The order of modifiers is irrelevant to their meaning your older can vary and is really a matter of taste. Here, is the recommended order:

```
<access> static abstract synchronized final native <unusual>
where,          <access> can be public, protected or private
                <unusual> includes volatile and transient.
```

- We have also seen that the variables and methods of a class are visible everywhere in the program. However, it may be necessary in some situations to restrict the access to certain variables and methods from outside the class.
- For example, we may not like the objects of a class directly alter the value of the variable or access a method. We can achieve this in Java by applying visibility modifiers to the instance variables and methods. The visibility modifiers are also known as access modifiers.
- Java provides four types of visibility modifiers public, private, protected and default.

Table 6.4

Attribute	Permitted Access
Public	From methods in any class anywhere as long as the class has been declared as public.
private	Accessible only from methods inside the class. No access from outside the class at all.
Protected	From methods in any class in the same package and from any subclass anywhere.
Default	From method in any class in same package only.

- This table shows how the access attributes you set a class member determine the parts of the Java environment from which you can access it.

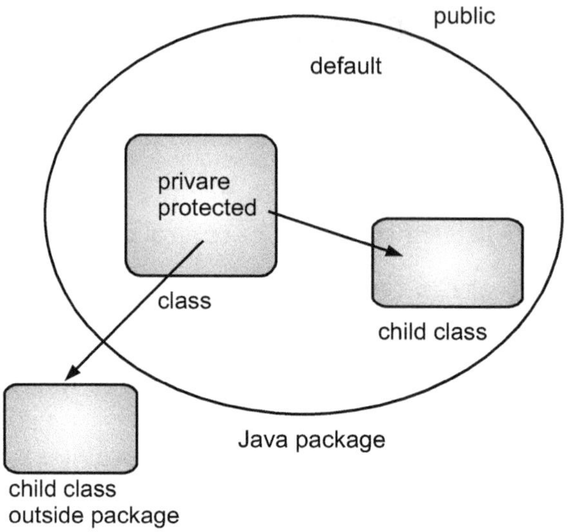

Fig. 6.2: Access Control

6.3.1 Public Access

- Any variable or method is visible to the entire class in which it is defined, but if you want to make it visible to all the classes outside this class, then simply declare that method or variable as public access.
- Example of public declarations:

```
public class public class
{
 public int a public int;
 public string a public string;
 public float a public method()
 {
    ...............
    ...............
 }
}
```

- A variable or method with public access has the widest possible visibility. Anyone can see it and anyone can use it. Of course, this may not always be what you want which brings us to be next level of protection.

Program 6.4: Program that shows the use of public access modifier.

```
class X
   {
      int a;
   X()
      {
         a= 60;
         System.out.println("the value of a is =" +a);
      }
```

```
    void display()
    {
       System.out.println("the value of a is =" +a);
    }
 }
  class Xtest
 {
    public static void main(String args[])
    {
       X ob1= new X();
       ob1.a=80;
       ob1.display();
    }
 }
```

Output:

```
the value of a is =60
the value of a is =80
```

6.3.2 Protected Access

- It lies between class and its present and future subclasses. These subclasses are much closer to a parent class than to any other "outside" classes for the following reasons:
    1. Subclasses are usually more intimately aware of the internals of a parent class.
    2. Subclasses are often written by you or by someone to whom you have given your source code.
    3. Subclasses frequently need to modify or enhance the representation of the data within a parent class.

Note that non-subclasses in other packages cannot access the "protected" members.

Program 6.5: Program that illustrates protected access modifier.

```
public class aprotectedclass
{
   protected int aprotectedint = 4;
   protected string aprotectedstring = "and a 3 and a";
   protected void aprotectedmethod()
   {
      system.out.println("aprotectstring + aprotectedint");
   }
}
```

```
public class aprotectedclasssubclass extends aprotectedclass
{
   public void testuse()
   {
      aprotectedclass apc = new aprotectedclass();
      System.out.println(apc.aprotectstring + apc.aprotectedint);
      apc.aprotectedmethod();
   }
}
public class anyclassinthesamepackage
{
   public void test_use()
   {
      aprotectedclass apc = new aprotectedclass();
      System.out.println(apc.aprotectedstring + apc.aprotectedint);
      apc.aprotectedmethod();
   }
}
```

- Even though anyclassinthesame package is in the same package as aprotectedclass, it is not a subclass of it. Only, subclasses are allowed to see, and use, protected variables and methods.

6.3.3 Private Access

- Private access has the highest degree of protection. They are accessible only with their own class. They cannot be inherited by subclasses and therefore not accessible in subclasses.
- The methods declared as private behaves like a method declared as final. Note that we cannot override a non-private method in a subclass and then make it private.

```
public class aprivateclass
{
 private int aprivateint;
 private string aprivatestring;
 private flaot aprivatemethod();
}
```

- If there is no access specifier and class is within package. Java applies a access specifier "Default", which enables class public within a package and private outside the package.

Program 6.6: Program that demonstrates private access modifier.

```
class X
 {
  private int a;
   X()
     {
       a= 60;
       System.out.println("the value of a is =" +a);
        }
   public void display()
       {
          System.out.println("the value of a is =" +a);
       }
   }
class Xtest
{
  public static void main(String args[])
  {
    X ob1= new X();
    ob1.a=80;
    ob1.display();
  }
}
```

Output:

```
the value of a is =60
the value of a is =60
```

6.4 Implementing interfaces

6.4.1 Defining an Interface

- An interface is defined similar to a class definition. The general form of the interface is given below:

```
access interface name {
return-type method-name(para_list);
return-type method-name(para_list);
type final-varname1 = value;
type final-varname2 = value;
//...
}
```

- If access is not defined, default access is considered and the interface only becomes available to the other members of the package in which it is declared.
- If the interface is declared as public, then it can be available by any other code. This must be the only public interface declared in a file. The name of the file should be same as the name of the public interface.
- The methods declared are abstract methods without method body. They just end with semicolon. Whenever any class implement this interface, the method definition is written according to the requirement of the class. All methods declared inside an interface must be defined by the class that implements the interface.
- Variables can also be defined inside interface. They are by default static and final. This means, they cannot be changed by the implementing class and they must be initialized. All methods and variables have public access by default.
- Let us look at following interface:

```
interface Callback
{
void callback(int param);
}
```

- This interface can be implemented by a class as follows:

6.4.2 Implementing Interfaces

- Once an interface is defined, one or more classes can implement that interface. 'implements' clause is used to implement an interface by the class. Interfaces are separated by comma, if any class implements more than one interface.
- The general form is as follows:

```
class classname [extends superclass][implements [, interface...]]
{ // class-body }
```

Program 6.7: Program that demonstrates use of interface

```
class Client implements Callback
{
public void callback(int p)
{
   System.out.println("callback called with " + p);
}
void nonIfaceMeth()
{
   System.out.println("Classes that implement interfaces " + "may
   also define other members, too.");
}
}
```

6.4.3 Applying interfaces

Program 6.8: Program that demonstrates how to apply interfaces in real applications.

```
// Define an integer stack interface.
interface IntStack {
void push(int item);
int pop();
}
private int stck[];
private int tos;
FixedStack(int size) {
stck = new int[size];
tos = -1;
}
public void push(int item) {
if(tos==stck.length-1)
System.out.println("Stack is full.");
else
stck[++tos] = item;
}
public int pop() {
if(tos < 0) {
System.out.println("Stack underflow.");
return 0;
}
else
return stck[tos--];
}
}
class IFTest {
public static void main(String args[])
{
FixedStack mystack1 = new FixedStack(5);
FixedStack mystack2 = new FixedStack(8);
for(int i=0; i<5; i++) mystack1.push(i);
for(int i=0; i<8; i++) mystack2.push(i);
System.out.println("Stack in mystack1:");
for(int i=0; i<5; i++)
System.out.println(mystack1.pop());
System.out.println("Stack in mystack2:");
for(int i=0; i<8; i++)
System.out.println(mystack2.pop());
}
}
```

6.4.4 Interfaces can be Extended

- One interface can inherit another by use of the keyword extends. The syntax is similar to that of inheriting classes. When a class implements an interface that inherits some other interface, it must provide implementation for all the methods defined within that interface inheritance chain.

6.5 User Defined Interfaces

- Interfaces are used a lot not only in JDK but also java design patterns, most of the frameworks and tools. Interfaces provide a way to achieve abstraction in java and used to define the contract for the subclasses to implement.
- For example, lets say we want to create a drawing consists of multiple shapes, here we can create an interface Shape and define all the methods that different types of Shape objects will implement. For simplicity purpose, we can keep only two methods – draw() to draw the shape and getArea() that will return the area of the shape.
- Based on above requirements, our Shape interface will look like this.

Program 6.9: Shape.java

```
package com.journaldev.design;
public interface Shape
{
 //implicitly public, static and final
 public String LABLE="Shape";

 //interface methods are implicitly abstract and public
 void draw()
 double getArea();
}
```

- An interface can't extend any class but it can extend another interface. public interface Shape extends Cloneable{} is an example of an interface extending another interface. Actually java provides multiple inheritance in interfaces, what is means is that an interface can extend multiple interfaces.
- Implements keyword is used by classes to implement an interface.
- A class implementing an interface must provide implementation for all of its method unless it's an abstract class. For example, we can implement above interface in abstract class like this:

Program 6.10: ShapeAbs.java

```
package com.journaldev.design;
public abstract class ShapeAbs implements Shape
{
    @Override
    public double getArea()
    {
      // TODO Auto-generated method stub
      return 0;
    }
}
```

- We should always try to write programs in terms of interfaces rather than implementations so that we know beforehand that implementation classes will always provide the implementation and in future if any better implementation arrives, we can switch to that easily.

Implementation of an interface:

- **Example:** Now lets see some implementation of our Shape interface.

Program 6.11: Circle.java

```
package com.journaldev.design;
public class Circle implements Shape
{
    private double radius;
    public Circle(double r)
    {
      this.radius = r;
    }
    @Override
    public void draw()
    {
       System.out.println("Drawing Circle");
    }
    @Override
    public double getArea()
    {
       return Math.PI*this.radius*this.radius;
    }
    public double getRadius()
    {
      return this.radius;
    }
}
```

- Notice that Circle class has implemented all the methods defined in the interface and it has some of its own methods also like getRadius(). The interface implementations can have multiple type of constructors. Lets see another interface implementation for Shape interface.

Program 6.12: Rectangle.java

```
package com.journaldev.design;
public class Rectangle implements Shape
{
   private double width;
   private double height;
   public Rectangle(double w, double h)
   {
     this.width=w;
     this.height=h;
   }
   @Override
   public void draw()
   {
      System.out.println("Drawing Rectangle");
   }
   @Override
   public double getArea()
   {
      return this.height*this.width;
   }
}
```

- Notice the use of override annotation
- Here is a test program showing how to code in terms of interfaces and not implementations.

Program 6.13: ShapeTest.java

```
package com.journaldev.design;
public class ShapeTest
{
   public static void main(String[] args)
   {
     //programming for interfaces not implementation
     Shape shape = new Circle(10);
     shape.draw();
     System.out.println("Area="+shape.getArea());
```

```
        //switching from one implementation to another easily
        shape=new Rectangle(10,10);
        shape.draw();
        System.out.println("Area="+shape.getArea());
    }
}
```

Output:

```
Drawing Circle
Area=314.1592653589793
Drawing Rectangle
Area=100.0
```

- If the implementation class has its own methods, we can't use them directly in our code because the type of Object is an interface that doesn't have those methods. For example, in above code we will get compilation error for code shape.getRadius(). To overcome this, we can use typecasting and use the method like this:
  1. Circle c = (Circle) shape;
  2. c.getRadius();

6.6 Adapter classes

- To handle the events, we have to define the class which implements the specific listener interface. When a class implements an interface, it has to define all the methods of the interface.
- Some of the listener interface contains one or more methods for specific events. For example, MouseListener interface contain five different methods like mousePressed(), mouseReleased(), mouseClicked() etc. However, If we just want to handle the event like mouse click, we may not be interested in defining rest of the methods. If we implement MouseListener interface, we are forced to define all five methods in our class. To avoid this problem, java provides special classes called 'Adapter Classes'. These classes make our event handling much simpler. These adapter classes implement listener interface which has empty definitions for all the methods of that interface. We can extend adapter class and override only those methods which are of our interest.
- Adapter classes are :
  - ComponentAdapter,
  - ContainerAdapter,
  - FocusAdapter,

- KeyAdapter,
- MouseAdapter,
- MouseMotionAdapter
- WindowAdapter.

Program 6.14: An application program that demonstrates how to make use of adapter classes

The DemoAdapter class extends WindowAdapter class which in turn implements WindowListner interface. The application creates a frame with suitable title and adds WindowListener interface to the class. The program only implements a single windowClosing() method out of all the methods defined by the WindowListener interface.

File: DemoAdapter.java

```
import java.awt.*;
import java.awt.event.*;
class DemoAdapter extends WindowAdapter implements WindowListener
{
   public DemoAdapter ()
   {
      Frame f = new Frame("Window");
      f.setVisible(true);
      f.setSize(400,400);
      f.setTitle("Demonstration of Adapter class");
      f.addWindowListener(this);
   }
   public void windowClosing(WindowEvent e)
   {
      System.exit(0);
   }
   public static void main(String[] args)
   {
      new  DemoAdapter();
   }
}
```

Practice Questions

1. How to import a class in JAVA?
2. What is a Java package and how is it used?
3. Explain Java API packages in detail.
4. Write a short note on User Defined Packages with suitable example
5. Which package is always imported by default?
6. Explain the following terms.
   (a) Accessing a Package
   (b) Package Visibility
7. What do you understand by package Access Specifier?
8. What is interface? Write correct syntax to define an interface.
9. What is wrong with the following interface?

```
public interface SomethingIsWrong {
    void aMethod(int aValue) {
        System.out.println("Hi Mom");
    }
}
```

10. What is the use of interface?
11. Write a short note on User Defined Interface.
12. What is Adapter class? Explain with example.

■■■

Chapter 7...

EXCEPTION HANDLING

Contents ...

7.1 Introduction

- It is usual to make mistakes while writing a program. These mistakes lead to an error. These errors produce unexpected results or incorrect output. It may terminate the program abruptly. Therefore it is necessary to handle all the possibilities of error conditions that may occur during the program execution. Errors can be classified as:
  - Compile-time Errors
  - Run-time Errors
- **Compile-time Errors:** Java compiler detects all the syntactical errors in your program. It displays a list of errors on the monitor to let the programmer know about the errors present in the program. A programmer fixes all these errors and when the program is bug free, Java compiler generates a .class file of the java program. Most of the compile time errors are due to typing mistakes.
- **Run-time Errors:** Once the program compiles successfully, Java creates a .class file which is a Java byte code file that should be executed while running Java program. The program may produce wrong result or terminate abruptly if program logic goes wrong at some place. Such errors are called **'run-time errors'**. Divide by zero, accessing an array element outside the array boundary defined etc are some of the examples of run-time errors. When such errors are encountered, Java generates error messages and terminates the program.

7.2 Types of Exceptions

- An **'Exception'** is a condition that is caused by a run-time error in the program. It is an abnormal condition that arises in a sequence of code at run-time. In early computer languages that do not have mechanisms for handling exceptions, errors must be checked and handled manually. But this is a troublesome approach. Java's exception handling avoids such types of problems. A Java exception is an object that describes an exceptional condition occurred in a program. When an exceptional condition arises, an object which represents that exception is created and is thrown in the method that caused the error. This means, it lets us know about the exceptional condition. That method may choose to handle the exception by itself or it passes it on. At some point, the exception is caught and processed. If the exception is not caught and handled, the Java interpreter displays an error message and terminates the program. If we want the program to continue execution of the remaining code, we should try to catch the exception object thrown and displays an appropriate message for correcting errors. This task is called as 'Exception Handling'.
- The following are the necessary steps for exception handling.

  0. Identify the problem or error(Exception)
  0. Inform the programmer that error has occurred. (Throw the exception)
  0. Get the information about the error (Catch the exception)
  0. Take the necessary actions (Handle the exception)

- Java exception handling is managed by five keywords- try, catch, throw, throws and finally.
- All exceptions are subclasses of built-in class Throwable. Class Throwable has two subclasses-Exception and Error. Below the branch, Exception, an important subclass RuntimeException that automatically defines exceptions such as divide by zero or an invalid array index. Other branch is Error which defines exceptions that are not expected to be caught under normal circumstances. Stack overflow is an error of such kind.
- Exceptions in Java can be categorized by two types:
- **Checked Exceptions:** The exceptions that are explicitly handled with the help of try-catch blocks are checked exceptions. Checked exceptions are extended from Exception class.
- **Unchecked Exceptions:** Exceptions that are not handled in the program code; instead, Java Virtual Machine handles such exceptions are unchecked exceptions. Unchecked exceptions are extended from RuntimeException class.

- Common Java exceptions are as follows:

Table 7.1: Common Java Exceptions

Exception Type	Cause of Exception
`ArithmeticException`	Caused by math errors such as division by zero
`ArrayIndexOutOfBoundsException`	Caused by bad array indexes
`ArrayStoreException`	Caused when a program tries to store the wrong type of data in an array
`FileNotFoundException`	Caused by an attempt to access a non-existent file.
`IOException`	Caused by general I/O failures, such as inability to read from a file.
`NullPointerException`	Caused by referencing a null object.
`NumberFormatException`	Caused when a conversion between strings and number fails.
`OutOfMemoryException`	Caused when there is not enough memory to allocate a new object.
`SecurityException`	Caused when an applet tries to perform an action not allowed by the browser's security setting.
`StackOverFlowException`	Caused when the system runs out of stack space.
`StringIndexOutOfBoundsException`	Caused when a program attempts to access a non-existent character position in a string.

7.3 Keywords in Exception Handling

7.3.1 Using try-catch

- The basic exception handling concept is throwing an exception and then catching it. Java uses a keyword **try** that encloses a block of code which is likely to cause an error and throw an exception. Java uses a keyword 'catch' that catches the exception thrown by the try block and handles it appropriately. The catch block is added immediately after the try block. The following example, illustrates the use of try-catch statements.

```
.....
try
{
   statement; // generates an exception.
}
catch(Exception-type e)
{
   statement; // processes an exception.
}
......
```

- The following diagram shows the exception handling mechanism.

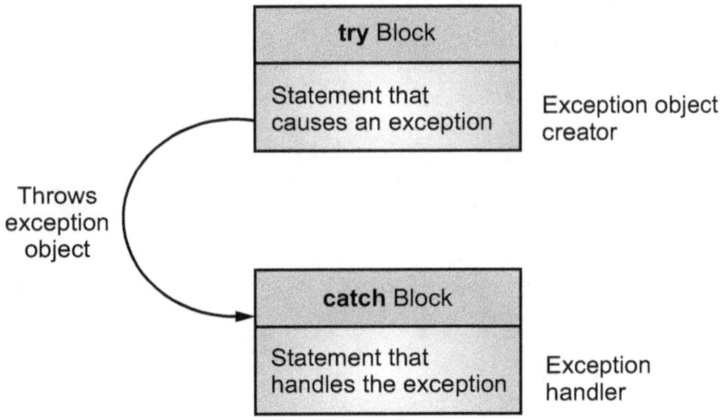

Fig. 7.1: Exception handling mechanism

- The try block can have one or more statements. If any statement generates an exception, the remaining statements in a try block are skipped and program control directly jumps to the catch block to handle that exception.
- The catch block also can have one or more statements to process the exception.
- Every try should be followed by at least one catch block. Otherwise compilation error will be generated.
- Catch statement is like a method definition. The parameter passed to the catch statement is the reference to the exception object thrown by the try block. If the parameter matches with the exception type, the exception is caught and the statements in the catch block are executed. If the exception is not caught, the default exception handler terminates the program.

Program 7.1: The following program illustrates the use of try-catch block to catch the exception.

The program catches divide by zero exception. It accepts two integer values from the user m and n. If the number n is zero, it should raise an arithmetic exception saying cannot divide by zero. The catch block is executed only if try block throws an exception. In this program, the catch block will be able to catch all arithmetic exceptions.

```
import java.util.Scanner;
class Divisionerrorhandling
{
    public static void main(String[] args)
    {
    int m, n, res;
    Scanner input = new Scanner(System.in);
```

```
    System.out.println("Input two integers");
    m = input.nextInt();
    n = input.nextInt();
    // try block
    try {
    res  = m / n;
    System.out.println("Result = " + res);
}
// catch block
catch (ArithmeticException e) {
System.out.println("Exception caught: Division by zero.");
}
}
}
```

Output:

```
Input two integers
20 4
Result = 5
Input two integers
20 0
Exception caught: Division by zero.
```

Program 7.2: The following program demonstrates the use of Exception class to catch all the exceptions.

The program defines an array of languages. It throws an ArrayIndexOutofBoundsException as it is trying to access an index out of the array boundaries. As the catch clause creates an object of Exception, program catches all types of exceptions including an ArrayIndexOutofBoundsException as it is a subclass of Exception class.

```
class Except
{
public static void main(String[] args)
{
String languages[] = { "Sandy ", "Maddy ", "Candy ",
                                        "Pillu ", "Rambo " };
```

```
try {
    for (int c = 1; c <= 5; c++) {
    System.out.println(languages[c]);
}
}
catch (Exception e) {
System.out.println(e);
}
}
}
```

Output:

```
Maddy
Candy
Pillu
Rambo
java.lang.ArrayIndexOutOfBoundsException: 5
```

7.3.2 throw Statement **[Oct. 2010]**

- We have been catching exceptions thrown by the Java run-time system. But it is also possible that program throws an exception explicitly using throw statement.
- General form of throw is shown here:

  `throw ThrowableInstance;`

- ThrowableInstance must be an object of type Throwable or a subclass of Throwable. There are two ways to obtain object of Throwable class.
  1. Using a parameter in a catch clause.

     For example, `throw e;`
  2. Creating one with new operator.

     For example, `throw new ArithmeticException();`
- The flow of execution stops immediately after the throw statement. All other statements after throw statement are skipped.

Program 7.3:

```
class ThrowDemo {
static void demoproc() {
try {
throw new NullPointerException("demo");
} catch(NullPointerException e) {
System.out.println("Caught inside demoproc.");
throw e;
}
}
public static void main(String args[]) {
try {
demoproc();
} catch(NullPointerException e) {
System.out.println("Recaught: " + e);
}
}
}
```

Output:

```
Caught inside demoproc.
Recaught: java.lang.NullPointerException: demo
```

7.3.3 throws statement

- If a method is capable of causing an exception that it does not handle, it must specify this so that caller of this method can guard themselves against that exception. You can do this by inserting a throws statement in method declaration. A throws statement enlists all the exception that a method might throw. This is necessary for all the exception except those are subclasses of Error or RuntimeException classes. Rest all other exceptions must be lised in a throws statement. If they are not reported in a throws statement, then you will get compile-time error. The general form of throws statement is given as follows:

```
type method-name(parameter-list) throws exception-list
{
// method body
}
For example,
void throwMethod() throws IllegalAccessException
{
}
```

7.3.4 finally block

- Java supports another statement known as finally statement. This can be used to handle exception that is not caught by any of the previous catch statements. Finally block may be added immediately after the try block or after the last catch block. When the method is about to return to the caller, from inside a try-catch block, finally clause is also executed just before the method returns.
- Finally clause is optional. However, each try statement requires at least one catch or a finally clause.

Program 7.4: The program illustrates the use of finally clause.

```
// Demonstrate finally.
class FinallyDemo {
static void procA() {
try {
System.out.println("inside procA");
throw new RuntimeException("demo");
} finally {
System.out.println("procA's finally");
}
}
static void procB() {
try {
System.out.println("inside procB");
return;
} finally {
System.out.println("procB's finally");
}
}
```

```
static void procC() {
try {
System.out.println("inside procC");
} finally {
System.out.println("procC's finally");
}
}
public static void main(String args[]) {
try {
procA();
} catch (Exception e) {
System.out.println("Exception caught");
}
procB();
procC();
}
}
```

7.4 Creating Your Own Exception

- There may be times when we would like to throw our own exceptions. We can do this by using the keyword throw as follows:

  ```
  throw new Throwable subclass;
  ```

  Examples:

  ```
  throw new ArithmeticException( );
  throw new NumberFormatException( );
  ```

- Below program demonstrates the use of a user-defined subclass of Throwable class. Note that Exception is a subclass of Throwable and therefore MyException is a subclass of Throwable class. An object of a class that extends Throwable can be thrown and caught.

Program 7.5: Creating our own exception.

```
import java.lang.Exception;
class MyException extends Exception
   MyException(String message)
   {
      super(message);
   }
class TestMyException
public static void main(Strings args[])
{
   int x = 5, y = 1000;
   try
   {
      float z - (float} x / (float) y;
      if(z < 0.01)
      {
         throw new MvException("Number is too small");
      }
   }
   catch (MyException e)
   {
      System.out.println("Caught my exception");
      System.out.println(e.getMessage( ) );
   }
   finally
   {
      System.out.println ("I am always here");
   }
}
```

Output:

```
Caught my exception
Number is too small
I am always here
```

- The object e which contains the error message "Number is too small" is caught by the catch block which then displays the message using the getMessage( ) method.
- Note that Program 7.5 also illustrates the use of finally block. The last fine of output is produced by the finally block.
- There could be situations where there is a possibility that a method might throw certain kinds of exceptions but there is no exception handling mechanism prevalent within the method. In such a case, important that the method caller is intimated explicitly that certain types of exceptions could be exception from the called method, and the caller must get prepared with some catching mechanism to deal with it.
- The throws clause is used in such a situation. It is specified immediately after the method declaration statement and just before the opening brace. The Program 7.6 shows an example of using the clause:

Program 7.6: Use of throws

```
class Examplethrows
{
static void divide_m() throws ArithmeticException
int x=22, y=0, z;
z = x/y;
}
public static void main(String args[])
try
divide_m();
}
catch(ArithmeticException e)
{
System.out.println("Caught the exception " + e);
}
}
}
```

Output:

```
Caught the exception java.lang.ArithmeticException: / by zero
```

7.5 Nested Try Statement Blocks

- try statements can be nested. try statement can be inside a block of another try. Each time a try statement is encountered, the context of that try is pushed on to the stack. If an inner try block does not have a catch block for the particular exception then the stack is popped and the next try block's catch block is examined for the same exception. This is continued until one of the catch statements succeeds, or until all the statements are exhausted and no catch statement matches, then the Java run-time system handles the exception.

Program 7.7:

```
class NestTry {
public static void main(String args[]) {
try {
int a = args.length;
the following statement will generate
   a divide-by-zero exception. */
int b = 42 / a;
System.out.println("a = " + a);
try { // nested try block
if(a==1) a = a/(a-a); // division by zero
if(a==2) {
int c[] = { 1 };
c[42] = 99;
}
} catch(ArrayIndexOutOfBoundsException e) {
System.out.println("Array index out-of-bounds: " + e);
}
} catch(ArithmeticException e) {
System.out.println("Divide by 0: " + e);
}
}
}
```

Output:

```
C:\>java NestTry
Divide by 0: java.lang.ArithmeticException: / by zero
C:\>java NestTry One
a = 1
Divide by 0: java.lang.ArithmeticException: / by zero
C:\>java NestTry One Two
a = 2
Array index out-of-bounds:
java.lang.ArrayIndexOutOfBoundsException:42
```

7.6 Multiple Catch Statements

- In some of the cases, more than one exception can be thrown by the piece of code embedded in a try block. To handle this type of situation, you can include more than one catch blocks for a single try block. Each catch clause catches a different excpetion. When an exception is thrown, it is matched with every catch statement in an order. The one whose type matches, is executed. Once the catch statement is executed, all other catch statements are bypassed and execution continues after the try-catch block.

Important:

- When you use multiple catch statements, exception subclasses must come bore any of their super classes. This is because, catch statement with exception super class catches all exceptions of that type as well as all its subclass exceptions. Thus a subclass would never be caught if super class comes before it.

Program 7.8:

```
class MultiCatch {
public static void main(String args[]) {
try {
int a = args.length;
System.out.println("a = " + a);
int b = 42 / a;
int c[] = { 1 };
c[42] = 99;
} catch(ArithmeticException e) {
```

```
System.out.println("Divide by 0: " + e);
} catch(ArrayIndexOutOfBoundsException e) {
System.out.println("Array index oob: " + e);
}
System.out.println("After try/catch blocks.");
}
}
```

Output:

```
a = 0
Divide by 0: java.lang.ArithmeticException: / by zero
After try/catch blocks.
C:\>java MultiCatch TestArg
a = 1
Array index oob: java.lang.ArrayIndexOutOfBoundsException:42
After try/catch blocks.
```

7.7 User Defined Exceptions

Java's built-in exceptions

- Inside a standard package java.lang, java defines several exception classes. The most general exceptions are subclasses of RuntimeExeception class. These exceptions need not be included in any of the methods throws list. In Java, these are called 'unchecked exceptions'. Some of the exceptions defined by java.lang must be included in a method's throws list if that method generates any one of these exceptions and does not handle it by itself. These exceptions are called 'checked exceptions'. Although Java's built-in exceptions handle most common errors, you can also create your own exception types suitable to your own application.

User defined exceptions

- You define a subclass of Exception which in turn is a subclass of Throwable. Thus all exceptions including those that you have created will inherit all methods of Throwable class.
- Exception class has the following constructors:

```
Exception()          //Creates an exception without any description.
Exception(String msg)
                //Creates an exception with description of an exception
```

Program 7.9: A program that illustrates user defined exception.

```
class MyException extends Exception {
private int detail;
MyException(int a) {
detail = a;
}
public String toString() {
return "MyException[" + detail + "]";
}
}
class ExceptionDemo {
static void compute(int a) throws MyException {
System.out.println("Called compute(" + a + ")");
if(a > 10)
throw new MyException(a);
System.out.println("Normal exit");
}
public static void main(String args[]) {
try {
compute(1);
compute(20);
} catch (MyException e) {
System.out.println("Caught " + e);
}
}
}
```

Output:

```
Called compute(1)
Normal exit
Called compute(20)
Caught MyException[20]
```

Practice Questions

1. What are Exceptions?
2. Differentiate between Error and Exception.
3. Explain different types of Exceptions.
4. Explain the following terms with example.
   (a) Using try-Catch
   (b) throw Statement
   (c) Multiple catch statements

5. Explain Nested try Statement block with example
6. How can we create our Own Exception?
7. State User Defined Exception in detail.
8. What is the use of Throws Statement?
9. How Throw Statement is used in Handling Exceptions?
10. Write a short note on Keywords in Exception Handling.

■■■

Chapter 8...

JAVA INPUT OUTPUT

Contents ...

8.1 Java IO package

- We can make use of variables and arrays for storing data in the program. But this data will be lost if variable goes out of scope or if the program itself is terminated. To overcome this problem, we can store data on secondary storage devices like hard disk. Here data is stored in files. This data is called as **'persistent data'**.
- A **file** is a collection of records placed on secondary storage device.
- Storing and managing data in files is called **'File Processing'**. Java supports various powerful features for manipulation of data in files.
- java.io package provides support for I/O operations. This package has built-in classes for reading and writing data in bytes, characters, fields and even objects.
- Some of the frequently used I/O classes defined by java.io package are listed here.

Table 8.1

BufferedInputStream	FileReader	RandomAccessFile
BufferedOutputStream	FileWriter	Reader
BufferedReader	InputStream	StringReader
BufferedWriter	InputStreamReader	StringWriter
DataInputStream	ObjectInputStream	Writer
DataOutputStream	ObjectOutputStream	
File	OutputStreamWriter	
FileInputStream	PrintStream	
FileOutputStream	PrintWriter	

- java.io package has a class File which can be used for creating files and directories. Class contains several methods for creating a file, deleting a file, opening a file, closing a file, getting name of the file etc.
- Each I/O statement or group of I/O statements must have an exception handler around it or the method must declare that it throws an IOException.
- Some of the IO exception classes are EOFException, FileNotFoundException, IOException, InterruptedException.
- If we want to create and use a file, we should decide first the name given to the file, data type to be stored in a file, purpose of opening the file and method of creating a file.
- The input or output operation can be performed with files, network connections, memory buffers etc. You will not find any difference between input and output when you write Java programs. They are all treated same by the abstraction **stream.** These various sources and destinations are handled by the **stream**.
- A **stream** is nothing but a logical entity that is linked with the data source or destinations. Data flows through this logical entity from source(input) to destination(output).

8.2 File Class

- Although most of the classes defined by java.io operate on streams, File class does not operate on streams. It directly deals with files and file system.
- File class does not specify how the information is retrieved from or stored in files. It also describes the properties of file. File object is used to manipulate such type of information associated with a disk file.
- For example, size, permission, date and time of creation and modification of file, directory path etc. Files are the main source for storing persistent information.
- You must have seen a list of files using a dir command. The list includes all the files along with their attributes in the specified directory.
- A directory in Java, simply is treated as a file with one additional property- a list of filenames in that directory that can be seen with the help of list() method.
- The following are the constructors of the File class.
    - File(String directoryPath)
    - File(String directoryPath, String fileName)
    - File(File dirObj, String fileName)
    - File(URI uriObj)
- Here,
    - directoryPath is the path name of the file.
    - fileName is the name of the file or subdirectory.

- dirObj is the name of the file object that specifies the directory.
- uriObj is the name of the URI object that describes a file.
- All of these constructors throw NullPointerException if filename is null.

Examples:

```
File f1 = new File("/");              // A directory path as an argument.
File f2 = new File("/", "test.dat");  // A directory path and a filename.
File f3 = new File(f1, "test.dat");   // refers to the same file as f2.
```

- The methods of File class are as follows:

Table 8.2

Method	Description
`String getName()`	Returns name of the file.
`String getParent()`	Returns name of parent directory.
`long length()`	Returns length of the file.
`boolean exists()`	Returns true if the files exists Otherwise returns false.
`boolean isFile()`	Returns true if the invoking object is a file. If the invoking object is a directory, device driver, special file or named pipe, the method returns false.
`boolean isDirectory()`	Returns true if the invoking object is a directory. Otherwise returns false.
`boolean isAbsolute()`	Returns true if the path is absolute. If the path is relative, returns false.
`boolean canRead()`	Returns true if file can be read.
`boolean canWrite()`	Returns true if file can be written.
`String getAbsolutePath()`	Returns absolute path of the file.
`String getPath()`	Returns relative path of the file.
`boolean rename(File newName)`	Renames the file. Returns true if file is renamed successfully. If for some reasons like attempts to overwrite files, or move them to unauthorized locations, the method returns false.

contd. ...

`boolean delete()`	Returns true if the file is deleted successfully. Otherwise, returns false. This method can also be used for directories. Before making an attempt to delete a directory, you must ensure that it is empty.
`boolean deleteOnExit()`	Deletes the file when the invoking object goes out of scope. You will find this method useful for working with temporary file.
`boolean isHidden()`	Returns true for hidden files and false for others.
`boolean setLastModified(long msec)`	Sets the time of last modification of the file. The argument specifies the number of milliseconds from Jan 1, 1970.
`boolean setReadOnly()`	Makes the file read only.
`String[ ] list()`	Returns the files and sub directories stored in the directory.
`boolean createNewFile()`	Creates a new file and returns true if the file is created successfully. Returns false, if for some reasons like file already exists, file is not created.
`boolean mkdir()`	Creates a directory and returns true if the directory is successfully created.
`boolean mkdirs()`	Creates a directory and its parent directories in the path. Returns true if the creation is successful.

Program 8.1: A program to illustrate the use of methods of File class that displays information about the file.

```
import java.io.*;
public class FileDemo
{
    public static void main(String[] args)
    {
    try {
    File f = new File("DrawApplet.java");
```

```
        System.out.println("\nCan read? " + f.canRead());
        System.out.println("\nCan write? " + f.canWrite());
        System.out.println("\nAbsolute path " + f.getAbsolutePath());
        System.out.println("\nLength " + f.length());
        System.out.println("\nParent " + f.getParent());;
        System.out.println("\nIs file? " + f.isFile());
        System.out.println("\nIs directory? " + f.isDirectory());
        String []list = f.list();
        for(int i=0; i<list.length; i++)
        System.out.println(list[i]);
        }
        catch(NullPointerException e) { System.out.println("Error"); }
        }
    }
```

Output:

```
    Can read? true
    Can write? true
    Absolute path D:\Java Programs\DrawApplet.java
    Length 888
    Parent null
    Is file? true
    Is directory? false
```

Table 8.3: Common stream classes used for I/O operations

Source or Destination	Characters		Bytes	
	Read	Write	Read	Write
Memory	CharArrayReader	CharArrayWriter	ByteArrayInputStream	ByteArrayOutputStream
File	FileReader	FileWriter	FileInputStream	FileOutputStream
Pipe	PipedReader	PipedWriter	PipedInputStream	PipedOutputStream

8.3 Byte/Character stream

8.3.1 Concept of Streams

- In case of file processing, input means the data that flows into a program and output means data that flows out of the program. Input may come from mouse, keyboard, memory etc. whereas output may go to screen, memory, disk etc. Though these input and output tasks are independent of each other, they share a common characteristic as unidirectional movement of data and sequential access to the data.
- Java uses a concept of streams to represent ordered sequence of data. A stream in java is a path along which data flows. It is like a pipe through which water flows. It has a source and destination. The source and the destination may be the physical devices, programs or other streams in the same program. Java streams are classified into two streams- **input stream** and **output stream**.
- An **input stream** reads data from the source file and sends it to the program while **output stream** takes data from the program and sends it to the destination file.

8.3.2 Stream Classes

- Java's IO package contains variety of stream classes. These classes can be categorized into two groups based on the data type.
  - Byte stream classes provide support for I/O operations on bytes.
  - Character Stream classes provide support for I/O operations on characters.
- Java's stream based I/O has four abstract classes – InputStream, OutputStream, Reader and Writer.
- InputStream and OutputStream deal with bytes i.e. read/write bytes.
- Reader and Writer are designed for character streams. Character streams read or write characters. Character streams are high level streams. High level streams work with character data and primitive data types which provides meaningful data for programmers.

8.3.3 Byte Stream Classes

- As the name implies, byte streams handle reading and writing of bytes.
- InputStream and OutputStream are the abstract classes designed for byte streams. Each of these abstract classes has several concrete subclasses which can be used for reading from or writing to various devices like disk files, network connections, memory buffers etc.
- Byte streams are low level streams. Low level streams will work with raw data as stored by the file system. This type is useful for applications that read or write image data.
- All stream methods are synchronized. This implies that methods of these streams return only after reading or writing bytes. They will wait till the data is available and then perform the operation and return.
- You should note that the methods of byte streams return the integer. The lower eight bits of the integer will be used to represent the byte read.
- **InputStream**: It is an abstract class. We cannot create an instance of this class. Most of its methods throw an IOException in case of errors.

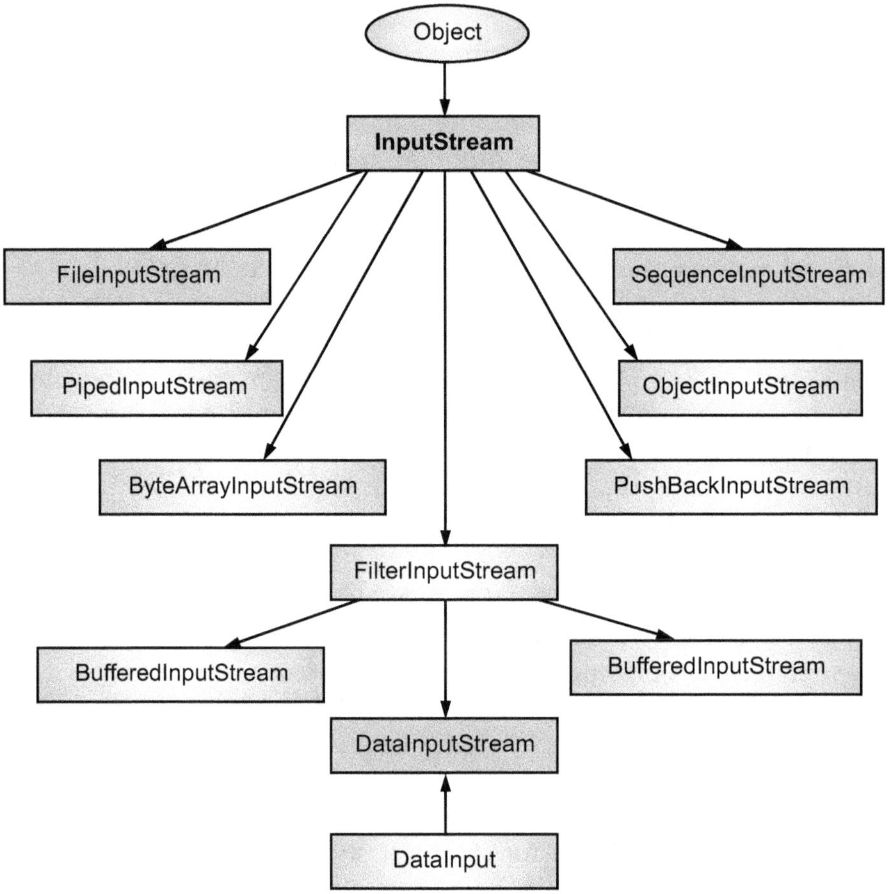

Fig. 8.1: Hierarchy of InputStream classes

- Table 8.4 shows methods in InputStream class.

Table 8.4

Method	Description
1. read()	it reads a byte from the input stream
2. read (byte b[ ])	it reads an array of bytes into b
3. read (byte b[ ], int n, int m)	it reads m bytes into b starting from n^{th} byte
4. available( )	it give number of bytes available in the input
5. skip(n)	it skips over n bytes from the inputs stream
6. reset( )	it goes back to the beginning of the stream
7. close( )	it closes the input stream

- Here are some of the popularly used concrete classes which are sub classes of InputStream abstract class.

FileInputStream

- This class extends InputStream class to read binary data from a file.

- The commonly used constructors are as follows:
  - FileInputStream(String path) throws FileNotFoundException
  - FileInputStream(File fileObject) throws FileNotFoundException
- Here,
  - path refers to the complete path of the file, and
  - fileObject refers to the object that describes the file.

Program 8.2: A program shows how FileInputStream class is used for reading bytes from file and FileOuputStream class is used to write bytes to a file.

```
File: FileRead.java
import java.io.*;
class FileRead
{
    public static void main(String[] args) throws IOException,
    FileNotFoundException
    {
        File f = new File("Ball.txt");
        FileInputStream fis = new FileInputStream(f);
        FileOutputStream fos = new FileOutputStream("NewBall.txt");
        int value;
        while((value=fis.read()) != -1)
        {
            System.out.print((char)value);
            fos.write(value);
        }
        fis.close();
        fos.close();
    }
}
```

Program reads an existing file and displays its bytes on the screen. It also writes data to the new file 'NewBall.txt'. We must first create the file named 'Ball.txt' before we run this program. The new file 'NewBall.txt' is created if it does not already exist. If the file exists, the previous contents are lost and data is written from the beginning of the file. In case if the file to be read or new file to be written is not found for any reason, FileNotFoundException is thrown.

ByteArrayInputStream

- This stream is similar to the FileInputStream but ByteArrayInputStream reads data from an array or from a portion of an array.
- The following are the constructors used to create byte array input streams:
  - ByteArrayInputStream(byte byteArray[])
- The above form constructs a stream to read from the specified byte array.
  - ByteArrayInputStream(byte byteArray[], int index, int size)

- The above form constructs a stream to read from a portion of the specified byte array that is from given index and of the given size.

Program 8.3: A program that demonstrates ByteArrayInputStream class.

We create two byte array streams- one to store sample string in bytes and the other to store a part of the sample byte stream.

```
import java.io.*;
class ByteArrayDemo
{
    public static void main(String args[])
    {
        String myString = "One Two Buckle my shoes";
        byte[] byteArray = myString.getBytes();
        byte b1[];
        int c;
        try
        {
        ByteArrayInputStream arrayInp1 = new ByteArrayInputStream
                                                          (byteArray);
        ByteArrayInputStream arrayInp2 = new
        ByteArrayInputStream(byteArray,0, 7);
        b1 = new byte[byteArray.length];
        for(int i=0; i<2; i++)
        {
        arrayInp1.read(b1);
        System.out.println(new String(b1));
        while ((c= arrayInp2.read())!= -1)
        System.out.print( ( char )c );
        System.out.println();
        arrayInp1.reset();
        arrayInp2.reset();
        }
        } catch(IOException e)
        {  System.out.println("Error in opening the stream");
        }
    }
    }
```

Output:

```
One Two Buckle my shoes
One Two
```

BufferedInputStream

- This class is extended from FilterInputStream. It is a high level stream. It reads data from a stream and associates a memory buffer to the stream. The reading will be done from this buffer and hence will be much faster as compared to reading directly from input streams. This enhances the performance and also supports operations like skipping, marking and resetting. The constructors are as follows:
  - o BufferedInputStream(InputStream ins)
  - o BufferedInputStream(InputStream ins, int bufferSize)
- The first form wraps the input stream into a buffered stream. The default size of the buffer is used here. The next form allows you to specify a buffer size. The optimum size of the buffer will depend on the host operating system. The smallest size enhances the performance of I/O stream.
- The following statement will wrap the FileInputStream to the buffered stream.
  - o FileInputStream fis = new FileInputStream("test.txt");
  - o BufferedInputStream bis = new BufferedInputStream(fis);
  - o bis.read() method will read data from the buffer and not from the file.

DataInputStream

This is a high level stream that permits reading of primitive data types. When you work with byte streams, you have to convert them to characters or strings to understand their meaning. But this stream provides methods to directly work with meaningful types. DataInputStream implements DataInput interface that defines methods to read the sequence of bytes and convert them into values of primitive data types. The following table shows commonly used methods. All these methods throw IOException.

Table 8.5

Method	Description
`boolean readBoolean()`	Reads and returns a boolean value from the stream.
`boolean readByte()`	Reads and returns a byte value from the stream.
`boolean readChar()`	Reads and returns a char value from the stream.
`boolean readDouble()`	Reads and returns a double value from the stream.
`boolean readFloat()`	Reads and returns a float value from the stream.
`boolean readInt()`	Reads and returns a integer value from the stream.

contd. ...

`Boolean readLong()`	Reads and returns a long value from the stream.
`boolean readshort()`	Reads and returns a short value from the stream.
`void readFully(byte buff[])`	Reads and fills the buffer buff with bytes.
`void readFully(byte buff[], int index, int number)`	Reads specified number of bytes and fills the buffer from buff[index].
`int skip Bytes(int n)`	Skips n bytes in the stream.
`void write (int j)`	Writes the byte in the lower 8 bits of j.
`void write (byte buff[ ])`	Writes contents of the buffer to the stream.
`void write (byte buff [ ], int index, int len)`	Writes a portion of the buffer to the stream (starting from index and of length len).
`void close ()`	Writes all data in the stream and closes the stream.
`void flush ()`	Flushes (writes) all data from the stream.

- **OutputStream:** OutputStream is an abstract class. Most of the methods of this class return void and throw IOException in case of errors.

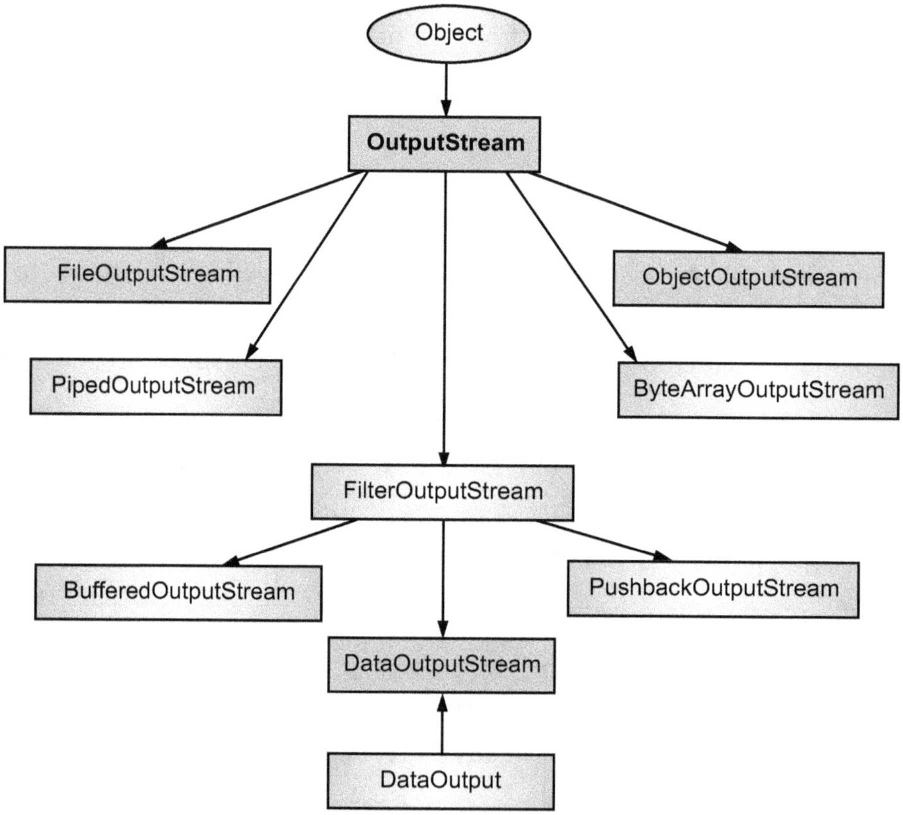

Fig. 8.2: Output Stream

- Table 8.6 shows methods in OutputStream class.

Table 8.6

Method	Description
1. write( )	it writes a byte to the output stream
2. write (byte b[ ])	it writes all bytes in the array b to the output stream
3. write (byte b[ ], int n, int m)	it writes m bytes from array b starting from nth byte
4. close( )	it closes the output stream
5. flush( )	it flushes the output stream

FileOutputStream

- This stream writes bytes to a file. The constructors are as follows:
  - FileOutputStream (String path) throws FileNotFound Exception
  - FileOutputStream (String path, boolean apppend) throws FileNot Found Exception
  - FileOutputStream (File fileOb)
- All these constructors throw FindNotFoundException. Parameter path indicates complete path to the file and fileOb indicates file object. Parameter append is true if the new data should be appended to the existing data and false if the old data should be overwritten.

Program 8.4:

```
import java.io.*;
class FileOutputStreamDemo
 {
     public static void main(String args[]) throws Exception
        {
             FileOutputStream fileOut = new
             FileOutputStream("sample.dat");
             int i;
             for(i=0;i<10;i++)
             fileOut.write(i%5);
             fileOut.close();
             FileInputStream fin = new
             FileInputStream("sample.dat");
             while ( (i = fin.read()) != -1)
             System.out.println(i);
             fin.close();
        }
 }
```

Output:

```
0 1 2 3 4 0 1 2 3 4
```

ByteArrayOutputStream

- This class is similar to the ByteArrayInputStream but only it writes bytes to the array. The default array length is 32 bytes. If required, you can also specify the byte array length. The constructors are as follows:
  - ByteArrayOutputStream()
  - ByteArrayOutputStream(int byteArLength)

Program 8.5:

```
import java.io. *;
class ByteArrayOutputStreamDemo
{
   public static void main(String [] arg) throws Exception
   {
      ByteArrayOutputStream b = new ByteArrayOutputStream();
      String myString = "One Two Buckle my shoes";
      byte[ ] byteArray = myString.getBytes();
      b. write(byteArray );
      byte[] ary = b.toByteArray();
      for (int i=0; i<ary.length; i++)
      System.out.print ((char) ary[i]);
      System.out.println("\n" + b.toString());
      b.reset();
      for(int i=0;i<ary.length;i++)
      b.write( '#' );
      System.out.println(b.toString());
   }
}
```

Output:

```
One Two Buckle my shoes
One Two Buckle my shoes
```

BufferedOutputStream

- This stream works with a buffer.
- It keeps data in buffer and then writes. flush() method writes data from the buffer to the output device.
- BufferedOutputStream helps to improve performance.
- The default size of the buffer is 512 bytes. If required, you can change the size of the buffer using an appropriate form of constructor. The constructors are as follows:
  - BufferedOutputStream(OutputStream os)
  - BufferedOutputStream(OutputStream os, int size)

PrintStream

- PrintStream extends from FilterOutputStream. PrintStream is one of the most used Java class. This class provides all of the output capabilities. The following are the constructors:
  - PrintStream(OutputStream os)
  - PrintStream(OutputStream os, boolean flushOnNewLine)
  - PrintStream(OutputStream os, boolean flushOnNewLine, String charSet) throws
- Here,
  - os defines the OutputStream that will receive output.
  - Unsupported encoding exception flushOnNewLine parameter is true, the output is automatically flushed every time a newline(\n) character is recognized or when println is called. If false, it is not flushed automatically.
  - charSet specifies character encoding scheme.

DataOutputStream

- This stream also extends from FilterOutputStream. This writes primitive data to a byte oriented output stream. It supports all of its methods defined by its superclasses. It implements DataOutput interface which define methods that convert values from primitive data type into a byte sequence and then writes to the underlying stream. writeDouble(), writeBoolean(), writeInt() are some of the examples of such methods.

8.3.4 Character Stream Classes

- Character streams can be used to read and write 16 bit Unicode characters. Like byte stream classes, character stream classes are reader stream and writer stream classes.

Reader

- Reader class is the base class for all the classes in this group. It is an abstract class. This class is quite similar to InputStream class in functionality. Methods of this class are also identical to those of InputStream class. The only difference is that the fundamental unit of data is character instead of byte.

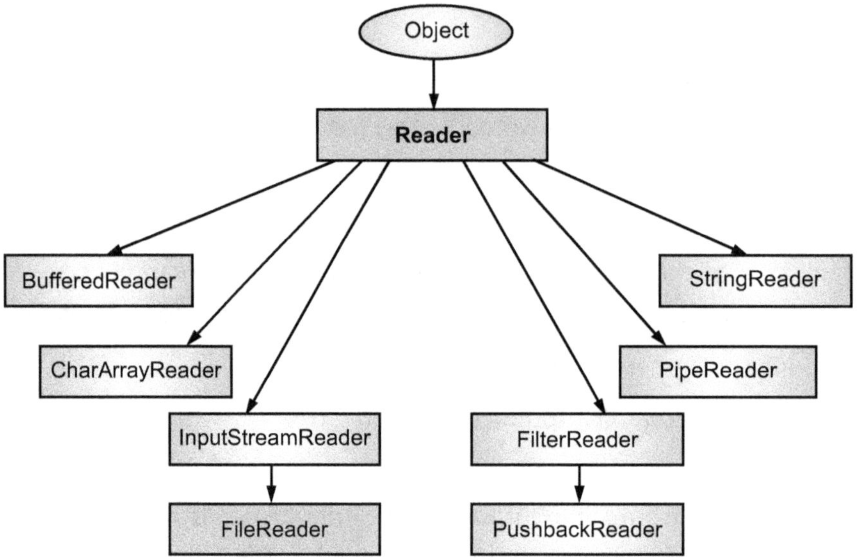

Fig. 8.3: Hierarchy of reader stream classes

Writer

- Writer class is the base class for all other writer classes in this group. It is an abstract class. This class is very similar to OutputStream class in functionality. Methods of this class are also identical to those of the OutputStream class. The only difference is that the fundamental unit of data is character instead of byte.

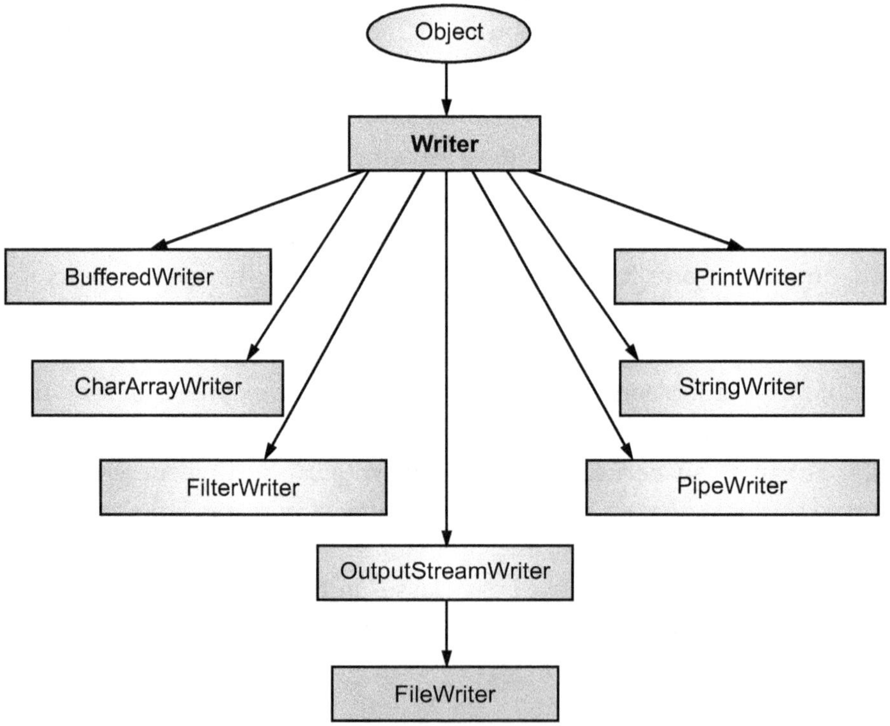

Fig. 8.4: Hierarchy of writer stream classes

8.4 Buffered Reader/Writer

8.4.1 BufferedReader

- It improves performance by buffering input. The contents of the stream can be read into a buffer to speed up the execution. The size of the buffer can be set explicitly, if required. In addition to the methods defined by the Reader class, this class has a method readLine() to read a line from the stream. It has two forms of constructors.
  - BufferedReader(Reader *inStream*): This form creates a buffered character stream with a default buffer size.
  - BufferedReader(Reader *inStream,* int *buffSize)*: The size of the buffer is passed in buffSize.

Program 8.6:

```
import java.io. *;
  class FileReaderDemo
  {
     public static void main(String args []) throws Exception
     {
        FileReader file = new FileReader(args[0] );
        BufferedReader buffer = new BufferedReader(file );
        int n = Integer.parseInt(args[1]);
        String line = " ";
        for(int i=0;i<n &and (line = buffer.readLine())!= null;i++ )
        System.out.println(line);
        file. close();
     }
  }
```

8.4.2 BufferedWriter

- It is a writer that buffers output. It improves performance by buffering output data and thus by reducing the number of times data is actually physically written to the output stream. It has two forms of constructors:
  - BufferedWriter(Writer *outStream*): This form creates a buffered character stream with a default buffer size.
  - BufferedWriter(Writer *outStream*, int *buffSize*): The size of the buffer is passed in buffSize.

8.5 File Reader/Writer

8.5.1 FileReader

- This class creates a Reader which you can use to read the characters from the file. This class is extended from InputStreamReader class. It has two forms of constructors.
  - FileReader(String *fPath*);
  - FileReader(File fileObject);
- Both these forms of constructors throw FileNotFound Exception.

Program 8.7:

```
import java.io. *;
class FileReaderDemo
{
    public static void main(String [] arg) throws Exception
    {
        char inpChars[] = new char[ 1024] ;
        FileReader inpFile = new FileReader (arg[01]);
        int charRead = inpFile.read(inpChars);
        String s = new String(inpChars, 0, charRead);
        System.out.println(s.toUpperCase());
        inpFile.close();
    }
}
```

8.5.2 FileWriter

- This class creates a Writer which can be used to write the contents to the file. It has four forms of constructors.
  - FileWriter(String fPath);
  - FileWriter(String fPath, boolean *append)*;
  - FileWriter(File *fileObject*);
  - FileWriter(File *fileObject*, boolean *append*);
- All these forms of constructors throw IOException. If *append* is true, then the output is appended to the end of the file.
- The following program uses two file stream classes to copy the contents of one file into the other file.

Program 8.8:

```
import java.io. *;
class CopyCharacter
{
   public static void main (Strings args[ ])
   {
      File FileIn = new File ("in.dat");
      File FileOut = new File ("out.dat");
      FileReader FileIn = null;
      FileWriter FileOut = null;
      try
      {
         in = new FileReader (FileIn);
         out = new FileWriter (FileOut);
         int ch;
         while ( (ch = In.read() ) != -1)
         {
            out.write(ch);
         }
      }
      catch(IOException e)
      {
         System.out.println(e);
         System.exit(-1);
      }
      finally
      {
         try
         {
            In.close();
            Out.close();
         }
         catch(IOException e) { }
      }
   }
}
```

8.6 Print writer

- It is a character oriented version of print stream. It has several constructors.
  - PrintWriter(OutputStream outStream);
  - PrintWriter(OutputStream outStream, boolean flushOnNewline);
  - PrintWriter(Writer outStream);
  - PrintWriter(Writer outStream, boolean flushOnNewline);
- OutStream specifies an open OutputStream that will receive output.
- FlushOnNewline parameter controls whether output buffer is flushed automatically with every println() or print() function. This parameter has value true if flushing takes place automatically. It has value false if flushing is not automatic. Constructors that do not have this parameter do not flush automatically.
- PrintWriter class has also a set of constructors that writes its output to a file:
  - PrintWriter(File outFile) throws FileNotFoundException
  - PrintWriter(File outFile, String charSet) throws FileNotFoundException, UnsupportedEncodingException
  - PrintWriter(String outFileName) throws FileNotFoundException
  - PrintWriter(String outFileName, String charSet) throws FileNotFoundException, UnsupportedEncodingException
- In all these cases, file is automatically created. Any pre-existing file with same name is destroyed.

8.7 Serialization and De Serialization

- Java provides a mechanism, called object serialization where an object can be represented as a sequence of bytes that includes the object's data as well as information about the object's type and the types of data stored in the object.
- After a serialized object has been written into a file, it can be read from the file and deserialized that is, the type information and bytes that represent the object and its data can be used to recreate the object in memory.
- Most impressive is that the entire process is JVM independent, meaning an object can be serialized on one platform and deserialized on an entirely different platform.
- Classes ObjectInputStream and ObjectOutputStream are high-level streams that contain the methods for serializing and deserializing an object.
- The ObjectOutputStream class contains many write methods for writing various data types, but one method in particular stands out:

```
public final void writeObject(Object x) throws IOException
```

- The above method serializes an Object and sends it to the output stream. Similarly, the ObjectInputStream class contains the following method for deserializing an object:

```
public final Object readObject() throws IOException,
ClassNotFoundException
```

- This method retrieves the next Object out of the stream and deserializes it. The return value is Object, so you will need to cast it to its appropriate data type.
- To demonstrate how serialization works in Java, I am going to use the Employee class that we discussed early on in the book. Suppose that we have the following Employee class, which implements the Serializable interface:

```
public class Employee implements java.io.Serializable
{
    public String name;
    public String address;
    public transient int SSN;
    public int number;

    public void mailCheck()
    {
        System.out.println("Mailing a check to " + name + " " +
        address);
    }
}
```

- Notice that for a class to be serialized successfully, two conditions must be met:
  - The class must implement the java.io.Serializable interface.
  - All of the fields in the class must be serializable. If a field is not serializable, it must be marked transient.
- If you are curious to know if a Java Standard Class is serializable or not, check the documentation for the class. The test is simple: If the class implements java.io.Serializable, then it is serializable; otherwise, it's not.

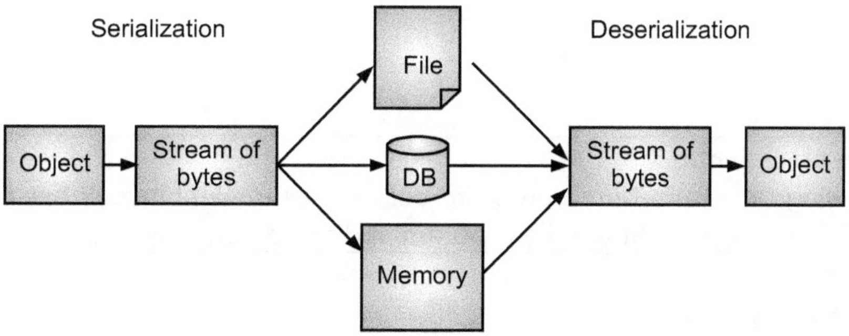

Fig. 8.5: Serialization and Deserialization

Serializing an Object:

- The ObjectOutputStream class is used to serialize an Object. The following SerializeDemo program instantiates an Employee object and serializes it to a file.

- When the program is done executing, a file named employee.ser is created. The program does not generate any output, but study the code and try to determine what the program is doing.
- Note: When serializing an object to a file, the standard convention in Java is to give the file a **.ser** extension.

Program 8.9:

```
import java.io.*;
public class SerializeDemo
{
   public static void main(String [] args)
   {
      Employee e = new Employee();
      e.name = "Reyan Ali";
      e.address = "Shivaji Nagar, Pune";
      e.SSN = 11122333;
      e.number = 101;

      try
      {
         FileOutputStream fileOut =
         new FileOutputStream("/tmp/employee.ser");
         ObjectOutputStream out = new ObjectOutputStream(fileOut);
         out.writeObject(e);
         out.close();
         fileOut.close();
         System.out.printf("Serialized data is saved in
                                        /tmp/employee.ser");
      }catch(IOException i)
      {
         i.printStackTrace();
      }
   }
}
```

Deserializing an Object:

- The following DeserializeDemo program deserializes the Employee object created in the SerializeDemo program. Study the program and try to determine its output:

Program 8.10:

```
import java.io.*;
public class DeserializeDemo
{
   public static void main(String [] args)
   {
      Employee e = null;
```

```
        try
        {
           FileInputStream fileIn =
                              new FileInputStream("/tmp/employee.ser");
           ObjectInputStream in = new ObjectInputStream(fileIn);
           e = (Employee) in.readObject();
           in.close();
           fileIn.close();
        }catch(IOException i)
        {
           i.printStackTrace();
           return;
        }catch(ClassNotFoundException c)
        {
           System.out.println("Employee class not found");
           c.printStackTrace();
           return;
        }
        System.out.println("Deserialized Employee...");
        System.out.println("Name: " + e.name);
        System.out.println("Address: " + e.address);
        System.out.println("SSN: " + e.SSN);
        System.out.println("Number: " + e.number);
    }
}
```

- This would produce the following output:

```
Deserialized Employee...
Name: Reyan Ali
Address: Shivaji Nagar, Pune
SSN: 0
Number:101
```

- There are following **difference between serialization and deserialization** in java:

Table 8.7

Serialization	Deserialization
Serialization is the process through which we can store the state of an object into any storage medium. We can store the state of the object into a file, into a database table etc.	Deserialization is the opposite process of serialization where we retrieve the object back from the storage medium.
An object is serialized by writing it an ObjectOutputStream.	An object is deserialized by reading it from an ObjectInputStream.

contd. ...

Example:	Example:

`FileOutputStream out = new FileOutputStream("abc.txt");`
`ObjectOutputStream oos = new ObjectOutputStream(out);`
`oos.writeObject(new String ());`
`oos.close ();`
	`FileInputStream in = new FileInputStream("abc.txt");`
	`ObjectInputStream ois = new ObjectInputStream(in);`
	`String s = (String) ois.readObject();`
	`ois.close();`

8.8 File Sequential / Random

- So far what we have discussed is that files are read or written sequentially only. These are known as 'sequential files'.
- RandomAccessFile class of java.io package allows us to create files that will be used for reading and writing bytes, text and Java data types with random access.
- A file can be created and opened for random access by giving a mode string as parameter. 'r' is the parameter used for read-only. 'rw' is the parameter used for read and write both. Random access file has a pointer known as 'file pointer' which can be moved to arbitrary position in the file before reading or writing. The file pointer is moved with the seek() method of RandomAccessFile class.
- When the file is opened with the following statement,

  f = new RandomAccessFile("test.dat","rw")

  the file pointer is moved at the beginning of the file.
- The following program is an example of random access.

Program 8.11:

```
//Random Access File Program.
import java.io.*;
public class RandomAccess
{
    public static void main(String[] args)
    {
        RandomAccessFile file;
        try
        {
            file = new RandomAccessFile("Ball.txt", "r");
            long size = file.length();
            long pos = size/2;
            file.seek(pos);
```

```
            while(true)
            {
               int data = file.read();
               if(data == -1)
                  break;
               System.out.print((char)data);
            }
            file.close();
         }
         catch(Exception e)
         {
            e.printStackTrace();
         }
      }
   }
```

- The program opens the file named 'Ball.txt' in random access mode. It gets the length of the file by using length() method. File pointer is moved to a position pos. Program starts reading a data character by character from that position and print it. When the end of file is reached, the value of the variable data becomes -1 and the loop breaks.

Few Sample Programs:

1. Reading and writing primitive data

Program 8.12:

```
import java.io.*;
class ReadWritePrimitiveData
{
   public static void main(String[] args)
   {
      try{
         FileOutputStream fos = new FileOutputStream("data.dat");
         DataOutputStream dos = new DataOutputStream(fos);
         //Writing primitive data to the data.dat file
         dos.writeInt(5000);
         dos.writeDouble(980.87);
         dos.writeChar('A');
         dos.writeBoolean(false);
         fos.close();
         dos.close();
```

```
        //Reading primitive data from the data.dat file
           FileInputStream fis = new FileInputStream("data.dat");
           DataInputStream dis = new DataInputStream(fis);
           System.out.println(dis.readInt());
           System.out.println(dis.readDouble());
           System.out.println(dis.readChar());
           System.out.println(dis.readBoolean());
           fis.close();
           dis.close();
           }catch(Exception e) {}
     }
  }
```

2. Reading ordinary text files

Program 8.13:

```
import java.io.*;
public class OrdFiles {
public static void main(String [] args) {
    // The name of the file to open.
    String fName = "temp.txt";
    // This will reference one line at a time
    String line = null;
    try {
      // FileReader reads text files in the default encoding.
      FileReader fReader =
      new FileReader(fName);
      // Always wrap FileReader in BufferedReader.
      BufferedReader buffReader =
         new BufferedReader(fReader);
      while((line = buffReader.readLine()) != null) {
         System.out.println(line);
      }
      // Always close files.
      buffReader.close();
    }
```

```
    catch(FileNotFoundException e) {
       System.out.println(
          "Unable to open file '" +
          fName + "'");
    }
    catch(IOException e) {
       System.out.println(
          "Error reading file '"
          + fName + "'");
          // Or we could just do this:
          // e.printStackTrace();
      }
    }
}
```

Practice Questions

1. Write a program which will read data from consol and display it using InputStream.
2. Write a program which will read data from Consol and display it using Reader till user enters 'q'.
3. Write a program which reads contents of file and display it on console using FileInputStream.
4. Write a program which reads contents of file and display it on console using FileReader.
5. Write a program which reads contents of a file and Store it in another file FileInputStream and FileOutputStream.
6. Write a program which reads a contains of a file and Store it in another file FileReader and FileWriter.
7. Write a program which will read number of lines of files.
8. Write a program which will read number of characters in a file.
9. What is Serialization in Java? Explain with example.
10. What is the difference between Serialization and De Serialization?

■■■

Chapter 9...

MULTITHREADING

Contents ...

9.1 Multithreading Concepts

9.1.1 Introduction

- Like many other programming languages, Java also supports multithreaded programming. A multithreaded program contains two or more parts which can execute concurrently. Each of this part is called a 'Thread'. Each thread defines a separate path of execution. Multithreading enables you to write very efficient programs. It helps in utilizing CPU at its maximum. By using multithreaded programming, we can keep, CPU's idle time minimum.

9.1.2 Process Based Multitasking and Thread Based Multitasking

- Multithreading is a specialized form of multitasking. Multitasking can be of two types. These are Process based multi tasking and Thread based multitasking.
- In process based multitasking, program is a smallest unit of dispatchable code. In Thread based multitasking, the thread that is, small part of a program is a smallest unit of dispatchable code. For example, you can use the text editor for typing the matter in it while it is printing some document. These two actions are carried out in two separate threads.
- Multitasking threads require less overhead than multitasking processes.
- Multitasking processes are heavy weight components that require separate address space. Therefore Inter-process communication is expensive and limited. On the other hand, threads that are light weight components share the same address space so inter-thread communication is inexpensive.
- Context switch between processes is costly. Context switch between the threads in low cost.

9.1.3 Java Thread Model

- Java runtime system depends on threads for many things. In a single threaded environment, when a thread is blocked when it is waiting for a resource. Because of this, the entire program stops running. The benefits of multithreading is that, one thread can pause without stopping the other parts of your program. All other threads continue to run. This helps in improving the efficiency by preventing the waste of CPU cycles.
- Thread can be in several states. A thread may be running. It can be ready to run. A running thread can be suspended temporarily. A suspended thread can be resumed. A thread can be blocked when waiting for a resource. At any time, a thread can be terminated. Once it is terminated, it cannot be resumed again.

9.1.4 Main thread

- When Java starts up, one thread begins running immediately. This thread is called a main thread of a program. This main thread is the one when your program begins its execution.
- It is a thread from which other child threads are spawned. It must be the last thread to finish an execution of a program.
- This thread is created automatically, when your program is started. But you can control it by calling a static currentThread() method of Thread object.
- By default, the name of this thread is 'main'. Its default priority value is 5.

9.2 Thread Life Cycle

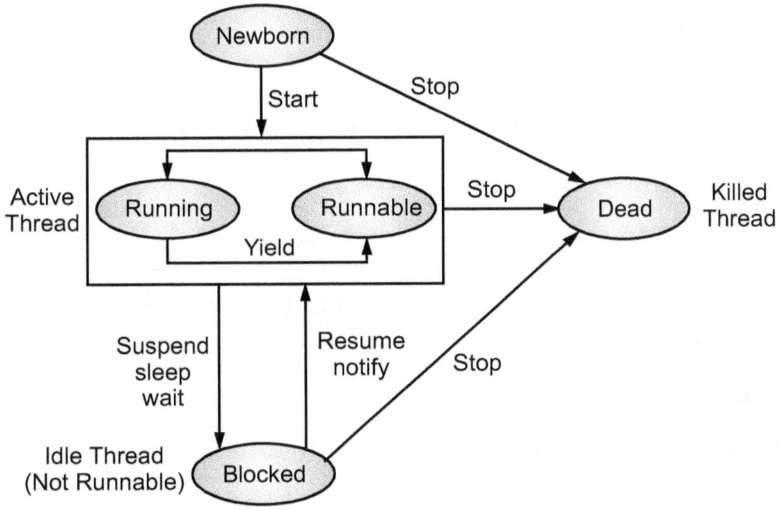

Fig. 9.1: Thread Life Cycle

- During the life time of a thread, it goes into several states mentioned below.
- **Newborn State:** When we create a Thread object, a thread is born and it goes into a new born state. We can schedule it for running using start() method or we can kill it by calling stop() method. If it is scheduled, it moves into runnable state.

- **Runnable State:** This means, a thread is ready for execution and is waiting for the processor. A thread enters into a queue of threads waiting for execution. If all threads are of equal priority then they are executed in round robin fashion. A thread can hand over control to another thread by calling the yield() method.
- **Running State:** A thread gets control of CPU for execution when it goes into a running state. The thread runs until it relinquishes control of its own or it is preempted by some higher priority thread. A running thread hands over control of CPU in one of the following situations.
  - It is suspended using suspend() method. A suspended thread can be restarted using resume() method.
  - We can put a thread to sleep for some specified amount of time using sleep() method. The thread enters into the runnable state as soon as the specified amount of time is elapsed.
  - The thread is notified to wait for some event to occur. This is done by using wait() method. The thread can be scheduled to run again using notify() method.
- **Blocked State:** A thread is said to be blocked when it is prevented from entering into the runnable state. This happens when the thread is suspended, sleeping or waiting. A blocked thread is not runnable. It cannot be called a dead thread as it fully qualified to run.
- **Dead State:** A running thread ends its life when it completes its execution. It is a natural death. We can also kill it by sending the stop() method when it is in any state. This is premature death.

9.3 Creating Multithreaded Application

- You create a thread by instantiating an object of type Thread. Java defines two ways for creating a thread.
  - You can extend Thread class.
  - You can implement the Runnable interface.

1. Using Thread class

- A Thread is created by creating a new class that extends Thread class. Then instance of that class can be created. The extending class must override the run() method. This method acts as an entry point for the new thread. It must call start() method to begin the execution of the new thread.

Program 9.1: The following program demonstrates how to create a thread by extending a Thread class.

Program starts its execution by starting the main thread. It creates an object of DemoThread class which extends Thread class. DemoThread calls start() method which in turn calls run() method of DemoThread class. Here, DemoThread also starts its execution. Main thread and demo thread are put to sleep for 1000 ms. Alternately. Finally main thread is the last thread which ends execution of the program.

```
File: DemoThread.java
class DemoThread extends Thread
{
   public void run()
   {
      for(int i=1; i<=5; i++)
      {
         System.out.println("run : " + i);
         try
         {
            Thread.sleep(1000);
         }
         catch (InterruptedException ie)
         {
            ie.printStackTrace();
         }
      }
   }
   public static void main(String[] args)
   {
      System.out.println("main thread starts");
      Thread t1 = new DemoThread();
      t1.start();
      for(int i=1; i<=5; i++)
      {
         System.out.println("main : " + i);
         try
         {
            Thread.sleep(1000);
         }
         catch (InterruptedException ie)
         {
            ie.printStackTrace();
         }
      }
      System.out.println("main thread ends");
   }
}
```

Output:

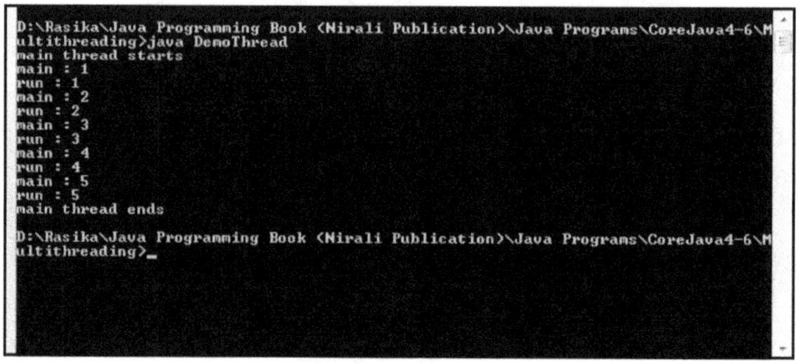

Fig. 9.2: Output

2. Using Runnable Interface

- The easiest way to create a thread is to implement the Runnable interface. You can construct a thread of any object that implements Runnable interface. The class needs to implement the run() method of Runnable interface.

```
public void run()
```

- We can define the code that constitutes new thread inside run() method. run() method can call other methods, declare variables and use other classes just like the main thread. This method is the entry point for other thread execution within a program. This thread ends when run() method returns.
- Once you create a class that implements Runnable interface, you have to create an instance of Thread class with this class. Thread class defines several constructors. The one we use here is:

```
Thread(Runnable runObject, String threadName)
```

- Where,
  - runObject is an instance of a class that implements Runnable interface
  - threadName is the name of the new thread.
- Once the new thread is created, it won't start running until it calls its start() method. This means, start() method executes a call to run() method. This is shown here.

```
void start()
```

Program 9.2: The following program shows how to create thread by implementing Runnable interface.

The program creates two threads t1 and t2 by creating objects of Thread class. Both threads start their execution by calling start() method which in turn give a call to run() method. currentThread() method returns the name of the current thread in execution. Both threads are put to sleep alternately for 1000 ms. Main thread creates an object of DemoRunnable class by calling its constructor.

```
File: DemoRunnable.java
class DemoRunnable implements Runnable
{
   Thread t1, t2;
   DemoRunnable()
   {
      t1 = new Thread(this, "t1");
      t2 = new Thread(this, "t2");
      t1.start();
      t2.start();
   }
   public void run()
   {
      if(Thread.currentThread() == t1)
      {
         for(int i=1; i<=5; i++)
         {
            System.out.println("run for t1 : " + i);
            try
            {
               Thread.sleep(1000);
            }
            catch (InterruptedException ie)
            {
               ie.printStackTrace();
            }
         }
      }
      else
      {
         for(int i=1; i<=5; i++)
         {
            System.out.println("run for t2 : " + i);
```

```
            try
            {
               Thread.sleep(1000);
            }
            catch (InterruptedException ie)
            {
               ie.printStackTrace();
            }
         }
      }
   }
   public static void main(String[] args)
   {
      DemoRunnable dr = new DemoRunnable();
   }
}
```

Output:

Fig. 9.3: Output

9.4 Thread Priorities

- In Java, Each thread is assigned a priority. Thread priorities are used by the thread scheduler to decide when each thread should be allowed to run. Theoretically, higher priority thread get more CPU time than lower priority thread. But in practice, the amount of CPU time each thread gets depends on several other factors besides its priority. Higher priority thread can also preempt lower priority thread. To set the threads priority, use setPriority() method. This method is a member of Thread class.

Final void setPriority(int level): level is an integer value which is the thread's priority. Thread class also defines several priority constants

MIN_PRIORITY = 1

NORM_PRIORITY = 5 //default priority

MAX_PRIORITY = 10

- When there are several threads ready for execution, JVM chooses the highest priority thread and executes it. If a lower priority threads wants to gain control of CPU, one of the following thing should happen:
  - It stops running at the end of run() method.
  - It is made to sleep using sleep() method.
  - It is told to wait using wait() method.
- However, if higher priority thread comes along, currently running thread will be preempted.

Program 9.3: The following program illustrates thread priorities.

```
File: DemoPriority.java
class DemoPriority  implements Runnable
{
   Thread t1, t2;
   DemoPriority()
   {
      t1 = new Thread(this, "t1");
      t2 = new Thread(this, "t2");
      t1.start();
      t2.start();
      t2.setPriority(Thread.MAX_PRIORITY);
      t1.setPriority(t2.getPriority()-3);
   }
   public void run()
   {
      if(Thread.currentThread() == t1)
         for(int i=1; i<=5; i++)
         {
            System.out.println("Run method of t1 = " + i);
         }
```

```
        else
            for(int i=1; i<=5; i++)
            {
                System.out.println("Run method of t2 = " + i);
            }
    }
    public static void main(String[] args)
    {
        DemoPriority d = new DemoPriority();
    }
}
```

Output:

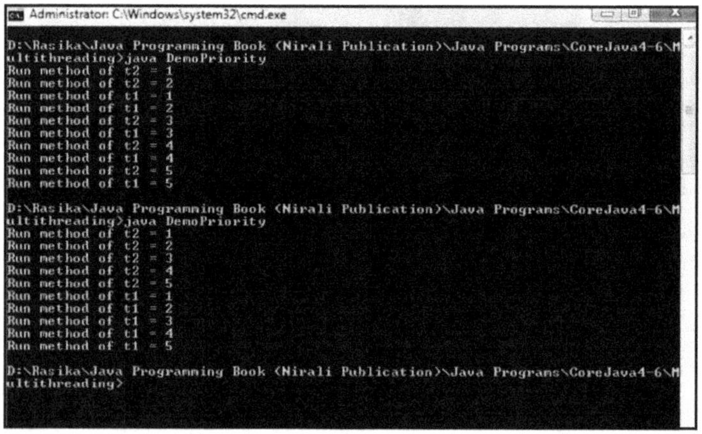

Fig. 9.4: Output

9.5 Thread Synchronization

- When two or more threads need access to a shared resource, it needs to ensure that the resource will be used by only one thread. The process by which this is achieved is called 'Synchronization'. For example, one thread is reading the contents of the file and other thread my want to write the contents to the same file. Results might be weird depending on the situation.
- In Java, keyword synchronized is used to solve such problems to keep a watch at such points in programs. For example, the method that will read information from the file and will write to it, is synchronized with the keyword synchronized.
- When we declare a method synchronized, Java creates a 'monitor' and hands it over to the thread that calls the method. It can be used as a mutually exclusive lock. Only one

thread can own a monitor at a given time. When a thread acquires a lock, it means, it has entered the monitor. All other threads attempting to enter the locked monitor will have to wait, until the first thread exits the monitor.

- When the thread that owns the monitor completes its task, it hands over the monitor to the next thread that is waiting to gain control of the same resource.
- We can synchronize a code in two ways

1. **Using Synchronized methods:** In Java, all objects have their own implicit monitor. To enter an object's monitor, you just need to call a method that is modified with synchronized keyword. When the thread is inside the synchronized method, all other threads that want to call it on the same instance have to wait.

   Synchronized void update()

```
{
---
---    // Code is synchronized here
}
```

Program 9.4: The following program shows how two threads call synchronized method while in execution so as to get the correct results.

```
class Account
{
   private long balance = 5000;
   public long getBalance()
   {
      return balance;
   }
   public void withDraw(int amount)
   {
      if(balance > amount)
      {
         balance = balance - amount;
         System.out.println("The amount is withdrawn by"
                                  + Thread.currentThread().getName());
      }
      else
      System.out.println(Thread.currentThread().getName() + " :
                                                Insufficient amount");
   }
}
```

```
public class  WithSync implements Runnable
{
   private Account a;
   private Thread t1, t2;
   WithSync()
   {
      a = new Account();
      t1 = new Thread(this, "Person1");
      t2 = new Thread(this, "Person2");
      t1.start();
      t2.start();
   }
public void run()
{
   doTransaction();
}
public synchronized void doTransaction()
{
   System.out.println(Thread.currentThread().getName() + "
                              is checking the balance = " + a.getBalance());
   a.withDraw(4500);
}
public static void main(String[] args)
{
   WithSync wo = new WithSync();
}

}
```

Output:

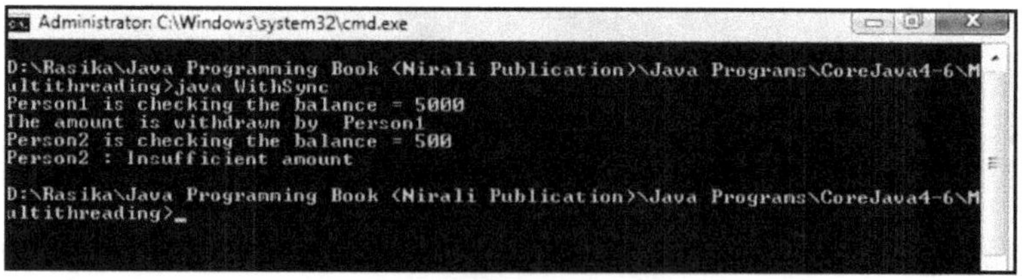

Fig. 9.5: Output

2. **Using Synchronized statement:** Creating synchronized methods within class is an effective way of achieving synchronization. But it will not be possible in all cases. Sometimes it is not possible to add the synchronized keyword to the method as you do not have access to the source code. The class is created by some third party. How an access to an object of this class be synchronized? The solution to this problem is to put calls to methods of this class inside a synchronized block.

   The general form is like this:

```
Synchronized(object) {
//statements to be synchronized
}
```

   Here, the object is a reference to the object being synchronized.

9.6 Inter-Thread Communication

- Inter-thread communication may be defined as an exchange of messages between two or more threads. Transfer of these messages take place, just before or after the thread changes its state.
- Polling is usually implemented by a loop that is used to check some condition repeatedly. Once the condition is true, appropriate action is taken. This wastes CPU time. So polling is definitely not desirable.
- To avoid polling, Java uses very elegant mechanism for inter-thread communication with the help of three methods – wait(), notify() and notifyAll().
- These methods are final methods of an Object class. Since all classes inherit from Object class, they have these methods.
- These three methods can be called only from synchronized context.
  - **wait():** This method tells the calling thread to give up the monitor and go to sleep. This thread can now be activated only be notify() or notifyAll() methods. One can also define the time for which the thread has to wait. To do this, an argument can be passed to the wait() method.

    ```
    final void wait()
    ```

  - **notify():** Resumes the thread that went into sleep mode.

    ```
    final void notify()
    ```

  - **notifyAll():** Resumes all the threads that went into sleep mode. One of the threads will be granted access.

    ```
    final void notifyAll()
    ```

Program 9.5: The following program illustrates the use of wait() and notify() method for inter-thread communication. It also demonstrates the use of synchronized block.

```
class WaitNotify
{
    public static void main(String [] args)
    {
        ThreadB b = new ThreadB();
        b.start();
        synchronized(b)
        {
            try
            {
                System.out.println("Waiting for b to complete...");
                b.wait();
            }
            catch (InterruptedException e)
            {
                e.printStackTrace();
            }
            System.out.println("Average is: " + b.total/100.0f);
        }
    }
}
class ThreadB extends Thread
{
    int total;
    public void run()
    {
        synchronized(this)
        {
            for(int i=1;i<=100;i++)
            {
                total += i;
            }
            System.out.println(total);
            notify();
        }
    }
}
```

Output:

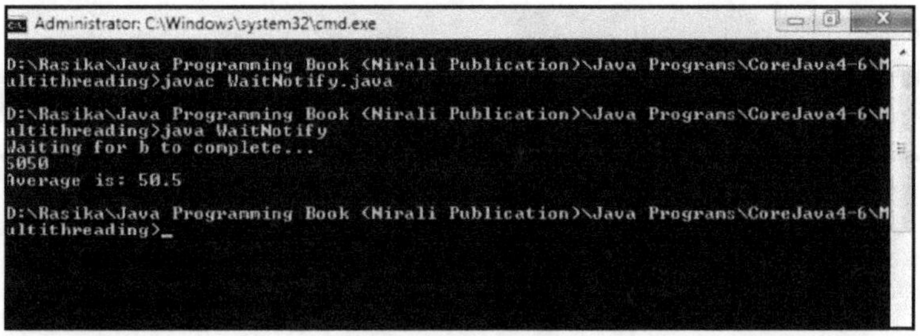

Fig. 9.6: Output

Practice Questions

1. What is a Thread?
2. Explain Thread Life Cycle in detail.
3. Explain the Thread Priorities.
4. What are two different ways used to implement threading in java programs?
5. What is Synchronization? Why it is used?
6. Explain the concept of inter-thread Communication.
7. Explain the following Methods.
   (a) Sleep()
   (b) resume()
   (c) getPriority()
   (d) getName()
   (e) wait()
   (f) notify()
8. Explain Method Wait.

Programming Questions

1. Write a program to display current system time on the left top corner of a GUI application.
2. Write a multithreaded program to create threads and use wait and notify methods to handle these threads.

■■■

Chapter 10...

ABSTRACT WINDOW TOOLKIT

Contents ...

- The Abstract Window Toolkit (AWT) is a set of Application Programming Interfaces (APIs) used by Java programmers to create Graphical User Interface (GUI) objects, such as buttons, scroll bars and windows. AWT is a part of Java Foundation Classes (JFC) from Sun Microsystems. The JFC are a set of GUI class libraries that make it easier to develop the user interface part of an application program.

10.1 Components and Graphics

10.1.1 Components

- A Graphical User Interface is designed with graphical elements called components. Typical components include buttons, scrollbars, text fields, labels etc.
- Components allow the user to interact with the program and provide the user with visual feedback about the state of the program.

- In AWT, all user interface components are instances of class Component or one of its subtypes.
- Components do not stand alone, but rather are found within containers.

10.1.2 Graphics

- AWT has Graphics class which is an abstract base class for all graphic contexts for various devices.
- Java's Graphics class includes methods for drawing different types of shapes and texts in different styles.
- All graphics are drawn relative to the window. Origin of the each window is at top left corner and is at 0, 0. Co-ordinates are specified in pixels.
- All output to the window is sent through a Graphics context.
- Following are some of the frequently used Graphics class methods to draw various shapes and texts.

Table 10.1

Method Name	Meaning
`void drawLine(int startX, int startY, int endX, int endY)`	Displays a line in the current drawing color beginning at startX, startY and ending at endX, endY.
`void drawRect(int top, int left, int width, int height)`	Displays an outlined rectangle.
`void fillRect(int top, int left, int width, int height)`	Displays a filled rectangle.
`void drawOval(int top, int left, int width, int height)`	To draw an ellipse.
`void fillOval(int top, int left, int width, int height)`	To draw a filled ellipse.
`void drawArc(int top, int left, int width, int height, int startAngle, int sweepAngle)`	The arc is drawn & is bounded by rectangle with specified width and height. It is drawn from startAngle through the angular distance specified by sweepAngle.
`void fillArc(int top, int left, int width, int height, int startAngle, int sweepAngle)`	The filled arc is drawn & is bounded by rectangle with specified width and height. It is drawn from startAngle through the angular distance specified by sweepAngle.

contd. ...

`void drawPolygon(int x[], int y[], int numPoints)`	It is possible to draw arbitrary shaped figures using this function. Polygon's endpoints are specified by the co-ordinate pairs contained within x and y arrays. The number of points is defined by numPoints.
`void fillPolygon(int x[], int y[], int numPoints)`	It is possible to draw filled arbitrary shaped figures using this function. Polygon's endpoints are specified by the co-ordinate pairs contained within x and y arrays. The number of points is defined by numPoints.

Program 10.1: The following applet program makes use of some of the above methods to draw lines, rectangles, oval and circle.

An applet can be executed by opening DrawShapes.html file in a browser or it can be executed in an applet viewer. HTML file name can be anything. It need not be same as that of the Java filename.

JavaFile:

Draw Shapes.java

```
import java.awt.*;
import java.applet.*;
public class DrawShapes extends Applet
{
    public void paint(Graphics g)
    {
        g.drawLine(95, 35, 240, 190);
        g.drawLine(65, 80, 300, 300);
        g.drawRect(30, 30, 50, 40);
        g.fillRect(110, 10, 50, 40);
        g.drawRoundRect(180, 10, 50, 60, 15, 15);
        g.drawOval(320, 20, 100, 100);
        g.fillOval(320, 180, 50, 70);
    }
}
```

HTML File: DrawShapes.html

```
<html>
    <body>
        <applet code="DrawShapes" width=500 height=500>
</applet>
    </body>
        </html>
```

Output:

Fig. 10.1: Output

Program 10.2: The following applet program uses some of the methods given in the above table to draw a polygon.

Java File: Poly.java

```
import java.awt.*;
import java.applet.*;
/* <applet code="Poly" width=300 height=300> </applet> */
public class Poly extends Applet {
public void paint(Graphics g) {
int xpoints[] = {40, 210, 35, 210, 40};
int ypoints[] = {40, 35, 210, 210, 40};
int num = 5;
g.drawPolygon(xpoints, ypoints, num);
}
}
```

HTML File: Poly.html

```
<html>
<body>
<applet code="Poly" width=300 height=300>
</applet>
</body>
</html>
```

Program Execution:

```
D:\finalprogram\final awt>javac Poly.java
D:\finalprogram\final awt>appletviewer Poly.html
```

Output:

Fig. 10.2: Output

10.2 Containers, Frames and Panels

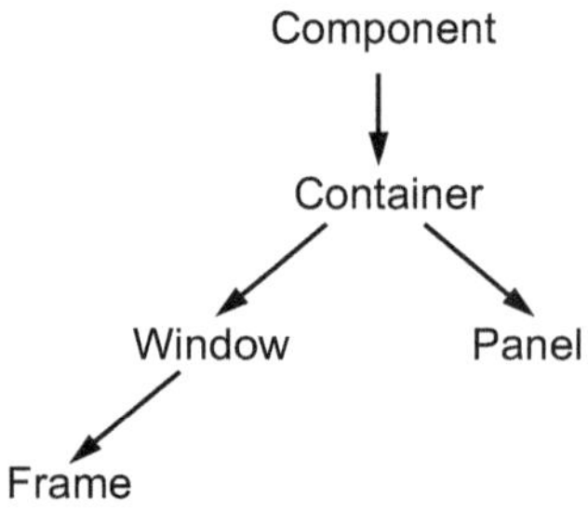

Fig. 10.3: Containers, Frames and Panels

- At the top of the AWT hierarchy, there is a Component class. All the user interface elements are displayed on the screen and interact with users.

Containers:

- Containers are integral part of AWT GUI components. A container provides a space where a component can be located. A Container in AWT is a component itself and it adds the capability to add component to itself. Following are noticable points to be considered.
- Sub classes of Container are called as Containter. For example Panel, Frame and Window.
- Container can add only Component to itself.
- A default layout is present in each container which can be overridden using setLayout method.
- The class Container is the super class for the containers of AWT. Container object can contain other AWT components.

- Following is the declaration for java.awt.Container class:

```
public class Container
   extends Component
```

- Following are the important methods of the Container class.
  1. **add():** This method is overloaded with which a component can be added to the container.
  2. **invalidate():** Used to invalidate the present set up of components in the container.
  3. **validate():** Used to revalidate the current set up of components after calling invalidate().
- Container class inherits methods from the following classes:
  1. java.awt.Component
  2. java.lang.Object

Program to Create Container

- In this program, you will see that three buttons have been added to the panel. The panel and a text area added to the frame. The position for the panel on the frame has been specified south of the frame by using BorderLayout.SOUTH since the position of the text area has been specified the center of the frame using BorderLayout.CENTER. Here, the add() method has been used for both operations (add buttons to the panel and add panel and text area to the frame).
  BorderLayout is the class of the java.awt.*; package which is used to arranging and resizing it's components to fit in five rigions: north, south, east, west and center. Each region may contain only one component. All regions are represented by the NORTH, SOUTH, EAST, WEST and CENTER constants of the BorderLayout class.

Program 10.3:

```
import java.awt.*;
import java.awt.event.*;
public class CreateContainer{
  public static void main(String[] args){
  Panel panel = new Panel();
  panel.add(new Button("Button 1"));
  panel.add(new Button("Button 2"));
  panel.add(new Button("Button 3"));
  Frame frame = new Frame("Container Frame");
  TextArea txtArea = new TextArea();
  frame.add(txtArea, BorderLayout.CENTER);
  frame.add(panel, BorderLayout.SOUTH);
  frame.setSize(400,400);
  frame.setVisible(true);
  frame.addWindowListener(new WindowAdapter(){
```

```
      public void windowClosing(WindowEvent we){
      System.exit(0);
      }
      });
      }
   }
```

Types of containers

- Panel The class Panel is the simplest container class. It provides space in which an application can attach any other component, including other panels. It uses FlowLayout as default layout manager.
- Following is the declaration for java.awt.Panel class:

```
public class Panel
   extends Container
      implements Accessible
```

Program 10.4: Create the following java program using any editor of your choice in say D:/ > AWT > com > tutorialspoint > gui >

AwtContainerDemo.java

```
package com.tutorialspoint.gui;
import java.awt.*;
import java.awt.event.*;
public class AwtContainerDemo {
   private Frame mainFrame;
   private Label headerLabel;
   private Label statusLabel;
   private Panel controlPanel;
   private Label msglabel;
   public AwtContainerDemo(){
      prepareGUI();
   }
   public static void main(String[] args){
      AwtContainerDemo  awtContainerDemo = new
                                              AwtContainerDemo();
      awtContainerDemo.showPanelDemo();
   }
```

```
    private void prepareGUI(){
        mainFrame = new Frame("Java AWT Examples");
        mainFrame.setSize(400,400);
        mainFrame.setLayout(new GridLayout(3, 1));
        mainFrame.addWindowListener(new WindowAdapter() {
            public void windowClosing(WindowEvent windowEvent){
                System.exit(0);
                }
        });
        headerLabel = new Label();
        headerLabel.setAlignment(Label.CENTER);
        statusLabel = new Label();
        statusLabel.setAlignment(Label.CENTER);
        statusLabel.setSize(350,100);
        msglabel = new Label();
        msglabel.setAlignment(Label.CENTER);
        msglabel.setText("Welcome to Abstract Window Toolkit");
        controlPanel = new Panel();
        controlPanel.setLayout(new FlowLayout());
        mainFrame.add(headerLabel);
        mainFrame.add(controlPanel);
        mainFrame.add(statusLabel);
        mainFrame.setVisible(true);
    }
    private void showPanelDemo(){
        headerLabel.setText("Container in action: Panel");
        Panel panel = new Panel();
        panel.setBackground(Color.magenta);
        panel.setLayout(new FlowLayout());
        panel.add(msglabel);
        controlPanel.add(panel);
        mainFrame.setVisible(true);
    }
}
```

- Compile the program using command prompt. Go to D:/ > AWT and type the following command.

```
D:\AWT>javac com\tutorialspoint\gui\AwtContainerDemo.java
```

- If no error comes that means compilation is successful. Run the program using following command.

```
D:\AWT>java com.tutorialspoint.gui.AwtContainerDemo
```

- Verify the following output:

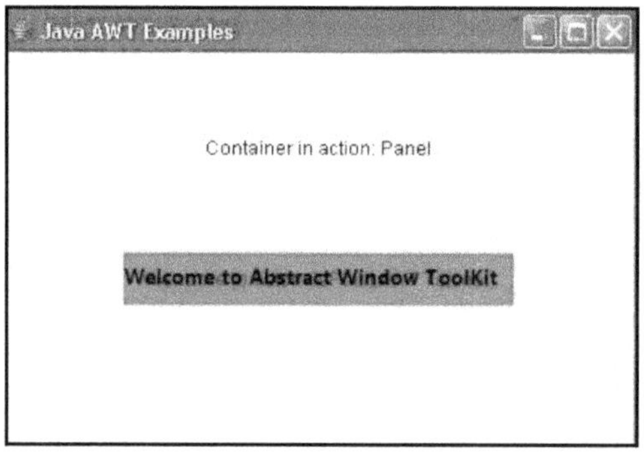

Fig. 10.4: Output

1. **Frame:**

- The class Frame is a top level window with border and title. It uses BorderLayout as default layout manager.
- Following is the declaration for java.awt.Frame class:

```
public class Frame
   extends Window
      implements MenuContainer
```

Program 10.5: An application program example for creating a frame window

The following program creates a frame window with the title 'My Frame' of width 300 and height 400. It displays Hello message and a blue color oval shape. It makes use of Font class to set the font of the text. The main() method creates an object of NewFrame class, calls its constructor & makes the frame visible in an application. NewFrame.java file should be compiled to create NewFrame.class file.

```
D:\Java_Programs\awt>javac NewFrame.java
```

This class file can be used while executing the program with the following command.

```
D:\Java_Programs\awt>java NewFrame
```

Java File: NewFrame.java

```
import java.awt.*;
class NewFrame extends Frame
{
   public NewFrame(String s)
   {
      super(s);
   }
   public void paint(Graphics g)
   {
      g.drawString("Hello" , 100 , 100);
      Font f = new Font("Courier New" , Font.BOLD , 15);
      g.setFont(f);
      g.drawString("Hello" , 50 , 50);
      Color c = new Color(123 , 145 , 234);
      g.setColor(c);
      g.fillOval(150 , 150 , 50 , 50);
   }
   public static void main(String[] args)
   {
      NewFrame n = new NewFrame("MyFrame");
      n.setSize(300 , 400);
      n.setVisible(true);
   }
}
```

Output:

Fig. 10.5: Output

2. Window

- The class Window is a top level window with no border and no menubar. It uses BorderLayout as default layout manager.
- Following is the declaration for java.awt.Window class:

```
public class Window
   extends Container
      implements Accessible
```

Program 10.6: Create the following java program using any editor of your choice in say D:/ > AWT > com > tutorialspoint > gui >

AwtContainerDemo.java

```
package com.tutorialspoint.gui;

import java.awt.*;
import java.awt.event.*;

public class AwtContainerDemo {
   private Frame mainFrame;
   private Label headerLabel;
   private Label statusLabel;
   private Panel controlPanel;
   private Label msglabel;

   public AwtContainerDemo(){
      prepareGUI();
   }

   public static void main(String[] args){
      AwtContainerDemo  awtContainerDemo = new AwtContainerDemo();
      awtContainerDemo.showFrameDemo();
   }

   private void prepareGUI(){
      mainFrame = new Frame("Java AWT Examples");
      mainFrame.setSize(400,400);
      mainFrame.setLayout(new GridLayout(3, 1));
      mainFrame.addWindowListener(new WindowAdapter() {
         public void windowClosing(WindowEvent windowEvent){
            System.exit(0);
         }
      });
      headerLabel = new Label();
      headerLabel.setAlignment(Label.CENTER);
      statusLabel = new Label();
      statusLabel.setAlignment(Label.CENTER);
      statusLabel.setSize(350,100);

      msglabel = new Label();
      msglabel.setAlignment(Label.CENTER);
      msglabel.setText("Welcome to TutorialsPoint AWT Tutorial.");

      controlPanel = new Panel();
      controlPanel.setLayout(new FlowLayout());
```

```
      mainFrame.add(headerLabel);
      mainFrame.add(controlPanel);
      mainFrame.add(statusLabel);
      mainFrame.setVisible(true);
   }

   private void showWindowDemo(){
      headerLabel.setText("Container in action: Window");
      final MessageWindow window =
         new MessageWindow(mainFrame,
         "Hello!this is window");

      Button okButton = new Button("Open a Window");
      okButton.addActionListener(new ActionListener() {
         public void actionPerformed(ActionEvent e) {
            window.setVisible(true);
            statusLabel.setText("A Window shown to the user.");
         }
      });
      controlPanel.add(okButton);
      mainFrame.setVisible(true);
   }

   class MessageWindow extends Window{
      private String message;

      public MessageWindow(Frame parent, String message) {
         super(parent);
         this.message = message;
         setSize(300, 300);
         setLocationRelativeTo(parent);
         setBackground(Color.gray);
      }

      public void paint(Graphics g) {
         super.paint(g);
         g.drawRect(0,0,getSize().width - 1,getSize().height - 1);
         g.drawString(message,50,150);
      }
   }
}
```

- Compile the program using command prompt. Go to D:/ > AWT and type the following command.

```
D:\AWT>javac com\tutorialspoint\gui\AwtContainerDemo.java
```

- If no error comes that means compilation is successful. Run the program using following command.

```
D:\AWT>java com.tutorialspoint.gui.AwtContainerDemo
```

- Verify the following output:

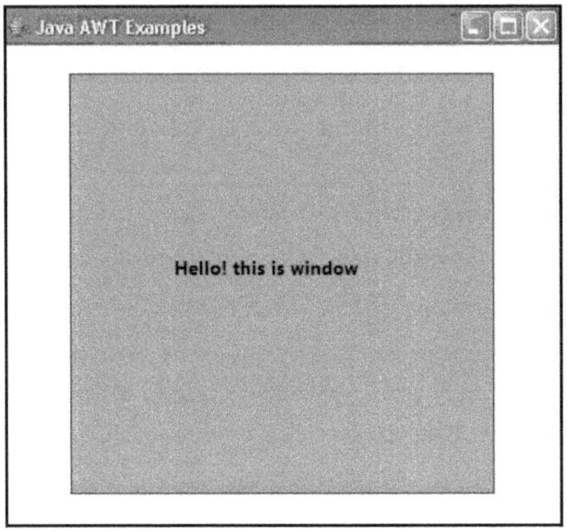

Fig. 10.6: Output

10.3 Layout Managers

- Java designers have come up with an efficient mechanism of arranging components. This responsibility of arranging components is delegated to another class called 'LayoutManager'. A Layout Manager is an object of any class that implements the LayoutManager interface.

How Layout Manager Works?

- Each container object has a layout manager associated with it. The layout manager keeps track of the components in the container. It is notified when the items are added or removed. It finds out the size of the parent window and then calculates the size of each components using the getPreferredSize() and getMinimumSize() methods. Using these values, it applies an algorithm to position components on the container.

Setting the Layout Manager:

- Each container has a Layout Manager associated with it. To change the layout manager for a container, use SetLayout() method.

```
setLayout(LayoutManager obj);
```

- If you pass NULL to this method, it disables the layout manager for the container.

  For example: Frame f = new Frame();

```
f.setLayout(new FlowLayout());
```

Predefined Layout Managers

Java has several predefined layout manager classes which implement Layout Manager interface. The predefined layout managers are listed below.

1. Border layout
2. Flow layout
3. Grid layout
4. Card layout

10.3.1 Border Layout [Oct. 2011]

- BorderLayout divides the container into five regions: NORTH, SOUTH, EAST, WEST, CENTER. BorderLayout Manager lets you choose where you want to place each component. **This is the default layout for JFrame.**

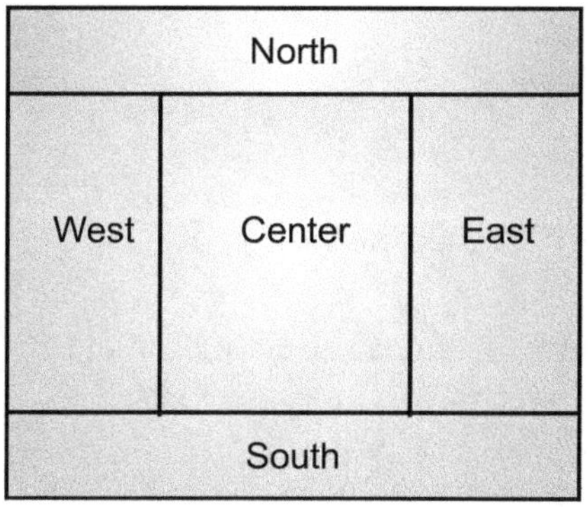

Fig. 10.7: Border Layout

Constructors:

- o BorderLayout();
- o BorderLayout(int hgap, int vgap);

Where,

- o hgap: The horizontal gap (in pixels) between components
- o vgap: The vertical gap (in pixels) between components

- BorderLayout class defines static constants to specify five positions. These are BorderLayout.NORTH, BorderLayout.SOUTH, BorderLayout.EAST, BorderLayout.WEST and BorderLayout.CENTER. These positions should be specified while adding components to the container.

Program 10.7: BorderLayout Demo Program.

The following applet program shows how to place components using BorderLayout in an applet window.

File: BorderLayout.java

```
Demonstrate BorderLayout.
import java.awt.*;
import java.applet.*;
import java.util.*;
/*
<applet code="BorderLayoutDemo1" width=500 height=500>
</applet>
*/
public class BorderLayoutDemo1 extends Applet {
public void init() {
setLayout(new BorderLayout());
add(new Button("NIRALI PRAKASHAN."),
BorderLayout.NORTH);
add(new Label("PRAGATI PRAKASHAN."),
BorderLayout.SOUTH);
add(new Button("Right"), BorderLayout.EAST);
add(new Button("Left"), BorderLayout.WEST);
String msg = "Address " +
"Abhyudaya Prgati;\n" +
"1312,  " +
"Shivaji Nagar.\n" +
"PUNE " +
"411002.\n\n" +
" www.pragationline.com\n\n";
add(new TextArea(msg), BorderLayout.CENTER);
}
}
```

File: BorderLayout.html

```
<html>
<body>
   <applet code="BorderLayoutDemo1" width=500 height=500>
</applet>
   </body>
</html>
```

Output:

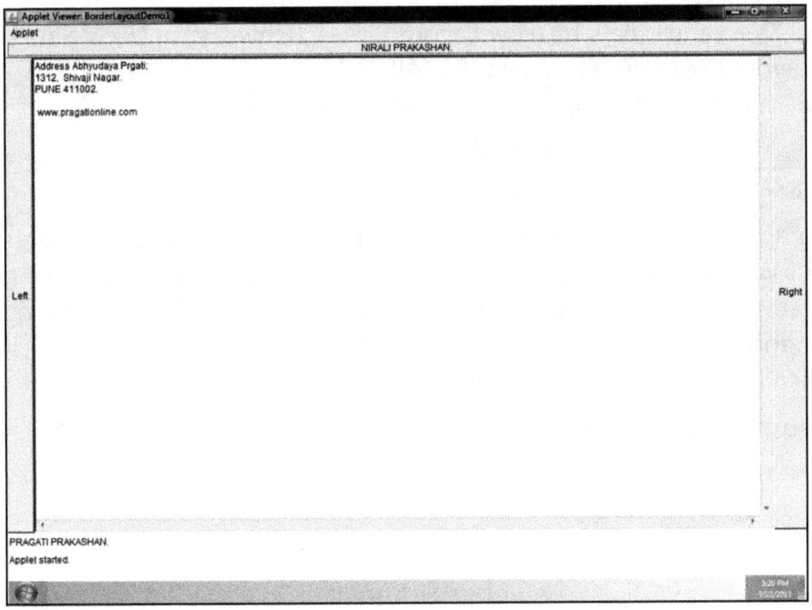

Fig. 10.8: Output

10.3.2 FlowLayout

- This is the default layout manager for Applet and Panel. In this components are added to the container from top left corner, left to right in the same row till no more components can be added in the same row. The remaining components are added in the next row in the same manner.

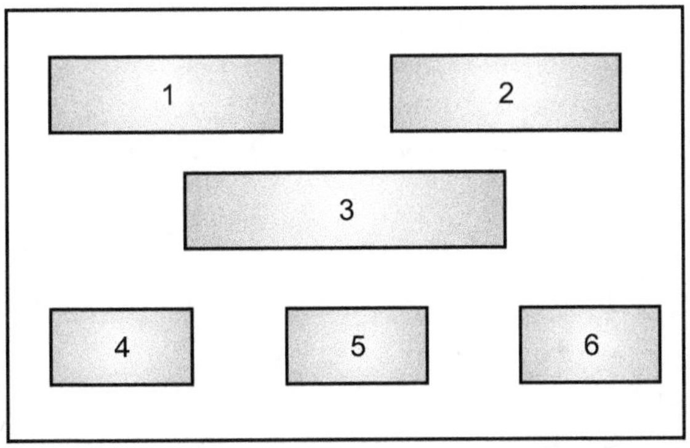

Fig. 10.9: FlowLayout

Constructors:

- FlowLayout();
- FlowLayout(int align);
- FlowLayout(int align, int hgap, int vgap);

Where,

- **align:** The values can be FlowLayout.RIGHT, FlowLayout.LEFT, FlowLayout.CENTER, FlowLayout.LEADING, FlowLayout.TRAILING.
- **hgap:** The horizontal gap (in pixels) between components
- **vgap:** The vertical gap (in pixels) between components

Program 10.8: FlowLayout Demo Program.

The following applet program shows how to set the Flow Layout for the applet window. The program has four checkbox components which are placed on an applet window using flow layout. Program also handles item events which are triggered when the check boxes are selected. To handle the events, an applet implements ItemListener interface. An appropriate message is displayed in the applet window.

File: FlowLayoutDempo1.java

```
import java.awt.*;
import java.awt.event.*;
import java.applet.*;
/* <applet code="FlowLayoutDemo1" width=250 height=200> </applet> */
public class FlowLayoutDemo1 extends Applet
implements ItemListener {
String msg = "";
Checkbox c, cpp, java, Advjava;
public void init() {
set left-aligned flow layout
setLayout(new FlowLayout(FlowLayout.LEFT));
c = new Checkbox("C PROGRMMING", null, true);
cpp = new Checkbox("CPP PROGRMMING ");
java = new Checkbox("java PROGRMMING");
Advjava = new Checkbox("Advjava PROGRMMING");
add(c);
add(cpp);
add(java);
add(Advjava);
register to receive item events
c.addItemListener(this);
cpp.addItemListener(this);
java.addItemListener(this);
Advjava.addItemListener(this);
}
Repaint when status of a check box changes.
public void itemStateChanged(ItemEvent ie) {
repaint();
}
```

```
Display current state of the check boxes.
public void paint(Graphics g) {
msg = "Current state: ";
g.drawString(msg, 6, 80);
msg = " c programming: " + c.getState();
g.drawString(msg, 6, 100);
msg = " cpp programming: " + cpp.getState();
g.drawString(msg, 6, 120);
msg = " java programming: " + java.getState();
g.drawString(msg, 6, 140);
msg = " Advjava programming: " + Advjava.getState();
g.drawString(msg, 6, 160);
}
}
```

HTML File: FlowLayoutDemo1:html

```
<html>
<body>
<applet code = "FlowLayoutDemo1" width = 300 height = 200>
</applet>
</body>
</html>
```

Output:

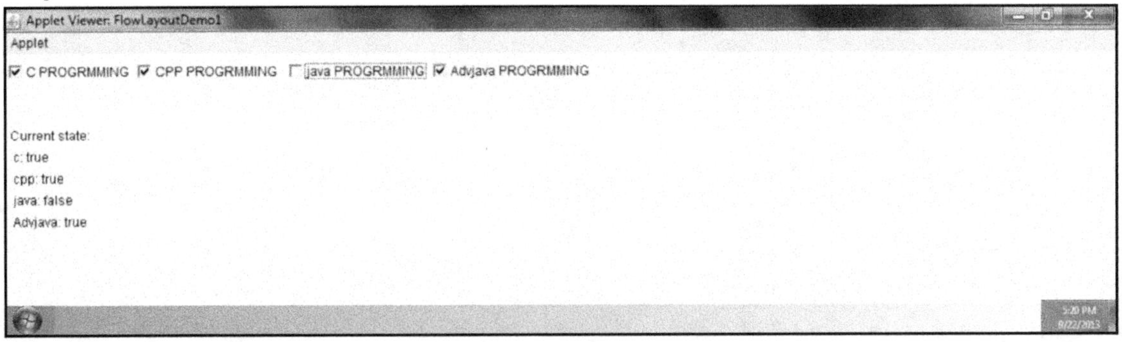

Fig. 10.10

10.3.3 GridLayout

- GridLayout arranges components in two dimensional grid. The number of rows and columns in the grid can be specified. The components are added to the grid row-wise. Each component is given the same size and dimensions. The gap between rows and columns of the grids can also be specified.

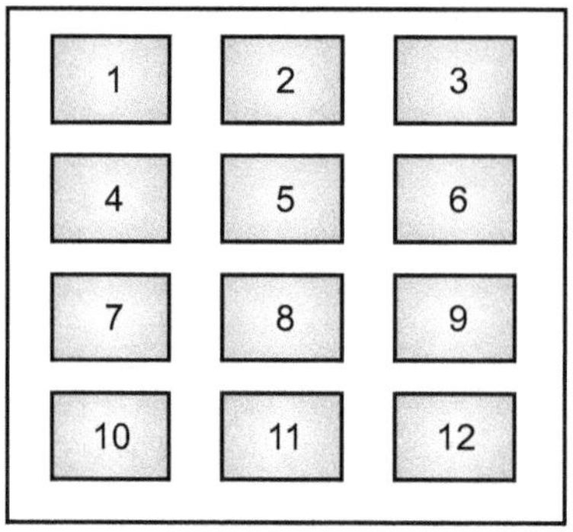

Fig. 10.11: GridLayout

- **Constructors:**
  - GridLayout();
  - GridLayout(int rows, int cols);
  - GridLayout(int rows, int cols, int hgap, int vgap);

Program 10.9: A GridLayout demo program

The following applet program shows how to place components using grid layout in an applet window.

File: GridLayoutDemo1.java

```
import java.awt.*;
import java.applet.*;
/* <applet code="GridLayoutDemo1" width=500 height=500>
</applet>    */
public class GridLayoutDemo1 extends Applet {
static final int m = 4;
public void init() {
setLayout(new GridLayout(m, m));
for(int i = 0; i < m; i++) {
for(int j = 0; j < m; j++) {
int p = i * m + j;
if(p > 0)
add(new Button("" + p));
}
}
}
}
```

File: GridLayoutDemo1.html

```
<html>
 <body>
  <applet code="GridLayoutDemo1" width=500 height=500>
</applet>
 </body>
</html>
```

Output:

Fig. 10.12: Output

10.3.4 CardLayout

- This layout handles several containers. The CardLayout display each container as cards. Each container can have different layout manager. Each card is assigned a name. You can move from card to card using the show() method.
- This layout is typically used in applications where containers have to be dynamically loaded depending on the user actions. You can prepare several cards which are added to Panel. The cards are initially hidden. A specific card can be selected using first(), last(), previous() and next() methods.

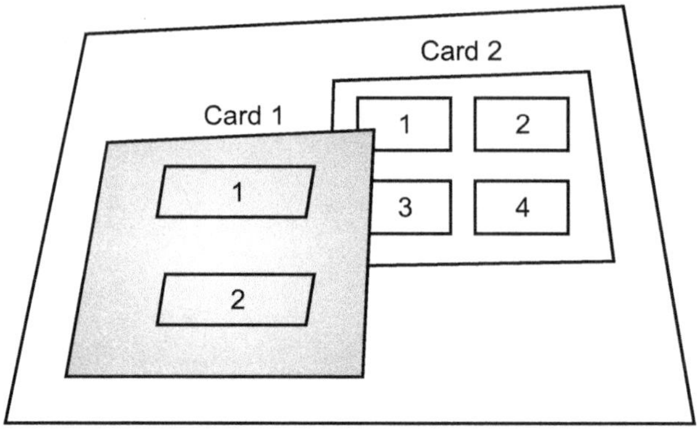

Fig. 10.13: CardLayout

- **Constructors:**
  - CardLayout();
  - CardLayout(int hgap, int vgap);
- **Methods:**
  - add(Panel oneCard, String name);
  - void first(Container deck);
  - void next(Container deck);
  - void previous(Container deck);
  - void last(Container deck);
  - void show(Container deck, String cardName);

10.4 AWT all Components

10.4.1 Control Fundamentals

- AWT supports the following types of controls.
  - Labels
  - Push buttons
  - Check boxes
  - Choice lists
  - Lists
  - Scroll bars
  - Text editing

  These controls are subclasses of Component class.

Adding and removing controls:

- We have to add the control in a window to make it a part of window. add() method of class Container is used to add components in a window.

  Syntax: `Component add(Component obj);`

  Here, obj is the instance of the control to add. Once the control is added to the window, it is automatically visible over the window.

Sometimes we may want to remove a control from a window. To do this, we have a remove() method of class Container.

Syntax: `void remove(Component obj);`

Here, obj is reference to the control which we want to remove.

removeAll() method will remove all the controls from the window.

1. **Labels:**

   A label is an object of class Label. It contains a text that is displayed on the label. Labels are called **passive controls** as they do not have any interaction with the user.

   - **Constructors:**
     - Label(); blank label
     - Label(String str); Label containing a string
     - Label(String str, int how); Label contains a string along with alignment of text – Label.LEFT, Label.RIGHT Label.CENTER.
   - **Methods:** We can set or edit the text in a label by using the setText() method. We can obtain the current label by using getText() method.
     - void setText(String str);
     - String getText();

Program 10.10: An applet program which shows handling of Label components.

The following program creates three label components by calling Label class constructor. The labels are added to the applet window by using add() method.

File: LabelDemo1.java

```
import java.awt.*;
import java.applet.*;
/* <applet code="LabelDemo1" width=500 height=500>
</applet> */
public class LabelDemo1 extends Applet {
public void init() {
Label one = new Label("OK ");
Label two = new Label("CANCEL ");
Label three = new Label("CLOSE ");
add labels to applet window
add(one);
add(two);
add(three);
}
}
```

File: LabelDemo1.html

```
<html>
 <body>
  <applet code="LabelDemo1" width=500 height=500>
</applet>
 </body>
</html>
```

Output:

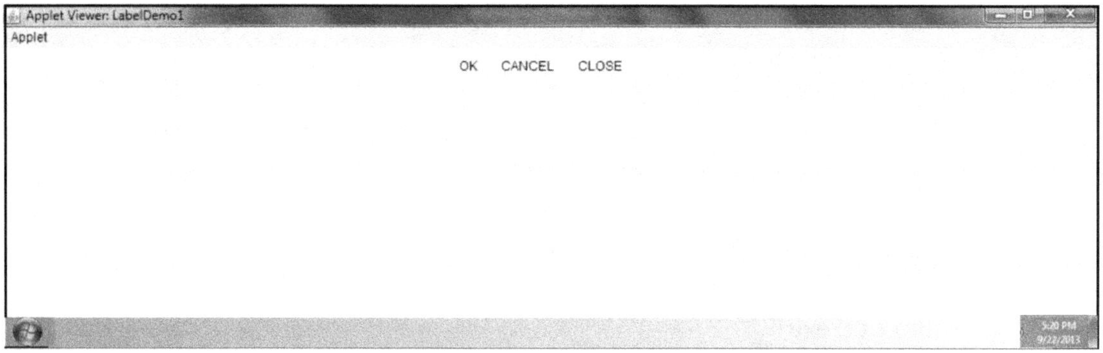

Fig. 10.14: Output

2. Buttons:

A push button is a component that has a label and when it is pressed, it generates an action event. Button is an object of class Button. Button is most widely used GUI control.

- **Constructors:**
    - Button(); Creates an empty button
    - Button(String str); Button that has a string as labels
- **Methods:**
    - void setLabel(String str); to set the label
    - String getLabel(); to obtain the current label

Program 10.11: An applet program which shows handling of Buttons

The following program creates three buttons by calling Button class constructor. It also handles Action event when any of the button is pressed. To handle the action event triggered by the buttons, an applet implements ActionListener interface.

File: ButtonDemo1.java

```
Demonstrate Buttons
import java.awt.*;
import java.awt.event.*;
import java.applet.*;
/* <applet code="ButtonDemo1" width=500 height=500> </applet> */
```

```
public class ButtonDemo1 extends Applet implements ActionListener {
String msg = "";
Button A, B, C;
public void init() {
A = new Button("A");
B = new Button("B");
C = new Button("C");
add(A);
add(B);
add(C);
A.addActionListener(this);
B.addActionListener(this);
C.addActionListener(this);
}
public void actionPerformed(ActionEvent ae) {
String str = ae.getActionCommand();
if(str.equals("A")) {
msg = "You pressed A.";
}
else if(str.equals("B")) {
msg = "You pressed B.";
}
else {
msg = "You pressed C.";
}
repaint();
}
public void paint(Graphics g) {
g.drawString(msg, 6, 100);
}
}
```

File: ButtonDemo1.html

```
<html>
 <body>
  <applet code="ButtonDemo1" width=500 height=500>
</applet>
 </body>
</html>
```

Output:

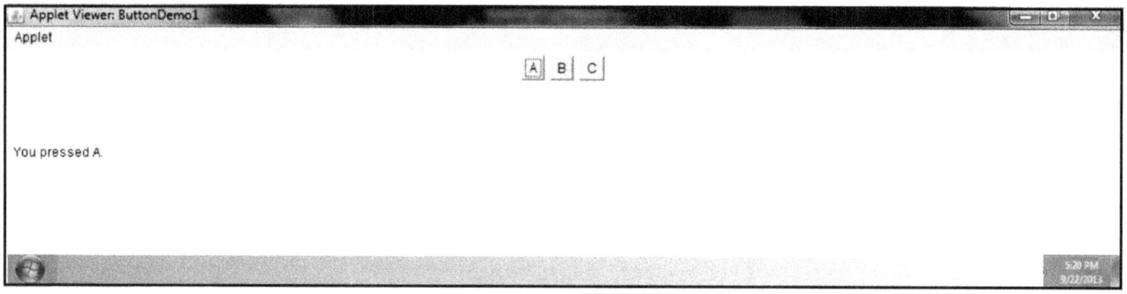

Fig. 10.15: Output

Fig. 10.16: Output

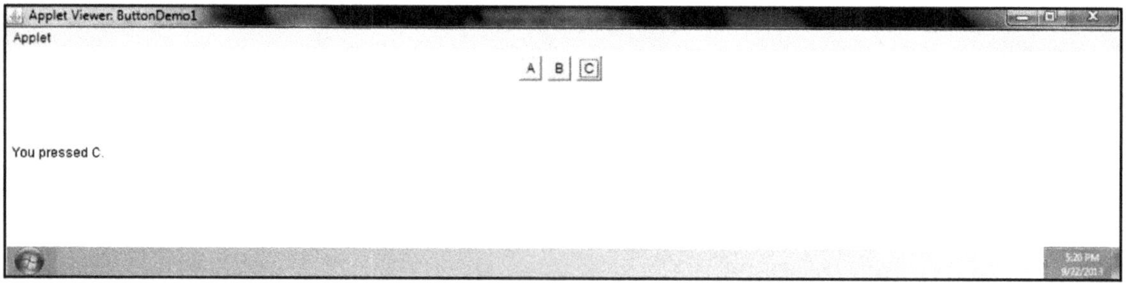

Fig. 10.17: Output

3. Check Boxes

- A check box is a GUI control that is used to turn the option on or off. It has two states-like yes or no, on or off, 1 or 0 etc. There is a label associated with check box. One can change the state by clicking on it. We can create a group of check boxes or use them as an individual item. Check boxes are the objects of class Checkbox. When a checkbox is selected or deselected, it causes an **ItemEvent**.
  - **Constructors:**
    - Checkbox(); Checkbox with blank label
    - Checkbox(String str); Checkbox with label
    - Checkbox(String str, boolean on); Checkbox with label and initial state either true(checked) or false(cleared)
    - Checkbox(String str, boolean on, CheckboxGroup grp); Checkbox with label, initial state and a checkbox group
    - Checkbox(String str, CheckboxGroup grp, boolean on); Checkbox with label, initial state and a checkbox group
  - **Methods:**
    - boolean getState();
    - void setState(boolean on);
    - String getLabel();
    - void setLabel(String str);

4. Radio Buttons

- It is possible to create a set of mutually exclusive check boxes in which one and only one checkbox in a group can be selected at a time. These checkboxes are often called as 'Radio Buttons'. We have to first create a group to which these checkboxes are added. Checkbox group is an object of class CheckboxGroup.
  - **Constructor:**
    - CheckboxGroup(); is the only default constructor.
  - **Methods:**
    - Checkbox getSelectedCheckbox(); to obtain which checkbox in a group is currenly selected.
    - void setSelectedCheckbox(Checkbox *chkbox*); to select a checkbox specified with *chkbox*.

Program 10.12: An applet program to show handling of radio buttons

The following program creates radio buttons by calling Checkbox class constructor. It first creates a radio button group by using CheckboxGroup class constructor and adds all the radio buttons in that group to make their selection mutually exclusive. An applet also implements ItemListener interface to handle the events triggered by the selection of the radio button.

File: RadioButton.java

```
Demonstrate radio group.
import java.awt.*;
import java.awt.event.*;
import java.applet.*;
/* <applet code="Radiobutton" width=500 height=400> </applet> */
public class Radiobutton extends Applet implements ItemListener {
String msg = "";
Checkbox c, cpp, java, Advjava;
CheckboxGroup cbg;
public void init() {
cbg = new CheckboxGroup();
c = new Checkbox("C Programming", cbg, true);
cpp = new Checkbox(" C++ Programming", cbg, false);
java = new Checkbox("java", cbg, false);
Advjava = new Checkbox("Advjava ", cbg, false);
add(c);
add(cpp);
add(java);
add(Advjava);
c.addItemListener(this);
cpp.addItemListener(this);
java.addItemListener(this);
Advjava.addItemListener(this);
}
public void itemStateChanged(ItemEvent ie) {
repaint();
}
Display current state of the check boxes.
public void paint(Graphics g) {
msg = "Current selection: ";
msg += cbg.getSelectedCheckbox().getLabel();
g.drawString(msg, 6, 100);
}
}
```

File: RadioButton.html

```
<html>
 <body>
  <applet code="Radiobutton" width=500 height=500>
</applet>
 </body>
</html>
```

Output:

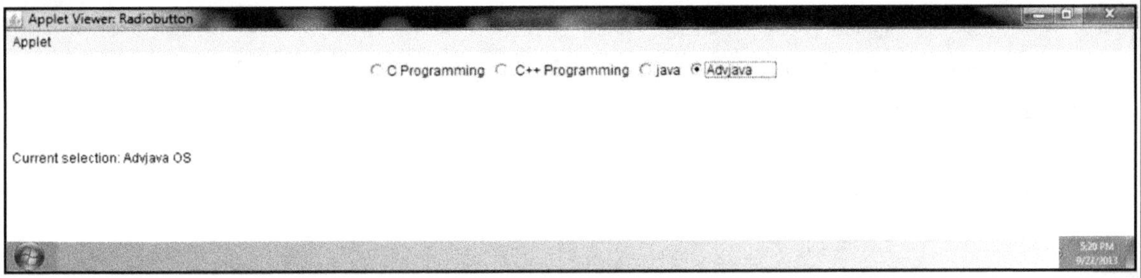

Fig. 10.18: Output

5. Choice

- To create a pop-up list of items, we can use Choice GUI control. When it is in inactive state, it occupies only the space needed for currently selected item. When it is clicked, the complete list of choices is displayed and a user can select a new item from the list. When an item from the list is selected an ItemEvent is generated.
    - **Constructor:**
        - Choice(); The only default constructor which creates an empty popup list;
    - **Methods:**
        - void add(String item); to add the items in the list.
        - String getSelectedItem(); to return the currently selected name of an item.
        - int getSelectedIndex(); to return the currently selected item index.
        - int getItemCount(); to obtain number of items in a list.
        - void select(int index); by passing index of an item to make the item as a currently selected item.
        - void select(String item); to make the item as a currently selected item by passing name of an item.
        - String getItem(int index); to obtain the name of an item of the specified index.

Program 10.13: An applet program that shows handling of pop-up lists

The following program creates a Pop-up list by calling Choice class constructor. It adds several items to the list. An Applet also implements ItemListener interface to handle the event triggered by the selection of the item from the given list.

File: Poplist.java

```
Demonstrate Choice lists.
import java.awt.*;
import java.awt.event.*;
import java.applet.*;
/* <applet code="Poplist" width=300 height=180> </applet> */
public class Poplist extends Applet implements ItemListener {
Choice language;
String msg = "";
public void init() {
language = new Choice();
language.add("C Programming");
language.add("C++ Programming ");
language.add("JAVA Programming");
language.add("Adv JAVA Programming");
add(language);
language.addItemListener(this);
}
public void itemStateChanged(ItemEvent ie) {
repaint();
}
Display current selections.
public void paint(Graphics g) {
msg = "Current Language: ";
msg += language.getSelectedItem();
g.drawString(msg, 6, 120);
msg = "Current Browser: ";
}
}
```

File: Poplist.html

```
<html>
 <body>
  <applet code="Poplist" width=500 height=500>
</applet>
 </body>
</html>
```

Output:

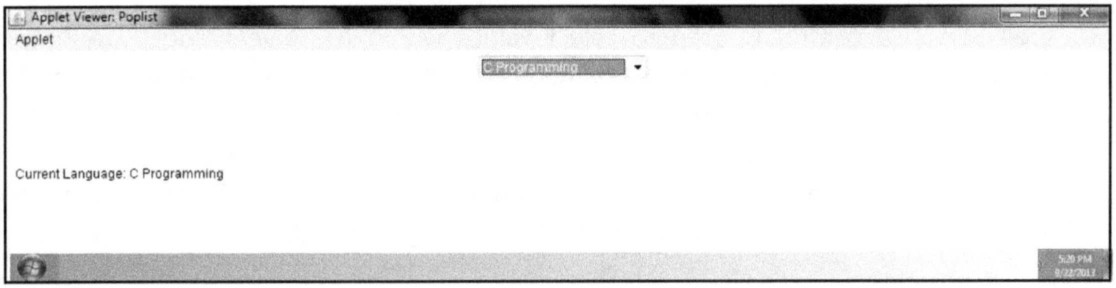

Fig. 10.19: Output

6. Lists

- List GUI control is a compact, multiple-choice, scrolling selection list. A List object displays possible number of list items in the visible window. It allows single selection as well as multiple selections. When list item is double clicked, an ActionEvent is generated. When it is single clicked, ItemEvent is generated.
- **Constructors:**
  - List(); Allows one item to be selected at a time.
  - List(int noRows); noRows value specifies the number of items in a list that would be visible at a time on list box.
  - List(int noRows, Boolean multiSelect); if multiSelect is true, user may select two or more items from the list.
- **Methods:**
  - void add(String *nm*); Adds item with name *nm* to the end of the list.
  - void add(String *nm*, int *index*); Adds item at the specified index. Index starts at 0. To add item to the end of the list, the value of the index should be -1.
  - String getSelectedItem(); Returns a string containing the list item. If multiple items are selected or selection is not made yet, NULL is returned.

- int getSelectedIndex(); Returns index of list item. If multiple items are selected or selection is not made yet, -1 is returned.
- String[] getSelectedItems(); for multiple selection of items, it returns an array of currently selected items.
- int[] getSelectedIndexes(); for multiple selection of items, it returns an array of currently selected items indices.
- int getItemCount(); to obtain number of items in a list.
- void select(int *index*); to set the currently selected item.
- getItem(int *index*); to obtain the name of an item at the specified index.

7. Scroll Bars

- Scroll Bars GUI control is used to select values within the given range specified by minimum and maximum. It can be oriented vertically or horizontally. At its both ends it displays arrows. If user clicks on it, it increments the current value by one unit. The slider box(or thumb) can be dragged to a new position. Scroll bar then displays the new value depending on the new position. Scroll bars are the objects of class Scrollbar. Whenever user interacts with the scroll bar, AdjustmentEvent is generated.
  - **Constructors:**
    - Scrollbar(); Creates a vertical scroll bar.
    - Scrollbar(int *style*); depending on the *style* a scroll bar is created. *style* can be wither Scrollbar.VERTICAL or Scrollbar.HORIZONTAL.
    - Scrollbar(int style, int *initValue*, int *thumbSize*, int *min*, int *max*); initial value for the scrollbar as *initValue*, number of units represented by *thumbSize*, *min* and *max* values for the scroll bar are specified at the time of creating scroll bar.
  - **Methods:**
    - void setValues(int *initValue*, int *thumbSize*, int *min*, int *max*).
    - int getValue(); to obtain the current value of the scroll bar.
    - void setValue(int *newValue*); to set a new value for scroll bar.
    - int getMinimum(); to retrieve minimum value of the scroll bar.
    - int getMaximum(); to retrieve maximum value of the scroll bar.
    - void setUnitIncrement(*int newIncr*); to change the default increment or decrement. By default it is 1.
    - void setBlockIncrement(*int newIncr*); to change the default page-up and page-down increment. By default it is 10.

8. Text Fields

- Text Field control is nothing but a single line text entry area. Text field control allows the user to enter the strings and to edit the text using arrow keys. TextField is a subclass of TextComponent class. Whenever user presses ENTER, an ActionEvent is generated.

- **Constructors:**
  - TextField(); Creates a default text field.
  - TextField(int *numChars*); Creates a text field with *numChars* wide.
  - TextField(String *str*); Creates a text field with given string.
  - TextField(String *str*, int *numChars*); Creates a text field by giving both a string as well as the width.
- **Methods:**
  - String getText(); to obtain the current string in the text field.
  - void setText(String str); to set the string specified by str to the text field.
  - String getSelectedText(); returns the selected text from the text field.
  - void select(int startIndex, int endIndex); selects the characters beginning at startIndex and ends with (endIndex-1).
  - boolean isEditable(); returns true if the text is changed else it returns false.
  - void setEditable(boolean canEdit); if canEdit is true, a text may be changed. If it is set to false, the text cannot be changed.

Program 10.14: An applet program to show handling of text fields.

The following program uses TextField class constructor to create text field components. It displays the text entered in the text field, the selected text and a password entered by the user. It implements ActionListener interface to handle the event generated by the text field.

File: TextField1.java

```
// Demonstrate text field.
import java.awt.*;
import java.awt.event.*;
import java.applet.*;
/* <applet code="TextField1" width=380 height=150> </applet> */
public class TextField1 extends Applet
implements ActionListener {
TextField n, p;
public void init() {
Label np = new Label("Name: ", Label.RIGHT);
Label pp = new Label("Password: ", Label.RIGHT);
n = new TextField(12);
p = new TextField(8);
p.setEchoChar('?');
add(np);
add(n);
add(pp);
add(p);
```

```
// register to receive action events
n.addActionListener(this);
p.addActionListener(this);
}
// User pressed Enter.
public void actionPerformed(ActionEvent ae) {
repaint();
}
public void paint(Graphics g) {
g.drawString("Name: " + n.getText(), 6, 60);
g.drawString("Selected text in name: "
+ n.getSelectedText(), 6, 80);
g.drawString("Password: " + p.getText(), 6, 100);
}
}
```

File: TextField1.html

```
<html>
 <body>
  <applet code="TextField1" width=500 height=500>
</applet>
 </body>
</html>
```

Output:

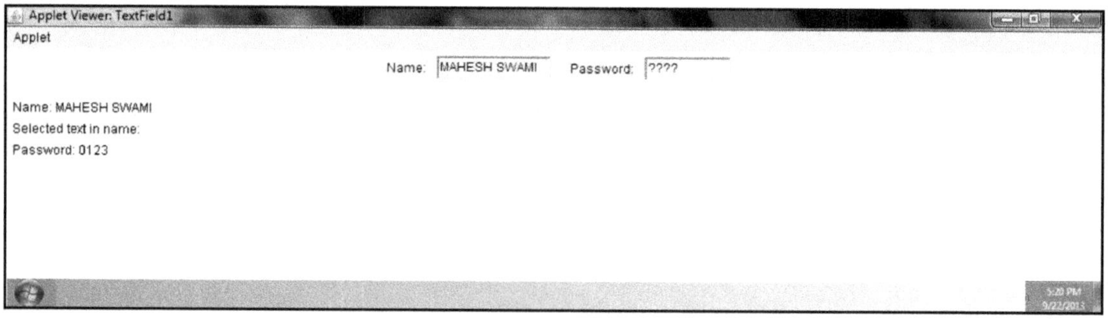

Fig. 10.20: Output

10.5 Event Delegation Model

Event Handling

- Event Handling is an integral part of GUI based applications. An event has to be captured that has generated by a GUI control. It has to be handled appropriately. Clicking of a button, moving a mouse, minimizing a window etc. are some of the examples of events. We will now learn event handling mechanism in Java.

Event

- An event is nothing but a signal given to inform an application that something has happened. The application may take some action or simply ignores an event. When an event occurs, information about that event is collected in an object of class EventObject. Events are supported by java.util, java.awt and java.awt.event packages.

Delegation Event Model

- Java uses delegation event model to handle events. The event handling mechanism follows these steps:
  - A source generates events.
  - A listener must register itself with an event source to receive event notification.
  - Event notification is sent to the listener.
  - Once the listener receives an event, an event handler processes it.
  - Event handler is an object of a class that implements the listener.

10.5.1 Event Source and Handler

Event Source

- The component which generates an event is called an **'Event Source'**. For example, when the user selects an item from the list, the list becomes the event source. A source may generate one or more events. For example, a list may generate an item event with a single click or action event with a double click.

Event Handler

- When an event occurs, an object of the event class is created and passed to the event handler.

10.5.2 Event Categories (Event classes)

- java.awt.event package defines several event classes. Following is the diagram which shows hierarchy of various event classes.

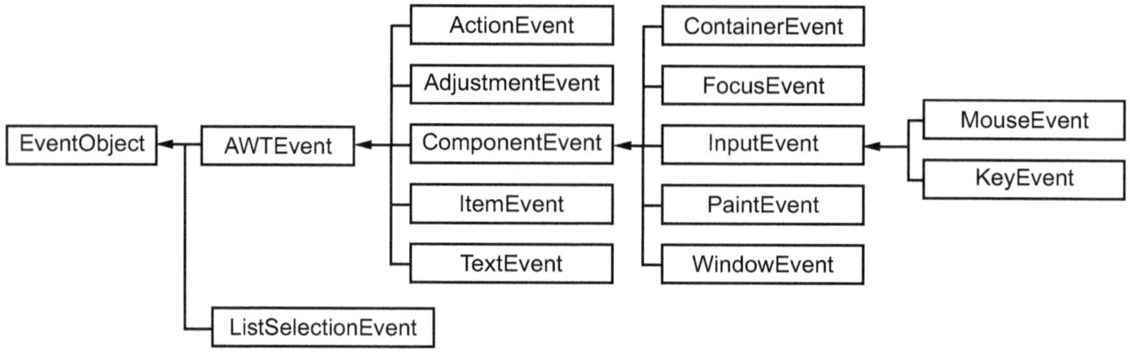

Fig. 10.21: Event Classes

Some of the event classes are:

ActionEvent:

- This event is generated when a button is pressed, a list item is double clicked or a menu item is selected.
    - **Methods:**
        - `String getActionCommand();` to obtain the command name for the event object.

          For example, when a button is clicked, the command name that gets stored in an event object is the label on that button.
        - `int getModifiers();`

AdjustmentEvent:

- This event is generated by a scrollbar. This class defines five integer constants which identify movements in a scrollbar. Those are BLOCK_DECREMENT, BLOCK_INCREMENT, UNIT_DECREMENT, UNIT_INCREMENT, TRACK.
    - **Methods:**
        - `Adjustable getAdjustable();`
        - `int getAdjustmentType();`
        - `int getValue();`

ItemEvent: **[April 2010]**

- This event is generated when checkbox or a list item is clicked or when a checkable menu item is selected or deselected. There are two types of item events SELECTED or DESELECTED. ITEM_STATE_CHANGED is an integer constant which signifies a change of state.
    - **Methods:**
        - `int getItem();`
        - `int getStateChange();`

ComponentEvent:

- This event is generated when size, position or visibility is changed. This class has 4 integer constants – COMPONENT_HIDDEN, COMPONENT_MOVED, COMPONENT_RESIZED, COMPONENT_SHOWN.
  - **Methods:**
    - `Component getComponent();`

ContainerEvent:

- This is generated when a component is added or removed from the container. Two types of events are generated COMPONENT_ADDED and COMPONENT_REMOVED.
  - **Methods:**
    - `Container getContainer();`
    - `Component getChild();`

FocusEvent:

- This event is generated when the component gains or loses foucus. This event is identified by integer constants like FOCUS_GAINED and FOCUS_LOST.

KeyEvent:

- Key event is generated when keyboard input occurs. Three types of key events are identified by integer constants like KEY_PRESSED, KEY_RELEASE and KEY_TYPED. First two events are generated when the key is pressed or released. Third event is generated when the character is generated. VK_0 to VK_9 and VK_A to VK_Z define ASCII equivalent of numbers and letters. These are called 'virtual key codes'. There are some other integer constant other that these like VK_ENTER, VK_ESCAPE, VK_SHIFT etc.

  KeyEvent is a subclass of InputEvent class.
  - **Methods:**
    - `char getKeyChar();`
    - `int getKeyCode();`

MouseEvent:

- This event is generated when the mouse is dragged, moved, cicked, pressed, released and when mouse enters or exits a component. Integer constants defined are MOUSE_CLICKED, MOUSE_MOVED, MOUSE_DRAGGED, MOUSE_PRESSED, MOUSE_RELEASED, MOUSE_ENTERED, MOUSE_EXITED.
  - **Methods:**
    - `int getX();`
    - `int getY();`
    - `Point getPoint();`

WindowEvent:

- This event is generated when a window is activated, closed, deactivated, iconified, deiconified, opened or closed. The integer constants are WINDOW_ACTIVATED, WINDOW_DEACTIVATED, WINDOW_ICONIFIED, WINDOW_DEICONIFIED, WINDOW_OPENED, WINDOW_CLOSED, WINDOW_CLOSING
    - **Methods:**
        - `Window getWindow();`

10.5.3 Event Listeners

- Listener is an object that is notified when an event occurs. It has two main requirements:
    - It must be registered with one or more event sources to receive event notification.
    - It must implement methods to receive and process these event notifications.
- The set of interfaces found in java.awt.event package has these methods for receiving and processing of an event. For example, ItemListener defines a method called itemStateChanged().

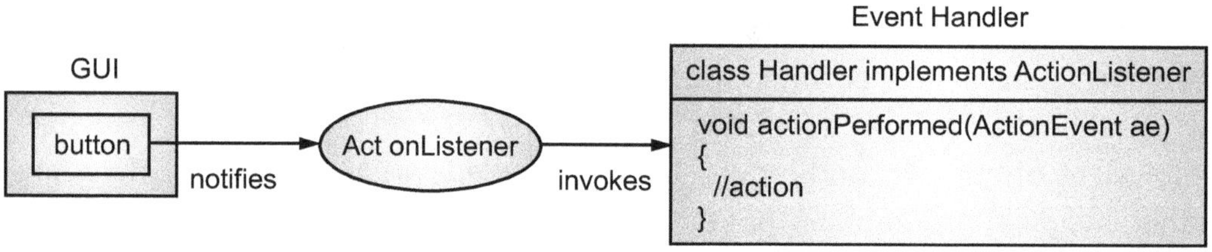

Fig. 10.22: Event Listeners

- In a diagram, a when a button is clicked, an action event is generated. This event should be notified to the listener interface that is registered with this button source. In this case, it is ActionListener. The action listener then delegates this event to event handler which is an object of a class which implements ActionListener interface. This event handler object calls an actionPerformed() method which specifies what action should be taken when action event occurs.

Interfaces

- Now that we know the event handling mechanism in java, we will try to understand which component generates what event and which listener interfaces listen to these events. The following table shows a list of Event Sources, events, listener interfaces and its methods.

Table 10.2

Event	Listener	Listener Methods	Generated when
ActionEvent	ActionListenor	actionperformed	Button click, a list item is double clicked, or menu items is elected
ItemEvent	ItemListener	itemStateChanged	A check box or list item is clicked; a choice selection is made or checkable menu item is selected or deselected.
MouseEvent	MouseListener	mouseClicked mousePressed mouseRealsed mouseEntered mouseExicted	The mouse is dragged, moved, clicked, pressed released; when the mouse enters or exits a component.
	MouseMotionListener	mouseDragged mouseMoved	
KeyEvent	KeyListener	keyTyped keyPressed keyReleased	Input is received from the keyboard.
TextEvent	TextListener	textValueChanged	Value of a text area of text field is changed
WindowEvent	WindowListener	windowOpened window windowClosed windowconified windowDeiconified windowActivated windowDeactivated	Window is activated, closed, deactivated, deiconified, iconified, opened or closed
ContainerEvent	ContainerListener	componentAdded componentRemoved	Component added or removed from container
ComponentEvent	ComponentListener	componentResized componentMoved componentShown componentHidden	The size, position or visibility of component is changed
FocusEvent	FocusListener	focusGained focusLost	Component gains or loses focus
AdjustmentEvent	AdjustmentListener	componentAdded componentRemoved	Scrollbar movements
ListSelectionEvent	ListSelectionListener	valueChanged	List items are selected

10.5.4 Event Adapters

- To handle the events, we have to define the class which implements the specific listener interface. When a class implements an interface, it has to define all the methods of the interface.
- Some of the listener interface contains one or more methods for specific events. For example, MouseListener interface contain five different methods like mousePressed(), mouseReleased(), mouseClicked() etc. However, If we just want to handle the event like mouse click, we may not be interested in defining rest of the methods. If we implement MouseListener interface, we are forced to define all five methods in our class. To avoid this problem, java provides special classes called 'Adapter Classes'. These classes make our event handling much simpler. These adapter classes implement listener interface which has empty definitions for all the methods of that interface. We can extend adapter class and override only those methods which are of our interest.
- Adapter classes are:
    - ComponentAdapter
    - ContainerAdapter
    - FocusAdapter
    - KeyAdapter
    - MouseAdapter
    - MouseMotionAdapter
    - WindowAdapter

Program 10.15: An application program that demonstrates how to make use of adapter classes

The DemoAdapter class extends WindowAdapter class which in turn implements WindowListner interface. The application creates a frame with suitable title and adds WindowListener interface to the class. The program only implements a single windowClosing() method out of all the methods defined by the WindowListener interface.

File: DemoAdapter.java

```
import java.awt.*;
import java.awt.event.*;
class DemoAdapter extends WindowAdapter implements WindowListener
{
    public DemoAdapter ()
    {
        Frame f = new Frame("Window");
        f.setVisible(true);
```

```
        f.setSize(400,400);
        f.setTitle("Demonstration of Adapter class");
        f.addWindowListener(this);
    }
    public void windowClosing(WindowEvent e)
    {
        System.exit(0);
    }
    public static void main(String[] args)
    {
        new  DemoAdapter();
    }
}
```

Output:

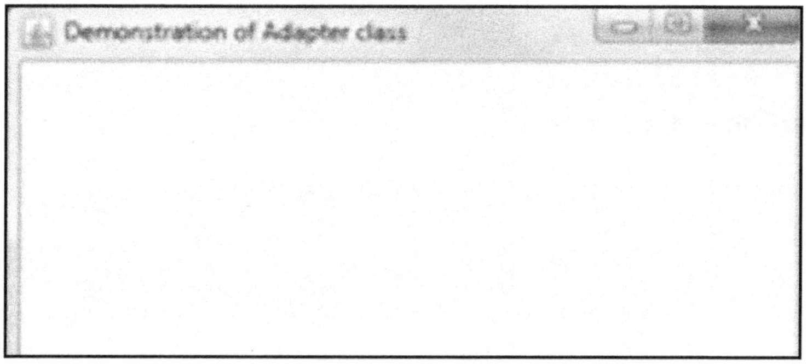

Fig. 10.23: Output

10.6 Anonymous Classes

- Anonymous class is one that is not assigned a name. An inner class is a class defined within another class or even within an expression. Anonymous inner class makes our job easy while writing code for event handlers. They can make our code simple as well as efficient.

Program 10.16: An applet program that shows how to write anonymous class.

The following applet program shows how to write anonymous class. Here, it creates an object of MouseAdapter class anonymously. It also displays 'Pressed' message in an applet window status bar when the mouse button is pressed.

File: AnonymousClass.java

```
import java.applet.*;
import java.awt.event.*;
```

```
/* <applet code="AnonymousClass" width=200 height=100> </applet> */
public class AnonymousClass extends Applet {
public void init() {
//Anonymous class MouseAdapter.
addMouseListener(new MouseAdapter() {
public void mousePressed(MouseEvent me) {
showStatus("Pressed");
}
});
}
}
```

File: AnonymousClass.html

```
<html>
 <body>
  <applet code="AnonymousClass" width=500 height=500>
</applet>
 </body>
</html>
```

Output:

Fig. 10.24: Output

Practice Questions

1. Explain following methods:
   (a) drawLine()
   (b) fillRect()
   (c) drawArc()
   (d) fillPolygon()
2. What is frame? Explain in detail.
3. What is Panel? Explain in detail.
4. Explain the concept of Layout Manager.
5. List out different layouts and explain any one in detail.
6. How components are placed in border layout?
7. Explain any three AWT components in brief.
8. Explain the concept of event delegation model.
9. What are event classes?
10. What are event listeners?
11. Explain the concept of anonymous class.
12. What are adapter classes?
13. "Adapter classes make our event handling much simpler." Comment.
14. What are the key features of swing library?
15. What are the disadvantages of swing?
16. What is dialog box? State its types and explain any one in detail.

Programming Questions

1. Write a program to design a form using components text field, checkbox, buttons, list and handle various events related to each component.
2. Write a program to design a calculator using Java components and handle various events related to each component and apply proper layout to it.
3. Write a program to demonstrate use of Grid Layout.
4. Write a program to demonstrate use of Flow Layout.
5. Write a program to demonstrate use of Card Layout.
6. Write a program to demonstrate use of Border Layout.
7. Write a program to display any string using available font and with every mouse click, change the size and style of the string. Make use of Font and FontMetrics classes and their methods.
8. Write a program to create a menu bar with various menu items and sub menu items. Also create a checkable menu item. On clicking a menu item display a suitable Dialog box.
9. Write a program to increase the font size of a font displayed when the value of thumb in scrollbar increases. It decreases the size of the font when the value of the font decreases.

■■■

Chapter 11...

APPLETS

Contents ...

11.1 Introduction

- Applets are small Java programs that are mainly used in Internet Applications.
- They can be transported over the Internet and can be executed using any web browser or an appletviewer.
- All Applets are subclasses of Applet class either directly or indirectly.
- An Applet is a subclass of Panel and Panel is itself a subclass of Container. The following figure shows hierarchy for Applet class.
- Applets which use **Swing** classes for GUI are inherited from class JApplet. But JApplet inherits Applet so all the features of Applet are also available to JApplet.

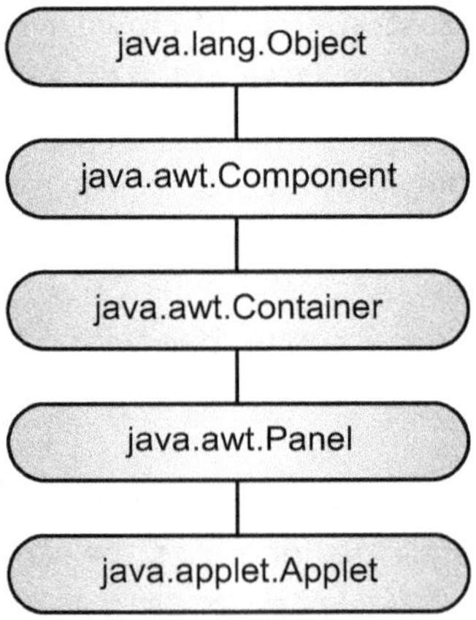

Fig. 11.1: Applet

- An Applet does not need to begin its execution with main().
- Applets are not stand alone programs. They can be executed either in any web browser or in an appletviewer provided by JDK.

11.2 Applet Life Cycle

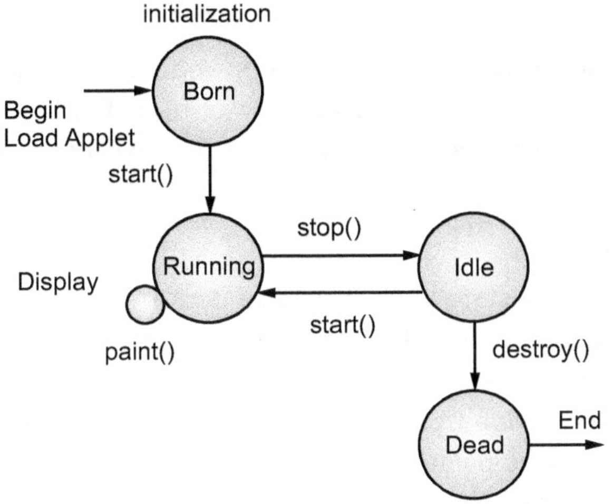

Fig. 11.2: Applet Life Cycle

- Every Applet inherits a set of default methods from Applet class. These methods are called **'life cycle methods'**. When an Applet runs, these methods are called by JVM(Java Virtual Machine).

11.2.1 Initialization

- Applet enters into an initialization state when it is first loaded. This can be done by calling init() method of an Applet class. Initialization occurs only once in Applet's life cycle. This method is also called to read the PARAM tag of HTML file. At this stage, we can set up initial values to variables, create objects needed by an Applet, load images, fonts, sound and declare variables required by an Applet. To provide this type of behavior, we must override an init() method.

11.2.2 Running State

- Applet enters the running state when system calls the start() method of Applet class. This method is called automatically after the initialization state. We may call start() method multiple times whenever we want to start or restart Applet. For example, if we leave the web page running an Applet temporarily, switch to some other page and return back to the same page again, the Applet starts running again. We may override the start() method.

11.2.3 Idle State

- An Applet becomes idle when it stops running. Stopping occurs when we leave the web page running an Applet. Methods like start(), stop() method can also be called more than once. We may override the stop() method.

11.2.4 Dead State

- An Applet is said to be dead when it is removed from memory. This is done by the destroy() method. This method is called only once in the life cycle of an Applet. This method is called automatically when we close the web browser in which an Applet is running.

11.2.5 Display State

- Applet moves to display state when it has to perform some output operations on the screen. This can happen only after Applet enters into running state. paint() method is called to do this task. Like all other life cycle methods, paint() method also has its default version. But we can override this method to display the desired output on the screen. It is important to note that paint() method is a method of Component class which is a super class of Applet class.

11.2.6 Program for Applet life cycle

- The following is an example of simple Applet.

Program 11.1: FirstApplet.java

```
import java.applet.*;
import java.awt.*;
/* <applet code = "FirstApplet.class" height = "500" width="500">
</applet> */
public class  FirstApplet extends Applet
{
    String message = "";
    public void init()
    {
        message = "In init method";
        System.out.println(message);
    }
    public void start()
    {
        message = "In start method";
        System.out.println(message);
    }
```

```
        public void stop()
        {
           message = "In stop method";
           System.out.println(message);
        }
        public void destroy()
        {
           message = "In destroy method";
           System.out.println(message);
        }
        public void paint(Graphics g)
        {
           g.drawString(message, 200, 200);
        }
     }
```

Output:

Fig. 11.3

- As paint() method will be called after start(), method 'message' will contain a string "In start method".

11.3 Applet Specific methods and Related HTML references

11.3.1 Methods of Applet class

- Applet class resides in java.applet package. Applet class defines the methods shown in the table 11.1. Applet provides all the necessary support for window based activities.

Table 11.1

Method	Description
void destroy()	Called by the browser just before an Applet is terminated.
AppletContext getAppletContext()	Returns the context associated with the Applet.
String getAppletInfo()	Returns the string that describes the Applet.

contd. ...

String getParameter(String paramName)	Returns the parameter associated with paramName. **Null** is returned if the specified parameter is not found.
void init()	Called when an Applet begins execution. It is the first method callrd for any Applet.
boolean isActive()	Returns true is the Applet has been started. It returns false is the Applet has been stopped.
void showStatus(String str)	Displays string in the status window of the browser or appletviewer. If the browser does not support status window, then no action takes place.
void start()	Called by the browser when an Applet should start an execution. It is automatically called after init().
void stop()	Called by the browser to suspend execution of an Applet.

11.3.2 Applet Display Methods

- Applets are displayed in a window. Methods to display output on Applet. To output a string to an Applet, use drawstring() method of Graphics class. This method is typically called from update() or paint() method. The following is the signature of:

1. drawString():

```
void drawString(String message, int x, int y)
```

   Here message is the String to be displayed in the appletviewer window or browser window beginning at position x,y.

2. To set the background color of an applet window, use setBackground() method of Component class.

```
void setBackground(Color newColor)
```

3. To set the foreground color of an applet window, use setForeground() method of Component class.

```
void setForeground(Color newColor)
```

   For Example, the following lines set the background color to blue & text color to yellow.

```
void setBackground(Color.blue);
void setForeground(Color.yellow);
```

11.4 Creating an Applet

- Let us create a small applet to accept two values from the user and display the product of it in an applet.

Program 11.2:

UserInput.java

```
import java.awt.*;
import java.applet.*;
import java.awt.event.*;
public class UserInput extends Applet implements ActionListener
{
   TextField tf1, tf2;
   int x =0, y = 0, prod = 0;
   String s1, s2 , s3;
   Button b1;
   public void init()
   {
      tf1 = new TextField(5);
      tf2 = new TextField(5);
      b1 = new Button("Click");
      add(tf1);
      add(tf2);
      add(b1);
      tf1.setText("0");
      tf2.setText("0");
      b1.addActionListener(this);
   }
public void actionPerformed(ActionEvent e)
{
if (e.getSource() == b1)
{
   s1 = tf1.getText();
   x = Integer.parseInt(s1);
   s2 = tf2.getText();
   y = Integer.parseInt(s2);
   prod = x * y;
   repaint();
}
}
public void paint(Graphics g)
{
g.drawString("Enter numbers in the given text boxes: ", 10,50);
g.drawString("The product of the two numbers is: "+ prod, 10,200);
}
}
```

UserInput.html

```
<html>
<body>
<applet code = "UserInput.class" width = 300 height = 300>
</applet>
</body>
</html>
```

Output:

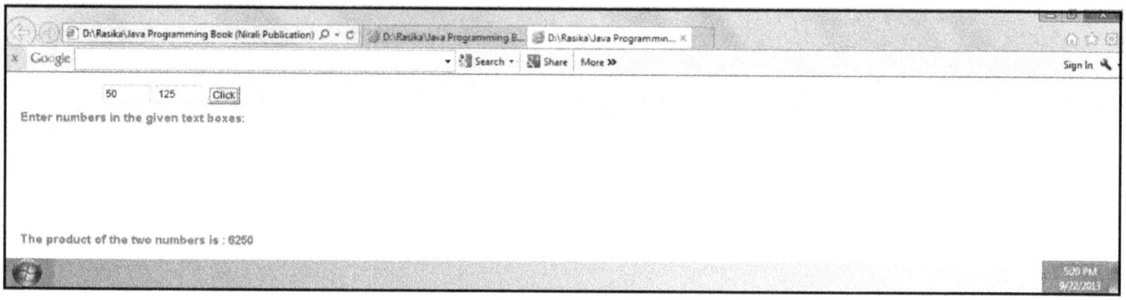

Fig. 11.4 Output

Program Analysis

- An Applet contains two text fields and a button. User enters two values into the text fields and when the user clicks on a button, the product of the two values is calculated and displayed in an applet window.
- Class UserInput extends Applet class and it implements ActionListener interaface to handle the event carried out by a button. It declares all the required variables. Applet's init() method declares all the GUI controls and it designs GUI for the applet. It also adds ActionListener interface to the button.
- When the button is clicked, it calls actionPerformed() method to handle the action event. actionPerformed() method is to be overridden by the code that should be executed to handle the event. repaint() method calls paint() automatically to display the updated information in the applet.
- paint() method is called by an Applet which displays initial informatation. It also displays product of the two numbers entered by the user when called again by repaint() method.

11.5 Displaying it using Web Browser, Applet Viewer.exe

- If you use Java enabled web browser, you will be able to see the entire webpage containing an applet. If you use AppletViewer tool, you will only be able to see the applet output. Since appletviewer is not a full-fledge web browser so it ignores all of the HTML tags except the part require dto run the applet. Appletviewer is available as part of Java Development Kit.

- When the browser finds the class file, it loads it over the network. The browser then creates an instance of the class. If you include an applet twice on one page, it loads the class file once and creates two instances of the class.

11.6 The HTML Applet Tag with all Attributes

- We have used Applet tag in its simplest form. The syntax of applet tag is a bit complex. It includes several attributes. The complete tag with all its attributes is shown below:

```
<APPLET [CODEBASE = codebase_url] CODE = appletfilename.class
[ALT = alternate_text]
[NAME = appletinstance_name]
WIDTH = pixels HEIGHT = pixels [ALIGN = alignment] [VSPACE = pixels]
[HSPACE = pixels] >
[ <PARAM NAME = name1 VALUE = value1> ]
[ <PARAM NAME = name2 VALUE = value2> ]
.......
</APPLET>
```

- The following table lists all the attributes along with their meaning.

Table 11.2

Attribute	Meaning
CODE=AppletFileName.class	Specifies the name of the applet class to be loaded. That is, the name of the already compiled, class file in which the executable Java bytecode for the applet is stored. This attribute must be specified.
CODEBASE=codebase_URL (Optinal)	Specifies the URL of the directory in which the applet resides. If the applet resides is the same directory as the HTML file, then the CODEBASE attribute may be omitted entirely.
WIDTH=pixels HEIGHT=pixels	These attributes specify the width and height of the space on the HTML page that will be reserved for the applet.
NAME=applet_instance_name (Optional)	A name for the applet may optionally be specified so that other applets on the page may refer to this applet. This facilitates inter-applet communication.

contd. ...

`ALIGN=alignment` (Optional)	This optional attribute specifies where on the page the applet will appear. Possible values for alignment are: TOP, BOTTOM, LEFT, RIGHT, MIDDLE, ABSMIDDLE, ABSBOTTOM, TEXTTOP and BASELINE.
`HSPACE=pixels (Optional)`	Used only when ALIGN is to set to LEFT to RIGHT, this attribute specifies the amount of horizontal blank space the browser should leave surrounding the applet.
`VSPACE=pixels (Optional)`	Used only when some vertical alignment is specified with the ALIGN attribute (TOP, BOTTOM etc.) VSPACE specifies the amount of vertical blank space the browser should leave surrounding the applet.
`ALT=alternate_text` (Optional)	Non-Java browsers will display this text where the applet would normally go. This attribute is optional.

11.7 Passing Parameters to Applet

- Many times, when we are writing Java applets, we may need to pass parameters. We can pass these parameters from an HTML page with the help of <param> tag. For example, we may want to tell the applet, which color should be set as a background to the applet.
- The benefit of passing parameter from HTML lies in its portability. If you pass parameters from HTML page, they can be passed from one webpage to the other and from one website to the other.
- We can make our applet more flexible and portable using this technique.
- Parameters are passed by placing them in a <PARAM> tag and placing this tag inside opening and closing of <APPLET> tag. For instance,

```
<APPLET> <PARAM name = 'name1' value = 'value1'> </APPLET>
```

Example of an applet: Passing parameters to an applet using <param> tag

Program 11.3:

DrawApplet.java

```
import java.applet.*;
import java.awt.*;
public class DrawApplet extends Applet
{
    String name;
    int age;
```

```
    public void init()
    {
        name = getParameter("nm");
        try
        {
            age = Integer.parseInt( getParameter("input_age"));
        }
        catch(NumberFormatException e){}
     }
    public void paint(Graphics g)
    {
        Font f = new Font("Helvetica", Font.BOLD, 20);
        g.setFont(f);
        g.setColor(Color.red);
        g.drawString("Name is "+ name + " & Age is " + age, 50,25);
    }
    }
```

DrawApplet.html

```
<html>
<body>
This is an Applet...
<applet code = "DrawApplet.class" width = 200 height = 200>
<param name = "nm" value = "Neeta Joshi">
<param name = "input_age" value = "20">
</applet>
</body>
</html>
```

Output:

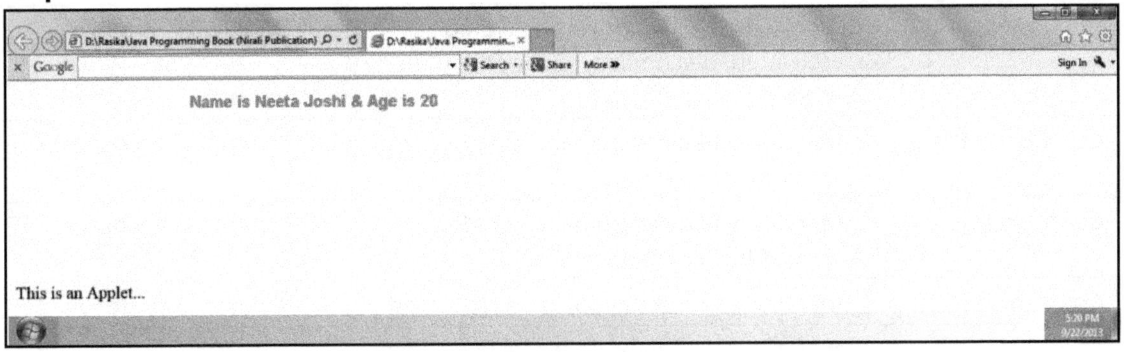

Fig. 11.5 Output

11.8 Event Handling in Applet

- Any program that uses GUI (graphical user interface) such as Java application written for windows, is event driven. Event describes the change of state of any object.

  Example: Pressing a button, Entering a character in Textbox.

Components of Event Handling

- Event handling has three main components,
  1. **Events:** An event is a change of state of an object.
  2. **Events Source:** Event source is an object that generates an event.
  3. **Listeners:** A listener is an object that listens to the event. A listener gets notified when an event occurs.

How Events are handled?

- A source generates an Event and send it to one or more listeners registered with the source. Once event is received by the listener, they processes the event and then return. Events are supported by a number of Java packages, like java.util, java.awt and java.awt.event.

Important Event Classe and Interface for Applet Event Handling

Table 11.3

Event Classe	Description	Listener Interface
ActionEvent	generated when button is pressed, menu-item is selected, list-item is double clicked	ActionListener
MouseEvent	generated when mouse is dragged, moved,clicked,pressed or released also when the enters or exit a component	MouseListener
KeyEvent	generated when input is received from keyboard	KeyListener
ItemEvent	generated when check-box or list item is clicked	ItemListener
TextEvent	generated when value of textarea or textfield is changed	TextListener
MouseWheelEvent	generated when mouse wheel is moved	MouseWheelListener
WindowEvent	generated when window is activated, deactivated, deiconified, iconified, opened or closed	WindowListener
ComponentEvent	generated when component is hidden, moved, resized or set visible	ComponentEventListener
ContainerEvent	generated when component is added or removed from container	ContainerListener
AdjustmentEvent	generated when scroll bar is manipulated	AdjustmentListener
FocusEvent	generated when component gains or loses keyboard focus	FocusListener

Example of Event Handling

Button event handling

- It is the most common event generating components in user interfaces. When we click on a button, an action is generated. In fact, the term action is used in button event handling.

Properties

- Some of the properties of a button event are:
  - It manages the list of button objects that implement the ActionListener interface.
  - The actionPerformed method is invoked when we click or press on a button, it is invoked for all of the ActionListener instances in its list.
  - The abstract actionPerformed method overrides the ActionListener classes to perform the task for the button.
  - As an argument of actionPerformed, an ActionEvent object is passed and from it you can extract information about the event such as which ActionListener initiated the event.
  - To add an instance of ActionListener to a button, we must invoke its addActionListener(ActionListener) method.
- The following example will help in the understanding of event handling in Applets.
- In this example, we perform event handling in an Applet that prints a message by clicking on the button.

Program 11.4

```
import java.awt.event.*;
import java.applet.*;
import java.awt.*;
public class EventApplet extends Applet implements ActionListener
  {
    Button bttn;
    TextField txtfld;
    public void init()
      {
        txtfld=new TextField();
        txtfld.setBounds(35,45,250,30);
        bttn=new Button("click me");
        bttn.setBounds(90,110,70,60);
        add(bttn);add(txtfld);
        bttn.addActionListener(this);
        setLayout(null);
      }
```

```
      public void actionPerformed(ActionEvent ae)
        {
          txtfld.setText("This is an example of Event Handling ");
        }
    }
  /*
  <applet code="EventApplet.class" width="400" height="400">
  </applet
  */
```

Output:

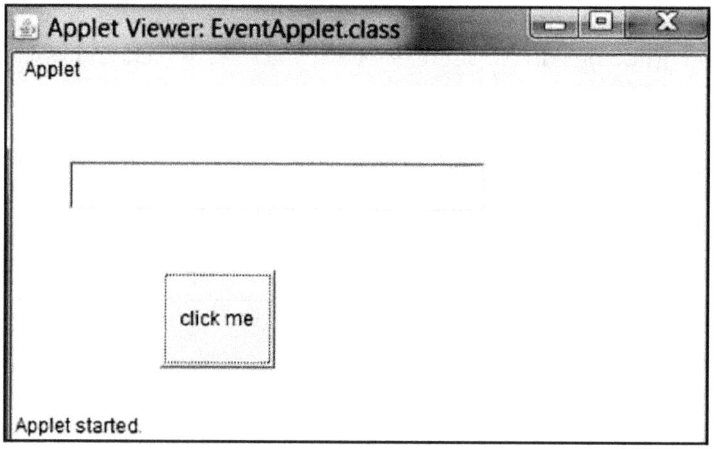

Fig. 11.6

- When we click on "click me" button an event is generated that displays the message that we pass in our program. The output is shown below.

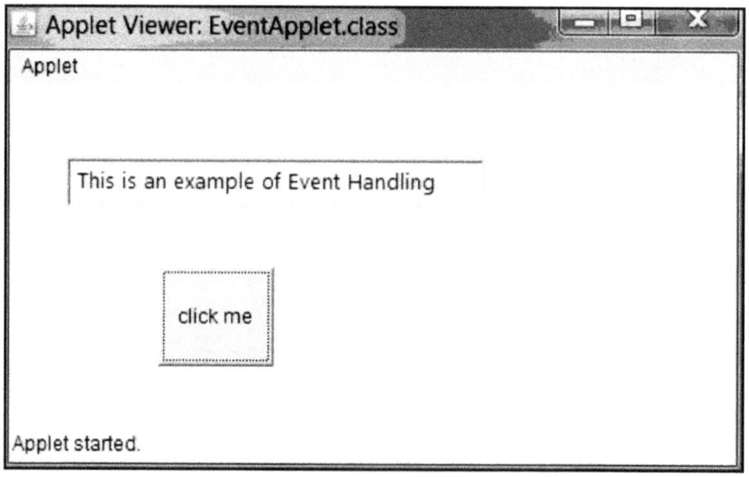

Fig. 11.7

11.9 Advantages and Disadvantages of an Applet vs. Applications

11.9.1 Advantages of Applets

- Applets are cross platform and can run on windows, MAC OS and Linux platform.
- Applets are supported by almost all the browsers.
- Applets are cached in most web browsers, so it can quickly be loaded when returning a webpage.

11.9.2 Disadvantages of Applets

- Java plug-in is required to run the applet.
- If the applet is not already present in the cache, it will be downloaded from Internet and so it will take time.
- Java applets require JVM, so first time it takes significant startup time.

11.9.3 Applets vs. Applications

Table 11.4

Applet	Application
They are not full featured application programs.	These are full featured application programs.
They are usually written as a small task. They are usually designed to use on Internet.	These are stand alone programs.
Applets do not use main() method to initiate the execution	Applications initiate their execution with main() method.
Applets do not run independently. They run from inside the webpage.	Applications can run independently.
Applets cannot read from or write to the files in the local computer.	Applications can read or write to the files in local computer.

Solved Examples of an Applets

1. An applet which accepts username and password from the user. If the user is valid, it displays 'Welcome' message. If the user is invalid, it displays 'Invaild' message.

Program 11.5:

Login.java

```
import java.awt.*;
import java.awt.event.*;
import java.applet.*;
```

```
public class  Login extends Applet implements ActionListener
{
   private Label l1, l2, l3;
   private Button ok, cancel;
   private TextField t1, t2;
   public void init()
   {
      l1 = new Label("USER NAME: ");
      l2 = new Label("PASSWORD: ");
      l3 = new Label("            ");
      t1 = new TextField(20);
      t2 = new TextField(20);
      t2.setEchoChar('*');
      ok = new Button("OK");
      cancel = new Button("CANCEL");
      add(l1); add(t1); add(l2); add(t2);
      add(ok); add(cancel);
      add(l3);
      ok.addActionListener(this);
      cancel.addActionListener(this);
   }
   public void actionPerformed(ActionEvent ae)
   {
      if(ae.getSource() == ok)
      {
         String user = t1.getText();
         String pass = t2.getText();
         String htmluser = getParameter("htmluser");
         String htmlpass = getParameter("htmlpass");
         if(user.equals(htmluser) && pass.equals(htmlpass))
            l3.setText("Welcome");
```

```
            else
            {
               l3.setText("Invalid");
               t1.setText("");
               t2.setText("");
            }
         }
         else
         {
            t1.setText("");
            t2.setText("");
            l3.setText("");
         }
      }
   }
```

Login.html

```
<html>
<body>
<applet code = "Login.class" width = 500 height = 300>
<param name = "htmluser" value = "mca1">
<param name = "htmlpass" value = "mca1">
</applet>
</body>
</html>
```

Output:

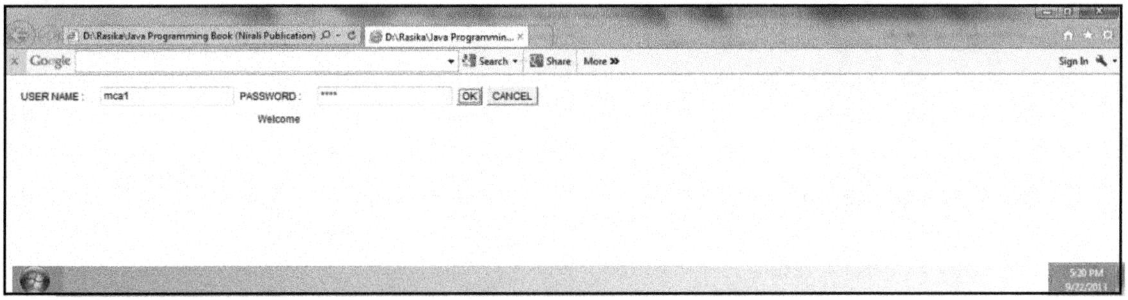

Fig. 11.8

An applet which handles events:

Program 11.6:

ButtonApplet.java

```
import java.awt.*;
import java.awt.event.*;
import java.applet.*;
public class  ButtonApplet extends Applet implements ActionListener
{
   private Button red, green, blue;
   private Color c;
   public void init()
   {
      red = new Button("RED");
      green = new Button("GREEN");
      blue = new Button("BLUE");
      add(red);      add(green);       add(blue);
      red.addActionListener(this);
      green.addActionListener(this);
      blue.addActionListener(this);
   }
   public void actionPerformed(ActionEvent ae)
   {
      AppletContext ac = getAppletContext();
      SquareApplet a = (SquareApplet)ac.getApplet("Square");
      if(ae.getSource() == red)
         c = Color.red;
      else
      if(ae.getSource() == green)
         c = Color.green;
      else
      if(ae.getSource() == blue)
         c = Color.blue;
      a.repaint();
   }
   public Color getColor()
   {
      return c;
   }
}
```

Program 11.7:

SquareApplet.java

```
import java.awt.*;
import java.applet.*;
public class  SquareApplet extends Applet
{
   public void paint(Graphics g)
   {
      AppletContext ac = getAppletContext();
      ButtonApplet a = (ButtonApplet)ac.getApplet("Button");
      g.setColor(a.getColor());
      g.fillRect(100, 100, 100, 100);
   }
}
```

Output:

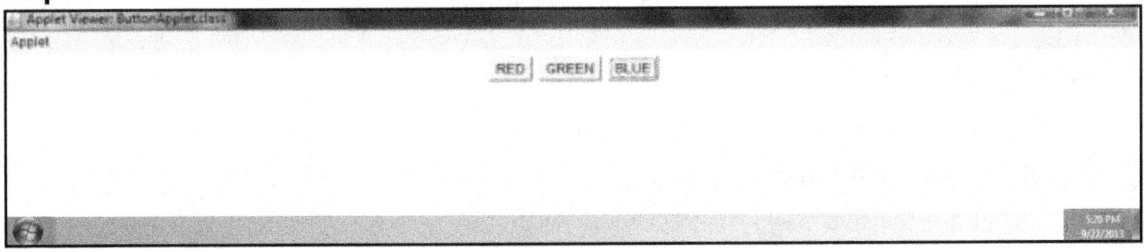

Fig. 11.9: Output

Red button press:

Fig. 11.10: Output

Green button press:

Fig. 11.11: Output

Blue button pressed:

Fig. 11.12: Output

Practice Questions

1. Write a note on Java's Applet Life Cycle.
2. Compare Applets and Applications
3. What are the two ways to execute an Applet?
4. Explain in brief, how to pass parameters to an Applet?
5. Write an importance of update() method.
6. Explain the following methods:
   (a) setForeground()
   (b) setBackground()
7. Explain how applets are included in HTML page?
8. Write a short note on Event Handling in Applets with suitable example.

Programming Questions

1. Create an Applet to display concentric circle.
2. Create an Applet to display concentric rectangle.
3. Create an Applet to display concentric circle filled with different colors.
4. Create an Applet to display concentric rectangle filled with different colors.
5. Create an Applet which displays numbers 1 to 10 in diagonal order having background color as red and foreground color as yellow.
6. Create an applet which display Olympic symbol.
7. Create an applet which displays Indian flag.
8. Create an applet which displays smiling face.
9. Create an applet which draw line chart.

10. Create an applet which will display a moving ball.
11. Create an applet which will display moving banner.
12. Create an applet which will take parameter from user and display it on status window.
13. Create an applet which will take parameter from user and display it.

■■■

Chapter 12...

SWING

Contents ...

12.1 Introduction

- We have seen how to build Graphical User Interfaces with AWT. Though AWT is very important aspect of Java, it is not widely used to design Graphical User Interface. Today most of the programmer use Swing for this purpose. Swing is a library of more powerful and flexible classes for designing GUI components as compared to AWT. Swing is not the complete replacement for AWT but it is built on top of AWT.
- Swing is a very large subsystem and uses many packages. Some of the important packages used by swing are javax.swing, javax.swing,event, javax.swing.filechooser, javax.swing.plaf etc. The main package is javax.swing. This package must be imported into a program that uses swing. This package contains basic swing components.

12.2 Features of Swing

- **Swing Components are lightweight**

  AWT translates its various visual components into platform specific equivalents or peers. Look and feel of each component is defined by platform and not by Java. This means that each component will look and act different on different platforms. This property threatens the signature statement of Java: Write once run everywhere. Look and feel of each component is fixed and cannot be changed. This makes the component heavyweight. Swing components are written entirely in java and do not translate into platform equivalents. Since they are not platform dependent, they are more efficient and more flexible. This makes these components lightweight.

- **Pluggable Look And Feel(PLAF)**

  Java supports Pluggable Look And Feel(PLAF). Look and Feel of a component is under the control of swing. It is possible to separate the look and feel of a component from the logic of component. It is possible to plug-in a new look and feel for a component without affecting its logical part. There are various GUI styles. We can plug-in any look and feel style and all components will be rendered in that style. Java SE 6 provides metal and motif look and feel styles. Metal is a default look and feel.

Disadvantages of Swing

1. Swing components appear slow as compare to peer-based components.
2. It is not an independent library. It is based on AWT library.
3. Since they look same on all platforms, user may be less familiar with them.

12.3 Model View Controller design pattern

- Model View Controller architecture is a well-known object oriented user interface design architecture. A visual component is a composite of three aspects:

  How component looks when it is rendered on the screen.

  How component reacts to the user

  The state information associated with that component.

- In general, components are broken down into three parts: Model, View and Controller. In MVC terminology, each component has three characteristics:

  1. Model corresponds to the state information associated with that component.
  2. View determines how the component is displayed on the screen.
  3. Controller defines how the component reacts to the user.

Model-Delegate Architecture

- Although the MVC architecture is conceptually sound, high level of separation between view and controller is not beneficial for swing components. Therefore, swing designers modified this MVC architecture a bit and combined view and controller into a single logical entity called as 'UI delegate'. For this reason, Swing's approach is called **'Model Delegate'** architecture. Most swing components contain two objects while supporting Model-Delegate architecture. Model delegates are defined by interfaces and UI delegates are the classes that inherit ComponentUI class. Normally user programs do not interact directly with UI delegates.

12.4 Swing Components

- Swing Framework contains a large set of components which provide rich functionalities and allow high level of customization. All these components are lightweight components. They all are derived from JComponentclass. It supports the pluggable look and feel.

12.14.1 JButton

- JButton class provides functionality of a button. JButton class has three constructors as follows:
  - JButton(Icon ic)
  - JButton(String str)
  - JButton(String str, Icon ic)
- It allows a button to be created using icon, a string or both. JButton supports ActionEvent. When a button is pressed an ActionEvent is generated.

Program 12.1: Write a program to create button.

```
import javax.swing.*;
import java.awt.event.*;
import java.awt.*;
public class testswing extends JFrame
{
    testswing()
    {
    JButton bt1 = new JButton("Yes");          //Creating a Yes Button.
    JButton bt2 = new JButton("No");           //Creating a No Button.
    setDefaultCloseOperation(JFrame.EXIT_ON_CLOSE)
                                              //setting close operation.
    setLayout(new FlowLayout());
                        //setting layout using FlowLayout object
    setSize(400, 400);  //setting size of Jframe
    add(bt1);           //adding Yes button to frame.
    add(bt2);           //adding No button to frame.
    setVisible(true);
}
```

```
public static void main(String[] args)
{
   new testswing();
}
}
```

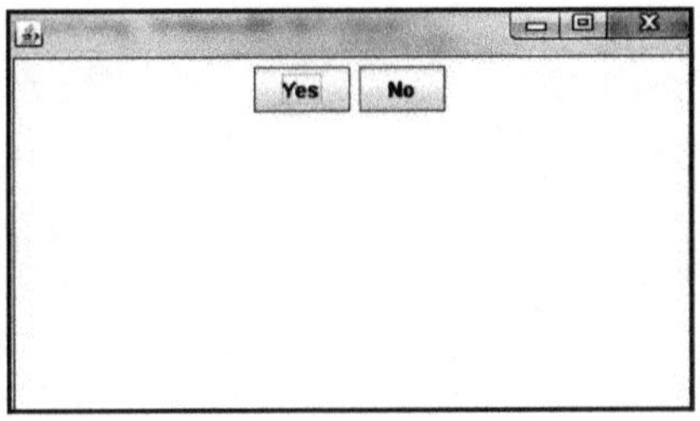

Fig. 12.1: Output

12.14.2 JTextField

- JTextField is used for taking input of single line of text. It is most widely used text component. It has three constructors as follows:

```
JTextField(int cols)
JTextField(String str, int cols)
JTextField(String str)
```

cols represent the number of columns in text field.

Program 12.2: Example using JTextField.

```
import javax.swing.*;
import java.awt.event.*;
import java.awt.*;
public class MyTextField extends JFrame
{
   public MyTextField()
   {
   JTextField jtf = new JTextField(20);      //creating JTextField.
   add(jtf);             //adding JTextField to frame.
   setLayout(new FlowLayout());
   setDefaultCloseOperation(JFrame.EXIT_ON_CLOSE);
   setSize(400, 400);
   setVisible(true);
   }
```

```
    public static void main(String[] args)
    {
        new MyTextField();
    }
}
```

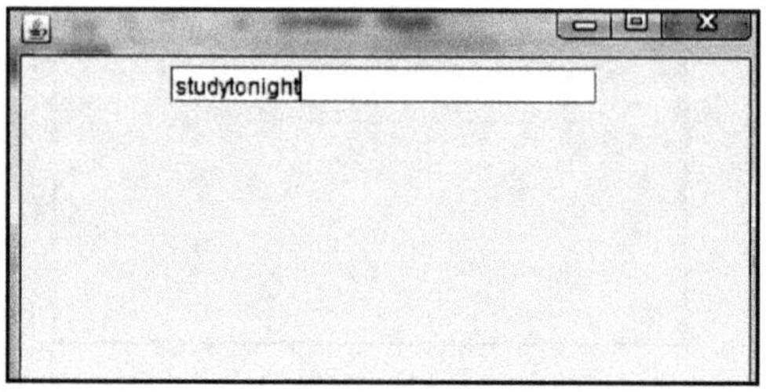

Fig. 12.2: Output

12.14.3 JCheckBox

- JCheckBox class is used to create checkboxes in frame. Following is constructor for JCheckBox,

  `JCheckBox(String str)`

Program 12.3: Example using JCheckBox

```
import javax.swing.*;
import java.awt.event.*;
import java.awt.*;
public class Test extends JFrame
{
    public Test()
    {
    JCheckBox jcb = new JCheckBox("yes"); //creating JCheckBox.
    add(jcb);                              //adding JCheckBox to frame.
    jcb = new JCheckBox("no");             //creating JCheckBox.
    add(jcb);                              //adding JCheckBox to frame.
    jcb = new JCheckBox("maybe");          //creating JCheckBox.
    add(jcb);                              //adding JCheckBox to frame.
    setLayout(new FlowLayout());
```

```
        setDefaultCloseOperation(JFrame.EXIT_ON_CLOSE);
        setSize(400, 400);
        setVisible(true);
    }
    public static void main(String[] args)
    {
        new Test();
    }
    }
```

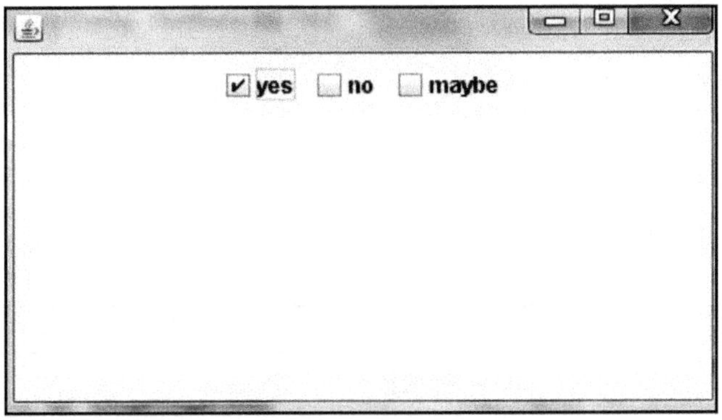

Fig. 12.3: Output

12.14.4 JRadioButton

- Radio button is a group of related button in which only one can be selected. JRadioButton class is used to create a radio button in Frames. Following is the constructor for JRadioButton,

```
JRadioButton(String str)
```

Program 12.4: Example using JRadioButton.

```
    import javax.swing.*;
    import java.awt.event.*;
    import java.awt.*;
    public class Test extends JFrame
    {
        public Test()
        {
        JRadioButton jcb = new JRadioButton("A"); //creating JRadioButton.
        add(jcb);                    //adding JRadioButton to frame.
        jcb = new JRadioButton("B");  //creating JRadioButton.
```

```
    add(jcb);                          //adding JRadioButton to frame.
    jcb = new JRadioButton("C");       //creating JRadioButton.
    add(jcb);                          //adding JRadioButton to frame.
    jcb = new JRadioButton("none");
    add(jcb);
    setLayout(new FlowLayout());
    setDefaultCloseOperation(JFrame.EXIT_ON_CLOSE);
    setSize(400, 400);
    setVisible(true);
    }
    public static void main(String[] args)
    {
    new Test();
    }
}
```

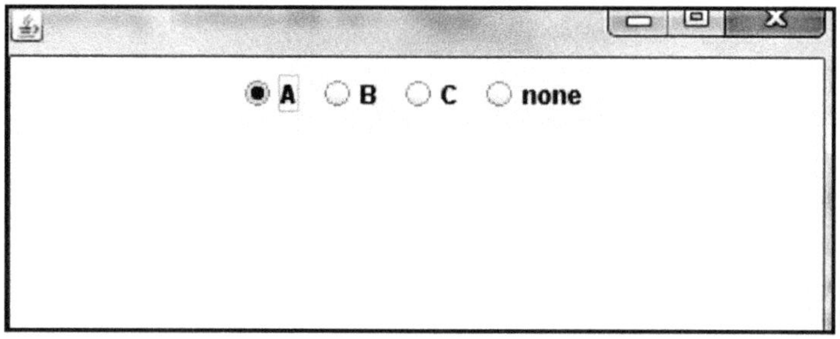

Fig. 12.4: Output

12.14.5 JComboBox

- Combo box is a combination of text fields and drop-down list.JComboBox component is used to create a combo box in Swing. Following is the constructor for JComboBox,

```
JComboBox(String arr[])
```

Program 12.5: Example using JComboBox.

```
import javax.swing.*;
import java.awt.event.*;
import java.awt.*;
public class Test extends JFrame
{
   String name[] = {"Abhi","Aliya","Anna","Ashkay"}; //list of name.
```

```
    public Test()
    {
       JComboBox jc = new JComboBox(name);
                              //initialzing combo box with list of name.
       add(jc);            //adding JComboBox to frame.
       setLayout(new FlowLayout());
       setDefaultCloseOperation(JFrame.EXIT_ON_CLOSE);
       setSize(400, 400);
       setVisible(true);
    }
    public static void main(String[] args)
    {
    new Test();
    }
}
```

Fig. 12.5: Output

12.4.6 JTextArea

- The class JTextArea is a multi-line area to display plain text. Following is the declaration for javax.swing.JTextArea class –

```
public class JTextArea
  extends JTextComponent
```

- Commonly used Constructors of JTextArea as follows:
    - **JTextArea():** Creates a text area that displays no text initially.
    - **JTextArea(String s):** Creates a text area that displays specified text initially.
    - **JTextArea(int row, int column):** Creates a text area with the specified number of rows and columns that displays no text initially..
    - **JTextArea(String s, int row, int column):** Creates a text area with the specified number of rows and columns that displays specified text.

Program 12.6: Write a program to create Text area.

```
import java.awt.Color;
import javax.swing.*;

public class TArea {
    JTextArea area;
    JFrame f;
    TArea(){
    f=new JFrame();

    area=new JTextArea(300,300);
    area.setBounds(10,30,300,300);

    area.setBackground(Color.black);
    area.setForeground(Color.white);

    f.add(area);

    f.setSize(400,400);
    f.setLayout(null);
    f.setVisible(true);
}
   public static void main(String[] args) {
   new TArea();
}
}
```

12.4.7 JTable

- The JTable class is used to display the data on two dimensional tables of cells.
- Following are the commonly used constructors of JTable:
    1. **JTable():** creates a table with empty cells.
    2. **JTable(Object[][] rows, Object[] columns):** creates a table with the specified data.

Program 12.7: Write a program to create a table.

```
import javax.swing.*;
public class MyTable {
    JFrame f;
MyTable(){
    f=new JFrame();
```

```
    String data[][]={ {"101","Amit","670000"},
             {"102","Jai","780000"},
                         {"101","Sachin","700000"}};
    String column[]={"ID","NAME","SALARY"};
    JTable jt=new JTable(data,column);
    jt.setBounds(30,40,200,300);

    JScrollPane sp=new JScrollPane(jt);
    f.add(sp);

    f.setSize(300,400);
//  f.setLayout(null);
    f.setVisible(true);
}
public static void main(String[] args) {
    new MyTable();
}
}
```

12.4.8 JProgressBar

- The JProgressBar class is used to display the progress of the task.
- Following are the commonly used Constructors of JProgressBar class:
  - **JProgressBar():** It is used to create a horizontal progress bar but no string text.
  - **JProgressBar(int min, int max):** It is used to create a horizontal progress bar with the specified minimum and maximum value.
  - **JProgressBar(int orient):** It is used to create a progress bar with the specified orientation, it can be either Vertical or Horizontal by using SwingConstants.VERTICAL and SwingConstants.HORIZONTAL constants.
  - **JProgressBar(int orient, int min, int max):** It is used to create a progress bar with the specified orientation, minimum and maximum value.
- Commonly used methods of JProgressBar class:
  1. **public void setStringPainted(boolean b):** It is used to determine whether string should be displayed.
  2. **public void setString(String s):** It is used to set value to the progress string.
  3. **public void setOrientation(int orientation):** It is used to set the orientation, it may be either vertical or horizontal by using SwingConstants.VERTICAL and SwingConstants.HORIZONTAL constants..
  4. **public void setValue(int value):** It is used to set the current value on the progress bar.

Program 12.8: Write a program to create progressbar.

```
import javax.swing.*;
public class MyProgress extends JFrame{
JProgressBar jb;
int i=0,num=0;

MyProgress(){
jb=new JProgressBar(0,2000);
jb.setBounds(40,40,200,30);

jb.setValue(0);
jb.setStringPainted(true);

add(jb);
setSize(400,400);
setLayout(null);
}

public void iterate(){
while(i<=2000){
  jb.setValue(i);
  i=i+20;
  try{Thread.sleep(150);}catch(Exception e){}
}
}
public static void main(String[] args) {
    MyProgress m=new MyProgress();
    m.setVisible(true);
    m.iterate();
}
}
```

12.4.9 JSlider

- The JSlider is used to create the slider. By using JSlider a user can select a value from a specific range.
- Following are the commonly used Constructors of JSlider class:
  1. **JSlider():** It creates a slider with the initial value of 50 and range of 0 to 100.
  2. **JSlider(int orientation):** It creates a slider with the specified orientation set by either JSlider.HORIZONTAL or JSlider.VERTICAL with the range 0 to 100 and initial value 50.

3. **JSlider(int min, int max):** It creates a horizontal slider using the given min and max.
4. **JSlider(int min, int max, int value):** It creates a horizontal slider using the given min, max and value.
5. **JSlider(int orientation, int min, int max, int value):** It creates a slider using the given orientation, min, max and value.

- Commonly used Methods of JSlider class:
  1. **public void setMinorTickSpacing(int n):** It is used to set the minor tick spacing to the slider.
  2. **public void setMajorTickSpacing(int n):** It is used to set the major tick spacing to the slider.
  3. **public void setPaintTicks(boolean b):** It is used to determine whether tick marks are painted.
  4. **public void setPaintLabels(boolean b):** It is used to determine whether labels are painted.
  5. **public void setPaintTracks(boolean b):** It is used to determine whether track is painted.

Program 12.9: Example using JSlider.

```
import javax.swing.*;
public class SliderExample1 extends JFrame{
public SliderExample1() {
JSlider slider = new JSlider(JSlider.HORIZONTAL, 0, 50, 25);
JPanel panel=new JPanel();
panel.add(slider);
add(panel);
}
public static void main(String s[]) {
SliderExample1 frame=new SliderExample1();
frame.pack();
frame.setVisible(true);
}
}
```

12.4.10 JDialog

- A Dialog is a top-level window with a title and a border that is typically used to take some form of input from the user. The default layout for a dialog is BorderLayout. JDialog is a sub class ofjava.awt.Dialog so all the methods in this are inherited to JDialog.
  1. A dialog can be either modal or modeless.

2. A modal dialog blocks user input to all other windows in the same application when it is visible. You have to close a modal dialog before other windows in the same application can get focus.
3. A modeless one does not block user input.
4. A dialog can belong to another dialog or a frame. Or, it can stand alone like a JFrame.

Program 12.10: A Simple Modal Dialog.

```
import java.awt.BorderLayout;
import java.awt.Dimension;
import java.awt.Point;
import java.awt.event.ActionEvent;
import java.awt.event.ActionListener;
import javax.swing.JButton;
import javax.swing.JDialog;
import javax.swing.JFrame;
import javax.swing.JLabel;
import javax.swing.JPanel;
public class AboutDialog extends JDialog implements ActionListener {
  public AboutDialog(JFrame parent, String title, String message) {
    super(parent, title, true);
    if (parent != null) {
     Dimension parentSize = parent.getSize();
     Point p = parent.getLocation();
     setLocation(p.x + parentSize.width/4, p.y + parentSize.height /4);
   }
   JPanel messagePane = new JPanel();
   messagePane.add(new JLabel(message));
   getContentPane().add(messagePane);
   JPanel buttonPane = new JPanel();
   JButton button = new JButton("OK");
   buttonPane.add(button);
   button.addActionListener(this);
```

```
        getContentPane().add(buttonPane, BorderLayout.SOUTH);
         setDefaultCloseOperation(DISPOSE_ON_CLOSE);
      pack();
      setVisible(true);
    }
    public void actionPerformed(ActionEvent e) {
      setVisible(false);
      dispose();
    }
    public static void main(String[] a) {
      AboutDialog dlg = new AboutDialog(new JFrame(), "title", "message");
    }
}
```

Fig. 12.6: Output

Practice Questions

1. What is Swing?
2. What are the key features of Swing Library?
3. Why Swing Components are lightweight?
3. Explain concept of Model View Controller Design Pattern.
4. What are the disadvantages of Swing?
5. Explain the following terms with example.
   (a) JButton
   (b) JTextArea
   (c) JComboBox
   (d) JTable
   (e) JDialog
6. Explain any two Swing Components with example.
7. State User defined exception in detail.
8. What is the use of JCheckbox, JRadioButton and JProgressBar?
9. What is the key difference between JTextArea and JTextField?
10. Write a short note on JSlider.

■■■

Chapter 13...

JAVA COLLECTION FRAMEWORK

Contents ...

13.1 Collections Overview

- Java.util is an important package which contains a large collection of classes and interfaces which supports a broad range of functionality. It contains Java's most powerful subsystem collections framework. Collection Framework is a sophisticated hierarchy of classes and interfaces for managing groups of objects.

Table 13.1: List of classes from java.util package

AbstractCollection	EventObject	Random
AbstractList	FormattableFlags	ResourceBundle
AbstractMap	Formatter	Scanner
AbstractQueue	GregorianCalendar	ServiceLoader (Added by Java SE 6.)

contd. ...

AbstractSequentialList	HashMap	SimpleTimeZone
AbstractSet	HashSet	Stack
ArrayDeque	Hashtable	StringTokenizer
ArrayList	IdentityHashMap	Timer
Arrays	LinkedHashMap	TimerTask
BitSet	LinkedHashSet	TimeZone
Calendar	LinkedList	TreeMap
Collections	ListResourceBundle	TreeSet
Currency	Locale	UUID
Date	Observable	Vector
Dictionary	PriorityQueue	WeakHashMap
EnumMap	Properties	
EnumSet	PropertyPermission	
EventListenerProxy	PropertyResourceBundle	

Table 13.2: List of interfaces defined by java.util package

Collection	List	Queue
Comparator	ListIterator	RandomAccess
Deque	Map	Set
Enumeration	Map.Entry	SortedMap
EventListener	NavigableMap	SortedSet
Formattable	NavigableSet	
Iterator	Observer	

- Java Collections is the standard way of groups of objects that are used by your program. Collections were not part of the initial Java release. It was added by J2SE 1.2. Before Collections framework, Java had ad hoc classes such as Dictionary, Vector, Stack and Properties for manipulating groups of objects.
- Collection Framework Goals:
  - Framework had to be high performance. Implementations for fundamental collections are highly efficient.
  - Framework had to allow different types of collections to work in a similar manner.
  - Extending and / or adapting a collection had to be easy. Entire Collection Framework is built upon a set of standard interfaces. Java has provided several implementations of these interfaces like LinkedList, HashSet, TreeSet etc. You can use these implementations as it is. But you can implement your own Collection as well.
  - Java provides mechanism for integrating standard arrays into the Collections Framework.

- Algorithm is another important part of Collection mechanism. They provide standard means of manipulating Collections.
- Iterator is also very closely associated with Collections Framework. Iterator interface offers a standard way of accessing elements within a collection.
- Framework also defines several map interfaces and classes. Map stores key and value pairs. Maps cannot be called as Collections though they come under Collections Framework. But you can obtain Collection view of Map.
- Collections altered the architecture of many utility classes. But it did not deprecate any of the previously used classes. It simply provides a better way of doing things.

13.2 Collection Interfaces

- The Collections Framework defines several interfaces. Collections interfaces determine the fundamental nature of Collection classes.
- Collection interfaces are summarized in the following table.

Table 13.3: Collection interfaces with their description

Interface	Explanation
Collection	Allow you to work with groups of objects; Collection interface is at the top of the collections hierarchy.
Deque	It extends **Queue** that handles a double-ended queue.
List	It extends **Collection** which handles sequences.
NavigableSet	Extends **SortedSet** to handle reclaimation of elements based on closest-match searches.
Queue	Extends **Collection** to handle special types of lists in which elements are to be removed only from the head.
Set	Extends **Collection** to handle sets that contain unique elements.
SortedSet	Extends **Set** to handle sorted sets.

13.2.1 Collection Interface

- Collection interface is the basis upon which the Collections Framework is built. Collection is a generic interface which extends Iterable interface. Collection has all the core methods that all collections will have.
- Several of these methods throw UnsupportedOperationException.
- ClassCastException is generated when one object is incompatible with another when an attempt is made to add these objects to the Collection.
- A NullPoinerEcception is thrown when n attempt is made to store null elements in the collection. IllegalArgumentException is thrown when an invalid argument is used. These methods are given in the following table.

Table 13.4: Methods defined by Collection interface

Method	Explanation of a method
boolean add(E *obj*)	Adds *obj* to the invoking collection. Returns **true** if *obj* is inserted to the collection. Returns **false** if *obj* is already a member of the collection and the collection does not allow duplicates.
boolean addAll(Collection<? extends E> *c*)	Adds all the elements of *c* to the invoking collection. Returns **true** if the operation succeeded (i.e., the elements were added). Otherwise, returns **false**.
void clear( )	Removes all elements from the invoking collection.
boolean contains(Object *obj*)	Returns **true** if *obj* is an element of the invoking collection. Otherwise, returns **false**.
boolean containsAll(Collection<?> *c*)	This method returns **true** if the invoking collection contains all elements of *c*. Otherwise, a method returns **false**.
boolean equals(Object *obj*)	Returns **true** if the call upon (invoking) collection and *obj* are equal. Otherwise, it returns **false**.
int hashCode ( )	Returns the hash code for the invoking collection.
boolean isEmpty( )	Returns **true** if the invoking collection is empty. Otherwise, returns **false**.
Iterator<E> iterator( )	Returns an iterator for the invoking collection.
boolean remove(Object *obj*)	Removes an instance of *obj* from the invoking collection. Returns **true** if the element was removed. Otherwise, returns **false**.
boolean removeAll(Collection<?> *c*)	Removes all elements of *c* from the invoking collection. Returns **true** if the elements were removed. Otherwise, returns **false**.
boolean retainAll(Collection<?> *c*)	Removes all elements from the invoking collection except those in *c*. Returns **true** if the elements were removed from the invoking collection. Otherwise, returns **false**.
int size( )	Returns the number of elements seized in the invoking collection.
Object[ ] toArray( )	Returns an array which contains all the elements stored in the invoking collection. The *array* elements are copies of the collection elements.
<T> T[ ] toArray(T *array*[ ])	Returns an *array* which contains the elements of the invoking collection. They *array* elements are copies of the collection elements. If the size of *array* is equal to the number of elements, these elements are returned in *array*. If the size of *array* is less than the number of elements, a new array of the required size is allocated and returned. If the size of *array* is greater than the number of elements, the array element following the last collection element is set to **null**. An **ArrayStoreException** is thrown if any collection element has a type that is not a subtype of *array*.

13.2.2 List Interface

- List interface extends Collection. This interface has a behavior that stores a sequence of elements. Elements can be inserted or accessed by their position in the list. A list may contain duplicate elements. In addition to the methods defined by Collection interface, List defines its own methods. It represents the ordered collection. (This order refers to the order in which items are added).

Table 13.5: Methods defined by List interface

Method	Explanation
void add(int *index*, E *obj*)	It adds *obj* into the invoking list at the given index passed in *index* parameter. Any previous elements at or after the point of insertion are shifted up. Thus, elements are not overwritten.
boolean addAll(int *index*, Collection<? extends E> *c*)	It adds all elements of *c* into the invoking list at given *index* passed in *index* parameter. Any previous elements at or after the point of insertion are shifted up. Thus, elements are not overwritten. Method returns **true** if the invoking list changes and returns **false** otherwise.
E get(int *index*)	Returns the *object* E stored at the specified *index* within the invoking collection.
int indexOf(Object *obj*)	Returns the *index* of the first instance of *obj* in the invoking list. If *obj* is not an element of the list, −1 is returned.
int lastIndexOf(Object *obj*)	Returns the *index* of the last instance of *obj* in the invoking list. If *obj* is not an element of the list, −1 is returned.
ListIterator<E> listIterator( )	Returns an iterator to the beginning of the invoking list.
ListIterator(E> listIterator(int *index*)	Returns an iterator that starts at the specified *index* of the invoking list.
E remove(int *index*)	Removes the element at the specified position *index* from the invoking list and returns the removed element. The resulting list is compressed. This means, the indexes of subsequent elements are decremented by one.
E set(int *index*, E *obj*)	Assigns *obj* to the position specified by *index* within the invoking list.
List<E> subList(int *start*, int *end*)	Returns a list which includes elements from *start* to (*end* −1) in the invoking list. Elements in the returned list are also referenced by the invoking object.

13.2.3 Set Interface

- The Set Interface defines a set. It extends Collection. Behavior of a collection is that it does not allow duplicate elements to store in the collection. It does not define any additional method of its own. It represents unordered collection.

13.2.4 SortedSet Interface

- SortedSet interface extends Set. The behavior of a collection is that a set is sorted in ascending order. SortedSet defines several methods that make set processing more convenient. SortedSet interface methods are summarized below in the table.

Table 13.6: Methods defined by SortedSet interface

Method	**Explanation**
Comparator<? super E> comparator( )	Returns the invoking sorted set's comparator. If the natural ordering is used for this set, **null** is returned.
E first( )	Returns the first element in the invoking sorted set.
SortedSet<E> headSet(E *end*)	Returns a **SortedSet** containing those elements less than given *end* that are contained in the invoking sorted set. Elements in the returned sorted set are also referenced by the invoking sorted set.
E last( )	Returns the last element in the invoking sorted set.
SortedSet<E> subSet(E *start*, E *end*)	Returns a **SortedSet** which includes those elements between *start* and (*end* –1). Elements in the returned collection are also referenced by the invoking object.
SortedSet<E> tailSet(E *start*)	Returns a **SortedSet** which contains those elements greater than or equal to *start* that are contained in the sorted set. Elements in the returned set are also referenced by the invoking object.

13.2.5 The Collection Classes

- Now let us look at the standard classes that implement these Collection interfaces. Standard Collection classes are summarized below.

Table 13.7: Standard collection classes

Class	Explanation
AbstractCollection	Implements **Collection** interface.
AbstractList	It extends **AbstractCollection** and implements **List** interface.
AbstractQueue	It extends **AbstractCollection** and implements parts of the **Queue** interface.
AbstractSequentialList	Extends **AbstractList** for use by a collection that uses sequential access of its elements.
LinkedList	Implements a linked list by extending **AbstractSequentialList.**
ArrayList	Implements a dynamic array by extending **AbstractList.**
ArrayDeque	Implements a dynamic double-ended queue by extending **AbstractCollection** and implementing the **Deque** interface.
AbstractSet	Extends **AbstractCollection** and implements most of the **Set** interface.
EnumSet	Extends **AbstractSet** for use with **enum** elements.
HashSet	Extends **AbstractSet** for use with a hash table.
LinkedHashSet	Extends **HashSet** to allow insertion-order iterations.
PriorityQueue	Extends **AbstractQueue** to support a priority-based queue.
TreeSet	Implements a set stored in a tree. Extends **AbstractSet.**

13.2.5.1 ArrayList Class

- ArrayList class extends AbstractList and implements the List interface. It supports dynamic arrays that can grow as and when needed.
- Difference between Standard Array and ArrayList:

Array	ArrayList
Fixed Length size.	Variable Length
Cannot grow or shrink as and when needed.	Can dynamically increase or decrease in size.
You must know in advance, how many elements an array stores.	The lists are created with initial size. When the size is exceeded, Collection is automatically enlarged.

ArrayList Constructors

- ArrayList(); An empty array list.
- ArrayList(Collection c); array list with the elements of collection c.
- ArrayList(int capacity); initial capacity of an array.

Program 13.1: The following program illustrates the use of class ArrayList.

We firstly create an object of ArrayList class and adds items to the array list using add() method. We can remove an item from the list by calling remove() method. We get the iterator with the help of iterator() method. Iterator iterates through the array list and display items from the list one by one using next() and hasNext() methods.

```
File: ArraylistDemo.java
import java.util.*;
class ArraylistDemo
{
   public static void main(String args[])
   {
      ArrayList arraylist = new ArrayList();
      arraylist.add("Item 3");
      arraylist.add("Item 4");
      arraylist.add("Item 5");
      arraylist.add("Item 6");
      arraylist.add("Item 0");
      arraylist.add("Item 2");
      arraylist.add(1, "Item 1");
      System.out.println("\nUsing the add method\n");
      System.out.println(arraylist);
      arraylist.remove("Item 5");
      System.out.println(arraylist);
      System.out.println("\nUsing the Iterator interface");
      String s;
      Iterator e = arraylist.iterator();
      while (e.hasNext())
      {
         s = (String)e.next();
         System.out.println(s);
      }
   }
}
```

Output:

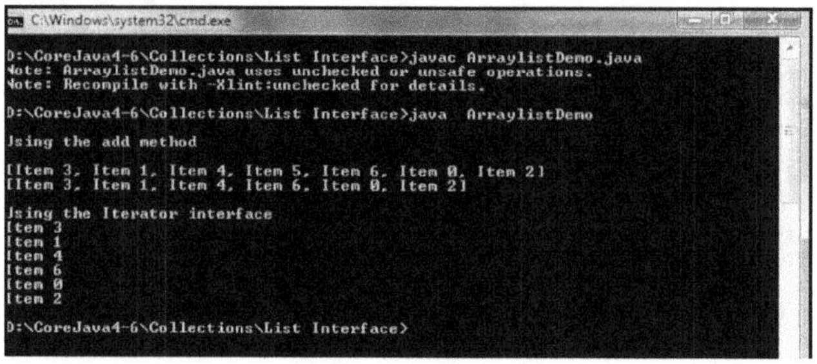

Fig. 13.1

- One can increase the capacity of storing objects into ArrayList by calling ensureCapacity() method.

```
void ensureCapacity(int capacity);
```

- We can call trimToSize() method which trims the capacity of this ArrayList instance to be the list's current size.

```
void  trimToSize();
```

- To obtain an array from ArrayList, we can call toArray() method. Below is the format for calling toArray() method.

```
T[] toArray(T array[]);
                    //T is the type of array, the method returns.
```

- For example,

```
Integer intAr[] = new Integer[al.size()];
intAr = al.toArray(intAr);
```

13.2.5.2 LinkedList Class

- LinkedList class extends AbstractSequentialList and implements List, Queue and Deque interfaces. It Provides a linked-list data structure.

LinkedList constructors:

- **LinkedList():** Constructs an empty list.
- LinkedList(Collection<? extends E> c): Constructs a list containing the elements of the specified collection, in the order they are returned by the collection's iterator.

  Because LinkedList implements Deque interface, you can access all the methods defined by Deque like addFirst(), addLast(), getFirst(), getLast(), removeFirst(), removeLast() etc.

  LinkedList also implement List interface, so it has access to all the methods defined by this List interface.

Program 13.2: The following program illustrates the use of class LinkedList.

The following program stores the contents in the linked list data structure. Program adds items to the linkedlist. Items can be removed from the linked list by calling remove() method. It uses set() method to update the items from the given list.

```
File : LinkedlistDemo.java
import java.util.*;
class LinkedlistDemo
{
   public static void main(String args[])
   {
      LinkedList linkedlist1 = new LinkedList();
      linkedlist1.add("Item 2");
      linkedlist1.add("Item 3");
      linkedlist1.add("Item 4");
      linkedlist1.add("Item 5");
      linkedlist1.addFirst("Item 0");
      linkedlist1.addLast("Item 6");
      linkedlist1.add(1, "Item 1");
      System.out.println(linkedlist1);
      linkedlist1.remove("Item 6");
      System.out.println(linkedlist1);
      linkedlist1.removeLast();
      System.out.println(linkedlist1);
      System.out.println("\nUpdating linked list items");
      linkedlist1.set(0, "Red");
      linkedlist1.set(1, "Blue");
      linkedlist1.set(2, "Green");
      linkedlist1.set(3, "Yellow");
      linkedlist1.set(4, "Purple");
      System.out.println(linkedlist1);
   }
}
```

Output:

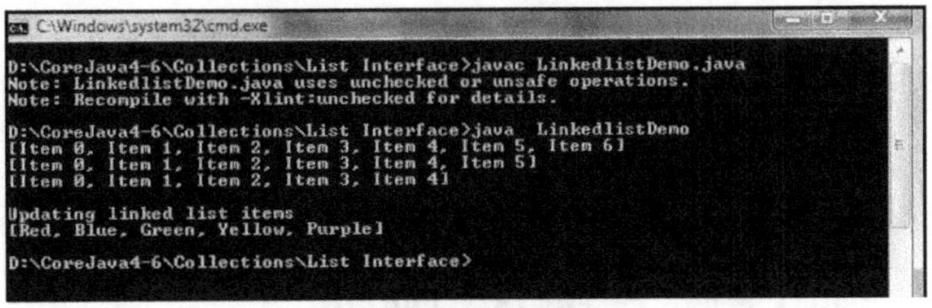

Fig 13.2: Output

13.2.5.3 HashSet Class

- HashSet extends AbstractSet and implements the Set interface. It creates a collection that uses a HashTable for storage. HashTable stores elements by using Hashing mechanism.
- Hashing: The information about the key value of each and every element is used to define a hash code. This has code is used as an index where the data associated with the key value is stored. Conversion of key value into hashcode is performed automatically. You cannot see the hash code by itself. Advantage of hashing is, the execution time of manipulation of elements remains constant even for large set of elements.

HashSet Constructors:

- **HashSet();** Constructs a default hash set.
- **HashSet(Collection<? extends E> c);** Hash set initialization using elements of c.
- **HashSet(int capacity);** Initializes the capacity of hash set (Default is 16)
- **HashSet(int capacity, float fillRatio);** Initializes capacity and fill ratio. The fill ratio must be between 0.0 and 1.0. It determines how full the hash set can be before it is resized upward. Constructors that do not accept fillRatio, default 0.75 fillRatio is used. Hash set does not provide extra methods other than defined by its super classes and interfaces. Hash set does not guarantee the order of elements.

Program 13.3: The following program demonstrates use of HashSet class.

```
File: HashsetDemo.java
import java.util.*;
class HashsetDemo
{
public static void main(String args[])
HashSet hashset1 = new HashSet();
hashset1.add("Item 0");
hashset1.add("Item 1");
hashset1.add("Item 2");
hashset1.add("Item 3");
hashset1.add("Item 4");
hashset1.add("Item 5");
hashset1.add("Item 5");
hashset1.add("Item 6");
hashset1.add("Item 6");
hashset1.add("Item 6");
System.out.println(hashset1);
    }
}
```

Output:

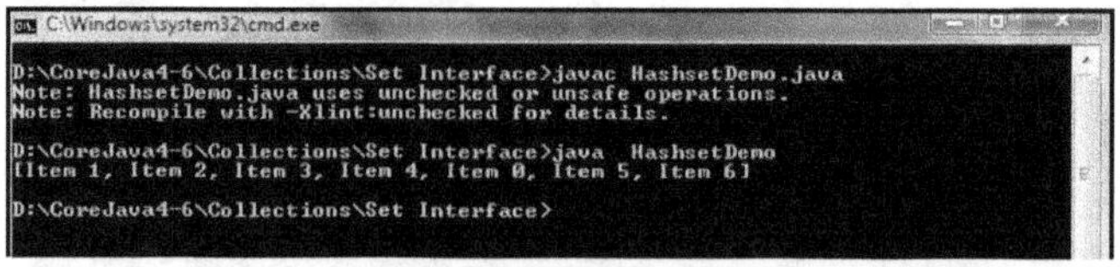

Fig 13.3: Output

13.2.5.4 TreeSet Class

- TreeSet extends AbstractSet and implements NavigableSet interface. It creates a colletion that uses a tree to store the elements. All the objects are stored in sorted , ascending order. Access time and retrieval time is really fast. TreeSet is an excellent choice when we want to store information in a sorted manner and need to be found quickly.

TreeSet Constructors:

- TreeSet(); empty tree set
- TreeSet(Collection<? extends E> c); Tree set which contains the elements of c.
- TreeSet(Comparator<? Super E> comp); Empty tree set which will be sorted according to the specified comparator comp.
- TreeSet(SortedSet<E> s); Tree set that contains the elements of s.
- TreeSet implements NavigableSet interface, so you can use all the methods defined by NavigableSet interface.

Program that demonstrates TreeSet class:

Program 13.4:

```
File: TreesetDemo.java
import java.util.*;
class TreeSetDemo
{
public static void main(String args[])
{
TreeSet treeset1 = new TreeSet();
treeset1.add("Item 3");
treeset1.add("Item 0");
treeset1.add("Item 1");
treeset1.add("Item 2");
treeset1.add("Item 4");
treeset1.add("Item 6");
treeset1.add("Item 5");
System.out.println(treeset1);
}
}
```

Output:

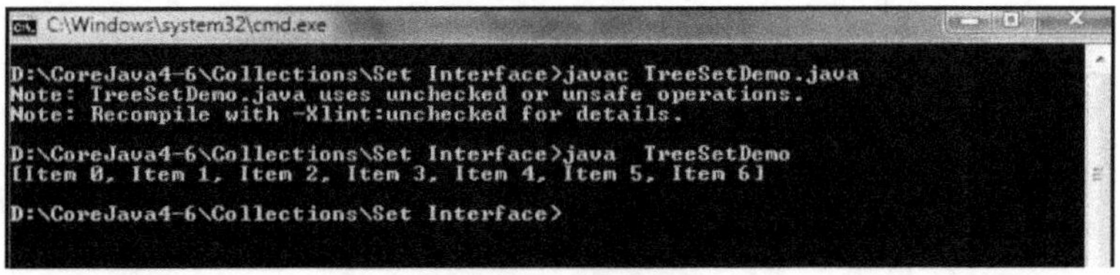

Fig 13.4: Output

13.2.5.5 Accessing a Collection via an Iterator

- If you want to cycle through the elements of collection, then the collection must have an iterator. Iterator enables you to cycle through the collection. ListIterator extends Iterator. With the help of ListIterator, we can traverse the elements of the list bi-directionally.
- Following table shows the methods from Iterator interface.

Table 13.8: Methods defined by Iterator

Method	Explanation
boolean hasNext( )	Returns **true** if there are more elements. Otherwise, returns **false**.
E next( )	Returns the next element. Throws **NoSuchElementException** if there is not a next element.
void remove( )	Removes the current element. Throws **IllegalStateException** if an attempt is made to call **remove( )** that is not preceded by a call to **next( )**.

- Following table shows the methods from ListIterator interface.

Table 13.9: Methods defined by ListIterator

Method	Explanation
void add(E *obj*)	Adds *obj* into the list in front of the element that will be returned by the next call to **next( )**.
boolean hasNext( )	Returns **true** if there is a next element. Otherwise, returns **false**.
boolean hasPrevious( )	Returns **true** if there is a previous element. Otherwise, returns **false**.
E next( )	Returns the next element. A **NoSuchElementException** is thrown if a next element is not present.
int nextIndex( )	Returns the index of the next element. If there is no next element, it returns the size of the list.
E previous( )	Returns the previous element. A **NoSuchElementException** is thrown if there is no such previous element.
int previousIndex( )	Returns the index of the previous element. If there is no such previous element, returns −1.
void remove( )	Removes the current element from the list. An **IllegalStateException** is thrown if **remove( )** method is called before **next( )** or **previous( )** is invoked.
void set(E *obj*)	Assigns *obj* to the current element. This is the element last returned by a call to either **next( )** or **previous( )**.

Steps to use an Iterator to cycle through the elements

- Obtain an iterator by calling the collections iterator() method.
- Write a loop that will give a call to hasNext() method. This method returns true, as long as there are elements in the collection.
- Obtain each element of collection by calling next() method.

- For collections which implement List interface, you can also obtain an iterator by calling listIterator() method. With list iterator, you can access the elements of a collection in both directions forward as well as backward.

For-Each alternative to Iterators

- If you do not want to modify the contents of collection or you do not want to obtain the elements in reverse order, then For-Each loop is convenient to use to cycle through a collection than iterator. The collection that implements Iterable interface, can operate upon by 'for' loop. Use of 'for' loop is shorter and simpler than Iterator approach. But you cannot modify the contents and you can cycle through the collection only in forward direction while using for loop.

13.3 The Map Interfaces

- A Map stores key-value pairs. If key is given, one can find its associated value. Key and value are objects. Key must be unique. Values may be duplicated. They do not implement Iterable interface. This means, you cannot cycle through a map using for-each loop.
- Map interface defines the nature of Map. The following interfaces supports maps.

Table 13.10: Interfaces that supports map

Method	Explanation
Map	Maps unique keys to values.
Map.Entry	Depicts an element (a key/value pair) in a map. This is an inner class of **Map**.
NavigableMap	Extends **SortedMap** to handle the retrieval of entries based on closest-match searches.
SortedMap	Extends **Map** so that the keys are maintained in ascending order.

13.3.1 Map Interface

- Map interface maps unique keys to values.
- A key is an object that you use to retrieve values. You can store the value in a Map object with keys associated with the value.
- You can retrieve it by using its key. Maps revolve around two basic operations: get() and put(). To put a value into the map, specify the key and value using put() method. To obtain a value, call get() method. Key is the argument that should be passed as an argument. The value is returned. Since Map do not implement Collection interface, they are not part of Collection Framework. But you can obtain a collection view of a map. To

do this, we can use entrySet() method. It returns a set that contains elements in the map. Collection view of keys can be obtained by keyset() method. Collection view of values can be obtained by using values() method.

- Methods of Map interface are summarized in the following table.

Table 13.11: Methods defined by Map

Method	Explanation
void clear( )	Removes all key/value pairs from the invoking map.
boolean containsKey(Object *k*)	Returns **true** if the invoking map contains *k* as a *key*. Otherwise, returns **false**.
boolean containsValue(Object *v*)	Returns true if the map contains *v* as a value. Otherwise, returns **false**.
Set<Map.Entry<K, V>> entrySet( )	Returns a **Set** that contains the entries in the map. The set contains objects of type **Map.Entry**. Thus, this method provides a set-view of the invoking map.
boolean equals(Object *obj*)	Returns **true** if *obj* is a **Map** and contains the same entries. Otherwise, returns **false**.
V get(Object *k*)	Returns the value associated with the key *k*. Returns **null** if the key is not found.
int hashCode( )	Returns the hash code for the invoking map.
boolean isEmpty( )	Returns **true** if the invoking map is empty. Otherwise, returns **false**.
Set<K> keySet( )	Returns a **Set** that contains the keys in the invoking map. This method provides a set-view of the keys in the invoking map.
V put(K *k*, V *v*)	Puts an entry in the invoking map, overwriting any previous value associated with the key. The key and value are *k* and *v*, respectively. Returns **null** if the *key* did not already exist. Otherwise, the previous value linked to the *key* is returned.
void putAll(Map<? extends K, ? extends V> *m*)	Puts all the entries from *m* into this map.
V remove(Object *k*)	Removes the entry whose *key* equals *k*.
int size( )	Returns the number of key/value pairs in the map.
Collection<V> values( )	Returns a collection containing the values in the map. This method provides a collection-view of the values in the map.

13.3.2 SortedMap Interface

- SortedMap extends Map. Entries are maintained in the ascending order of key. Methods of SortedMap are summarized in the table.

Table 13.12: Methods defined by SortedMap

Method	Explanation
Comparator<? super K> comparator( )	Returns the invoking sorted map's comparator. If natural ordering is used for the invoking map, **null** is returned.
K firstKey( )	Returns the first *key* in the invoking map.
SortedMap<K, V> headMap(K *end*)	Returns a sorted map for those map entries with keys that are less than end.
K lastKey( )	Returns the last key in the invoking map.

13.3.3 Map Classes

- Several classes provide implementation of the Map interface. AbstractMap is a super class for all Map implementations. These classes are summarized in the following table.

Table 13.13: Classes used for Map

Class	Explanation
AbstractMap	Implements most of the **Map** interface.
EnumMap	Extends **AbstractMap** for use with **enum** keys.
HashMap	Extends **AbstractMap** to use a hash table.
TreeMap	Extends **AbstractMap** to use a tree.
WeakHashMap	Extends **AbstractMap** to use a hash table with weak keys.
LinkedHashMap	Extends **HashMap** to allow insertion-order iterations.
IdentityHashMap	Extends **AbstractMap** and uses reference equality when comparing documents.

13.3.3.1 HashMap

- HashMap class extends AbstractMap and implements the Map interface. A HashTable is used to store the Map.
- HashMap Constructors:
  - o HashMap(); Default hash map
  - o HashMap(Map<? Extends K, ?extends V> m); Initializes the hash map using the elements of m.
  - o HashMap(int capacity); Initializes the hash map with defined capacity
  - o HashMap(int capacity, float fillRatio); Initializes hash map with capacity and fill ratio.

Program 13.5: A program that illustrates HashMap class.

- The program begins with creating a hash map and adds the mapping of items with values.
- The contents of map are displayed using set-view obtained by calling entrySet() method. The keys and values are displayed by calling getKey() and getValue() methods which are defined by Map.Entry.

Program 13.5:

```
File: HapMapDemo.java
import java.util.*;
class HashMapDemo
{
public static void main(String args[])
{
HashMap hashmap1 = new HashMap();
hashmap1.put("Item 0", "Value 0");
hashmap1.put("Item 1", "Value 1");
hashmap1.put("Item 2", "Value 2");
hashmap1.put("Item 3", "Value 3");
hashmap1.put("Item 4", "Value 4");
hashmap1.put("Item 5", "Value 5");
hashmap1.put("Item 6", "Value 6");
Set set = hashmap1.entrySet();
Iterator iterator = set.iterator();
while(iterator.hasNext())
{
    Map.Entry mapentry = (Map.Entry) iterator.next();
    System.out.println(mapentry.getKey()
                                        + " / " +mapentry.getValue());
}
}
}
```

Output:

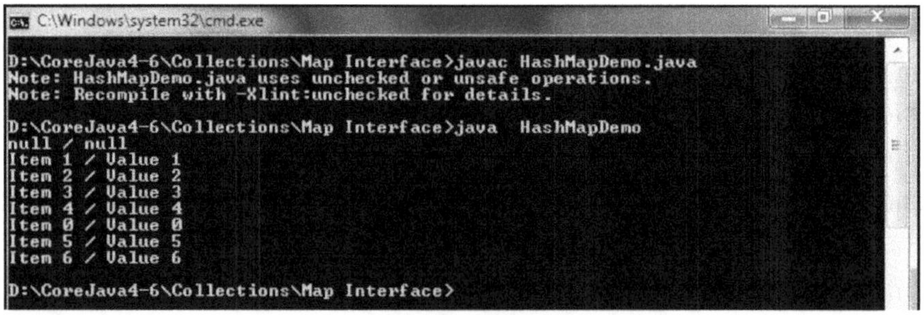

Fig 13.5: Output

13.3.3.2 TreeMap

- TreeMap extends AbstractMap and implements the NavigableMap interface. Map is stored in a tree structure. TreeMap stores key/value pair in sorted order. This allows fast retrieval. Its elements are stored in ascending key order.
- TreeMap Constructors:
  - o TreeMap(); Empty tree map
  - o TreeMap(Map<?Extends K, ?extends V> m); Tree map which contains the elements of m.
  - o TreeMap(Comparator<? Super E> comp); Empty tree map which will be sorted according to the specified comparator comp.
  - o TreeMap(SortedMap<K, ?extends V> sm); Tree map that contains the elements of sm.

Program 13.6: The following program illustrates TreeMap class.

Notice that the TreeMap sorts the keys.

```
File: TreeMapDemo.java
import java.util.*;
class TreeMapDemo
{
public static void main(String args[])
{
TreeMap TreeMap1 = new TreeMap();
TreeMap1.put("Item 6", "Value 6");
TreeMap1.put("Item 1", "Value 1");
TreeMap1.put("Item 2", "Value 2");
TreeMap1.put("Item 5", "Value 5");
TreeMap1.put("Item 3", "Value 3");
TreeMap1.put("Item 4", "Value 4");
TreeMap1.put("Item 0", "Value 0");
Set set = TreeMap1.entrySet();
Iterator iterator = set.iterator();
while(iterator.hasNext())
{
Map.Entry mapentry = (Map.Entry) iterator.next();
System.out.println(mapentry.getKey() + " / " +mapentry.getValue());
}
}
```

Output:

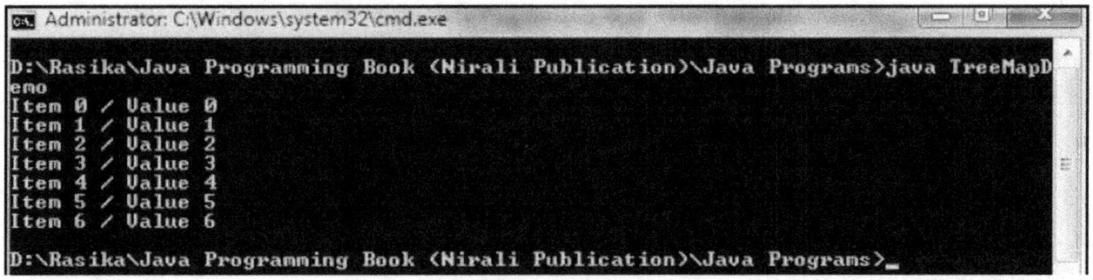

Fig 13.6: Output

13.4 Legacy Classes and Interfaces

- Early versions of java.util did not include the Collections Framework. It had several interfaces and classes that provided ad hoc methods for storing objects. When collections were added, several original Classes were re-engineered. They made fully compatible with collection framework. No classes are actually been deprecated. These legacy classes are still in existence as there are still some software codes that still use them. All legacy classes are synchronized. Collection classes are not synchronized.

13.4.1 Legacy Classes

- Dictionary, HashTable, Properties, Stack and Vector are legacy classes. There is one legacy interface called 'Enumeration'.

Dictionary:

- Dictionary is a abstract class, which holds the data as Key/value pair. It works as Map collection.
- The abstract methods and its description that are available in Dictionary class are in below Table 13.14.

Table 13.14

Method	Description
Enumeration elements()	Returns an enumeration of the values contained in the dictionary.
Object get(Object key)	Returns the object that contains the valued associated with key. If key is not in dictionary, a null object is returned.
boolean isEmpty()	Returns true if the dictionary is empty, and returns false if it contains atleast one key.
Enumeration keys()	Returns an enumeration of the keys contained in the dictionary.
Object put(Object key, Object value)	Inserts a key and its value into the dictionary. Returns null if key is not already in the dictionary; returns the previous value associated with key if key is already in the dictionary.
Object remove(Object key)	Removes key and its value. Returns the value associated with key. If key is not in the dictionary, a null is returned.
int size()	Returns the number of entries in the dictionary.

HashTable:

- HashTable is a part of java.util package and it is a concrete class which extends the Dictionary class.
- In Java 1.2 version on ward HashTable class implemented the Map interface and it is as part of Collection Framework.
- HashTable is synchronized.

Properties:

- Properties class will hold the set of properties in Key/value pair. Properties class extends HashTable class. This class is thread-safe, multiple threads can share single Properties object without making externally Synchronization.

Stack:

- Stack represents the Last-In-First-Out (LIFO). Stack class extends the Vector class.

Vector:

- Vector class is a grow-able array and is similar to ArrayList class with two difference.
- Vector is a Synchronized.
- It is used where programmer didn't have knowledge of what the size of the Array is. It means you can ignore the size of the Vector, even still Vector will work without any exceptions. We will learn vector stack and Hashtable in detail in next topic 13.5.

13.4.2 Enumeration Interface

- Enumeration interface defines methods by which you can obtain elements one at a time from the collection of objects. Though this interface is not deprecated it has been superseded by Iterator. It is still used by several legacy classes such as Vector and Properties.
- Enumeration has two methods:
  - boolean hasMoreElements(): Returns true if there are still more elements.
  - E nextElement(): Returns next object in enumeration.

13.5 Vector, Stack, HashTable

13.5.1 Vector

- Vector implements dynamic array. It is similar to ArrayList with two major differences. Vector class is reengineered to extend AbstractList and it implements List interface. It is also reengineered to implement Iterable interface. Means, Vector can have its elements traversed through the for loop. Vector is fully compatible with collections.
- Difference between Vector and ArrayList

Vector	ArrayList
Vector is synchronized.	ArrayList is not synchronized.
It contains legacy methods that are not part of the Collection Framework	Collection Framework defines ArrayList which has several methods that are part of collection framework.

Vector Constructors:

- Vector(); default vector with initial size 10
- Vector(int size); vector whose initial capacity is specified by size.
- Vector(int size, int increment); vector whose initial capacity is specified by size and increment is specified by increment. Increment is the number of elements allocated each time a vector is resized in upward direction. Constructors which do not accept increment, will resize vector with capacity 10 by default in upward direction.
- Vector(Collection<?extends E> c); vector that contains the elements of collection c.

- Some of the important methods defined by Vector class are summarized in the following table.

Table 13.15: Legacy methods defined by Vector

Method	Explanation
void addElement(E *element*)	The object specified by element is added to the vector.
int capacity( )	Returns the capacity of the vector.
Object clone( )	Returns a duplicate of the invoking vector.
boolean contains(Object *element*)	Returns **true** if elements is contained by the vector, and returns **false** if it is not.
E elementAt(int *index*)	Returns the element at the given location specified by index.
Enumeration<E> elements( )	Returns an enumeration of the elements in the vector.
void ensureCapacity(int *size*)	Sets the minimum capacity of the vector to size.
E firstElement( )	Returns the first element in the vector.
int indexOf(Object *element*)	Returns the index of the first occurrence of element. If the object is not in the vector, −1 is returned.
int indexOf(Object *element*, int *start*)	Returns the index of the first occurrence of element at or after start. If the object is not in that portion of the vector, −1 is returned.
void insertElementAt(E element, int *index*)	Adds element to the vector at the location specified by index.
boolean isEmpty( )	Returns **true** if the vector is empty, and returns **false** if it contains one or more elements.
E lastElement( )	Returns the last element in the vector.
int lastindexOf(Object *element*)	Returns the index of the last occurrence of element. If the object is not in the vector, −1 is returned.
int lastindexOf(Object *element*, int *start*)	Returns the index of the last occurrence of element before start. If the object is not in that portion of the vector, −1 is returned.
void removeAllElements( )	Empties the vector. After this method executes, the size of the vector is zero.
boolean removeElement(Object *element*)	Removes element from the vector. If more than one instance of the specified object exists in the vector, then it is the first one that is removed. Returns **true** if successful and **false** if the object is not found.
void removeElementAt(int *index*)	Removes the element at the given location specified by index.

... contd.

void setElementAt(E *element*, int *index*)	The location specified by index is assigned element.
void setSize(int *size*)	Sets the number of elements in the vector to size. If the new size is less than the old size, elements are lost. If the new size is larger than the old size, **null** elements are added.
int *size*( )	Returns the number of elements currently in the vector.
String to String( )	Returns the string equivalent of the vector.
void trimToSize( )	Sets the vector's capacity equal to the number of elements that it currently holds.

Program 13.7: The following program demonstrates Vector class.

A program uses a vector to store various types of numeric objects. It demonstrates several legacy methods defined by the Vector class.

```
File: VectorDemo.java
import java.util.*;
class VectorDemo
{
public static void main(String args[])
{
Vector vector = new Vector(5);
System.out.println("Size :   " + vector.size());
System.out.println("Capacity : " + vector.capacity());
vector.addElement(new Integer(0));
vector.addElement(new Integer(1));
vector.addElement(new Integer(2));
vector.addElement(new Integer(3));
vector.addElement(new Integer(4));
vector.addElement(new Integer(5));
vector.addElement(new Integer(6));
vector.addElement(new Integer(5));
vector.addElement(new Integer(6));
vector.addElement(new Double(3.14159));
vector.addElement(new Float(3.14159));
```

```
    System.out.println("Capacity : " + vector.capacity());
    System.out.println("Size : " + vector.size());
    System.out.println(vector);
    System.out.println("First item : " + (Integer)vector.firstElement());
    System.out.println("Last item :  " + (Float) vector.lastElement());
    if(vector.contains(new Integer(3)))
    System.out.println("Found 3");
    }
    }
```

Output:

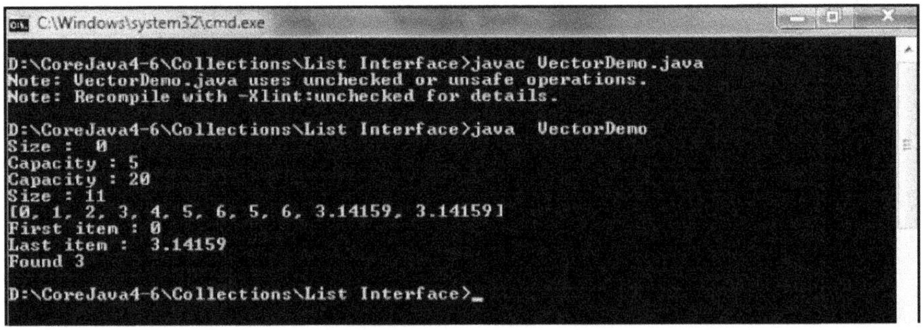

Fig 13.7: Output

13.5.2 Stack

- Stack is a subclass of vector. Stack has only one constructor which defines an empty stack. Stack has all the methods defined by Vector class. Along with them, it has its own methods.
- The following table shows methods of Stack class.

Table 13.16: Methods defined by Stack

Method	Explanation
boolean empty( )	Returns **true** if the stack is empty, and returns **false** if the stack contains elements.
E peek( )	Returns the element on the top of the stack, but does not remove it.
E pop( )	Returns the element on the top of the stack, removing it in the process.
E push(E *element*)	Pushes element onto the stack. element is also returned.
int search(Object *element*)	Searches for element in the stack. If found, its offset from the top of the stack is returned. Otherwise, –1 is returned.

Program 13.8: The following program demonstrates the Stack class.

Here is an example that pushes several integer objects onto the stack and then pops them off again.

```
File: StackDemo.java
import java.util.*;
class StackDemo
{
public static void main(String args[])
{
Stack stack1 = new Stack();
try
{
stack1.push(new Integer(0));
stack1.push(new Integer(1));
stack1.push(new Integer(2));
stack1.push(new Integer(3));
stack1.push(new Integer(4));
stack1.push(new Integer(5));
stack1.push(new Integer(6));
System.out.println("Pop->"+(Integer) stack1.pop());
System.out.println("Pop->"+(Integer) stack1.pop());
System.out.println("Pop->"+(Integer) stack1.pop());
System.out.println("Pop->"+(Integer) stack1.pop());
System.out.println("Pop->"+(Integer) stack1.pop());
System.out.println("Pop->"+(Integer) stack1.pop());
System.out.println("Pop->"+(Integer) stack1.pop());
}
catch (EmptyStackException e) {}
}
}
```

Output:

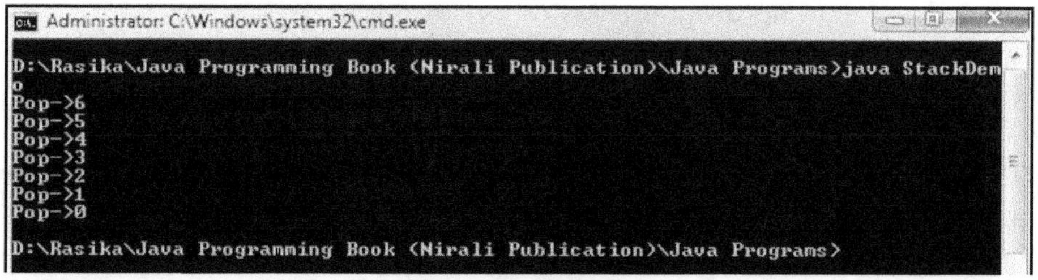

Fig 13.8: Output

13.5.3 HashTable

- HashTable is a concrete implementation of Dictionary but it was reengineered to also implement Map interface. So it is now similar to HashMap but it is synchronized.
- HashTable stores key/value pairs in a hash table. However neither keys nor values can be null. The key is hashed and the resulting hash code is used as index where the value is stored within the table.

HashTable Constructors:

- o HashTable(); Default constructor
- o HashTable(int size); Hash table with initial size.
- o HashTable(int size, float fillRatio); Hash table with initial size and fill ratio.
- o HashTable(Map<?extends K, ?extends V> m); Hash table with the elements in m.

- Here are some of the important HashTable methods:

Table 13.17: Methods defined by Hashtable

Method	Explanation
void clear()	Resets and empties the hash table.
boolean contains(Object *value*)	Returns true if some value which is equal to *value* present in the hash table, false otherwise.
boolean containsKey(Object *key*)	Returns true if some key which is equal to *key* present in the hash table, false otherwise.
boolean containsValue(Object *value*)	Returns true if some value which is equal to *value* present in the hash table, false otherwise.
Enumeration <V> elements()	Returns an enumeration of the values contained in the hash table.
V get(Object *key*)	Returns the object that contains the value associated with the *key*.
boolean isEmpty()	Returns true is the hash table is empty, false otherwise.
Enumeration <K> keys()	Returns an enumeration of the keys present in the hash table.
V put(K *key*, V *value*)	Inserts a *key* and a *value* in the hash table.
int size()	Returns the number of entries in the hash table.
V remove(Object *key*)	Removes key and its value from the hash table. It returns the value associated with *key*.

Program 13.9: The following program illustrates Hashtable class.

The program uses hash table to store the contents. Hash table does not directly supports iterators. Hence program uses enumeration to display the contents of the hash table. However, you can also obtain set-view of the hash table that permits the use of iterators. This can be done by calling entrySet() or keyset() method of Map interface like the one we have demonstrated in HashMap example.

```
File: HashTableDemo.java
import java.util.*;
class HashTableDemo
{
   public static void main(String args[])
   {
      Hashtable hashtable1 = new Hashtable();
      hashtable1.put("Item 0", "Value 0");
      hashtable1.put("Item 1", "Value 1");
```

```
            hashtable1.put("Item 2", "Value 2");
            hashtable1.put("Item 3", "Value 3");
            hashtable1.put("Item 4", "Value 4");
            hashtable1.put("Item 5", "Value 5");
            hashtable1.put("Item 6", "Value 6");
            Enumeration keys = hashtable1.keys();
            while(keys.hasMoreElements())
            {
               String key = (String) keys.nextElement();
               System.out.println(key + " / " + hashtable1.get(key));
            }
      }
   }
```

Output:

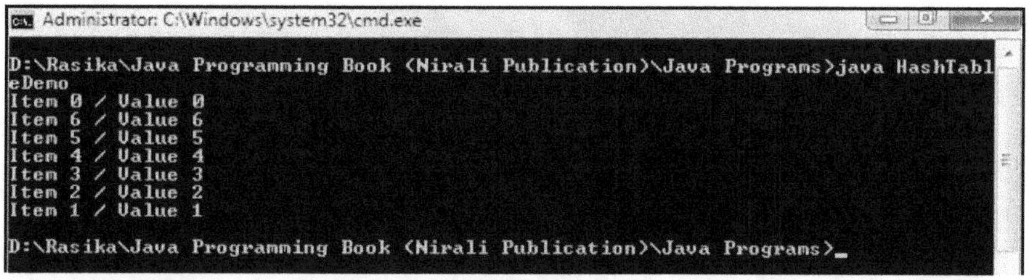

Fig. 13.9

Practice Questions

1. What is a Collection? Why Collections are used?
2. What are the advantages of Collections?
3. What is a Collection Framework?
4. What are the Interfaces available in Collection Framework?
5. What are the Components of Collection Framework?
6. Write a short note on Collection Interface.
7. What are the core Collection Interfaces? Explain any one of them.
8. Explain Collection Interfaces and Classes with the help of diagram.
9. What are the basic methods available in Collection Interface?
10. Write a short note on List Interface.
11. Write a short note on Set Interface.
12. State the Set Interface.
13. Explain Collection Classes in detail.
14. Write a note on :
    (a) ArrayList Class (b) LinkedList Class (c) HashSet Class (d) TreeSet Class
15. What is the use of LinkedList Class?
16. What is the use of Comparators?
17. Explain Iterator with the help of example.
18. What is a Vector? How many Constructors are supported by Vector?

■■■

www.ingramcontent.com/pod-product-compliance
Lightning Source LLC
LaVergne TN
LVHW082030051026
849532LV00011B/3318
* 9 7 8 9 3 8 6 0 8 4 7 2 9 *